MERI JHAAI

A Journey of Loss, Love and Divine Grace

(My Granny)

ANJALI NARINDER SETHI

notionpress.com

INDIA · SINGAPORE · MALAYSIA

ISBN

Hardcase 979-8-90479-823-9
Paperback 979-8-90392-333-5

जहाँ धर्म है, वहाँ श्री कृष्ण हैं।

और जहाँ श्री कृष्ण हैं, वहाँ विजय निश्चित है।

Guru Vandana

"Guru Brahma, Guru Vishnu, Guru Devo Maheshwara
Guru Sakshat Parabrahma, Tasmai Shri Gurave Namah
Akhanda Mandalaakaram Vyaptam Yena Characharam
Tatpadam Darshitam Yena Tasmai Shri Gurave Namah"

I bow in deep gratitude to all my Gurus who have entered my life in different forms and moments, and shaped me into who I am today. Each one has educated me, nurtured me, supported me, guided me, and corrected me—quietly building my understanding of life through their presence and wisdom.

My greatest Guru for the past eight years and many lifetimes has been Shri Krishna, who continues to guide me in every moment—as strength in weakness, clarity in confusion, and light in silence.

My late grandmother has been one of my most defining Gurus. She educated, nurtured, supported, guided, and corrected me in her lifetime, and even in her physical absence, she continues to live within me—shaping my thoughts, values, and path through her eternal presence.

To all my Gurus—known and unknown, past and present—I remain forever grateful.

Smt. Sumitra Devi Sethi Ji

Shri Jai Ram Sethi Ji

To the Souls That Never Leave Us

Meri Jhaai is my debut book—a soulful tribute to my late grandmother, Smt. Sumitra Devi Sethi Ji, my late grandfather, Shri Jai Ram Sethi Ji, and to all my ancestors whose love, sacrifices, and blessings continue to guide me beyond time.

This book is dedicated to every human soul that has endured the unbearable pain of losing a loved one; to every spirit that still believes in humanity and dreams of igniting a change—a revolution for the betterment of society and mankind.

It is dedicated to every parent who has suffered the heartbreaking loss of a child, to every wife who has learned to live with the silence left behind by her husband, to every husband carrying the emptiness left by the loss of his wife, to every daughter and son carrying the ache of losing their parents or grandparents, to every sibling grieving the absence of a brother or sister once cherished as a part of their own soul, and to every pet lover who has experienced the silent heartbreak of losing a companion that was never "just an animal," but family.

I hope this book brings peace to every wounded soul searching for comfort in the pain of loss. I may never be able to erase their sorrow or fill the emptiness left behind, but if these words can make even one person feel less alone, then this book has found its purpose.

Through these pages, I hope to offer warmth, strength, and a small ray of light to those walking through the darkness of grief—reminding them that love never truly dies, and that even after the deepest pain, life goes on and the show must go on

"For the soul there is neither birth nor death at any time.
It has not come into being, does not come into being, and will not come into being.
The soul is unborn, eternal, everlasting, and primeval.
It is not destroyed when the body is destroyed."

"आत्मा किसी भी काल में न जन्म लेती है और न मरती है। यह न तो कभी उत्पन्न हुई है, न ही आगे कभी उत्पन्न होगी। यह अजन्मा, नित्य, शाश्वत और पुरातन है। शरीर के नष्ट होने पर भी आत्मा का नाश नहीं होता।"

—Bhagavad Gita, Chapter 2, Verse 20

Contents

Author's Note

This book is a work of fiction, yet it is born from questions I have carried within me for a long time—questions about life, purpose, and the quiet journey inward.

It is not written to give answers, but to invite reflection. The characters and events are imagined, but the emotions, struggles, and realizations may feel familiar, perhaps even personal to you.

I would ask you to read this not as something to be analyzed, but experienced. Move through it slowly, and allow it to meet you where you are.

Take what resonates with you, and let go of what does not serve you. Both are equally valid.

In many ways, this story is not just mine.
It becomes yours too.

Introduction

Before I wrote a single word of this book, I knew it carried a purpose far greater than ink on paper. I knew it was meant to travel beyond these pages—to reach souls, to stir hearts, to awaken something long forgotten within us.

This is not merely a book. It is an encounter.

A quiet yet undeniable stirring of the spirit. It will ask you the questions you have long avoided. It will hold a mirror to your existence and gently, yet firmly, invite you to look deeper.

We live in a world that never truly pauses. We move endlessly between roles, responsibilities, relationships, ambitions, and expectations. In this constant motion, we lose clarity, stillness, and often, ourselves. We strive to build a place for ourselves, to prove our worth, to secure comfort—yet somewhere along the way, we drift away from who we truly are.

Who are you beneath the roles?
Beyond the responsibilities?
Beyond the expectations placed upon you?

Caught in Moh Maya—the beautiful yet blinding illusion of worldly attachment—we begin to measure life in achievements rather than awareness, in possessions rather than purpose.

This book is a nudge to your conscience and an awakening of your inner voice. It does not judge. It does not preach. It simply invites you to pause… to reflect… to question. Not to unsettle you—but to liberate you.

This will be a profound journey.

Some chapters will move you. Some will challenge you. Some will stretch your imagination. Some will confront your morals and principles, compelling you to look within more honestly. Some will reflect society itself. Some will demand surrender and ask you to embrace truths you once believed impossible.

There will be pages that break you—not to destroy you, but to strip away everything that is not real. And in that breaking, something truer will rise.

A clearer vision.
A quieter mind.
A self you may have long forgotten.

You may begin to realize that life is not as complicated as we believe—we are. When we stop resisting life and stop performing it, it reveals its quiet simplicity.

This book is a call back to your truth. As you read, trust its rhythm. Do not rush it. Do not resist it. Go with the flow. Every pause, every full stop, every silence between words is intentional—it is meant to be felt, not skipped.

At the end of this journey, you will experience Shri Krishna—not as mythology or distant divinity, but as consciousness, as guidance, as truth.

I have poured my soul into these pages—through despair, darkness, and fractured moments—with one intention: to uplift, to extend a hand, and to remind you that even in your most vulnerable moments, you are not alone.

This book is not meant to be dissected. It is meant to be experienced—beyond reason, beyond intellect—speaking directly to the part of you that has always known.

Wherever you are, whatever storm you are navigating, these pages will meet you there. They will not walk your path for you, but they may illuminate it when the way seems dark.

I am only a medium.
You are the protagonist of your life.

If even one soul emerges stronger, sees clearer, loves deeper, or awakens more fully after reading this, then this book has fulfilled its purpose.

You will meet yourself—raw, unarmored, awake—and for the first time, you will not look away.

Beyond fear, a life awaits—not louder, not grander, but truer. And you will not walk this path alone.

If a girl who lived through a thousand silent deaths before thirty could rise through faith alone, then ask yourself: what is truly stopping you?

Meri Jhaai is now yours.

I am with you in spirit. If you feel lost or overwhelmed, pause—but do not abandon the journey. Trust its unfolding.

Whether it is me, Anjali, or Sonia beside you—steady, unwavering—you will be reminded to keep moving forward.

Even if the world doubts you, I will not. I will believe in you and your dreams, even when you falter.

And now, I begin with my favorite character in this book.
I am certain you will not only fall in love with this character—you will rise in love

Sonia

In the late 1980s, Sonia was born on a crisp winter afternoon in Delhi, the eldest daughter of a simple, middle-class Punjabi family. From the very first moment, she was wrapped in love—her Jhaai cradling her in soft cotton and mul, humming lullabies that seemed to protect her tiny world. Her father called her his pride; her mother, her little star—until a younger sibling arrived two years later.

In 1994, at the age of five, life changed. The family moved to Mumbai, and the distance from her beloved Jhaai left Sonia adrift. Her body weakened, her spirit dimmed. Doctors insisted she return to Delhi, to the home that had nurtured her soul. For the next six months, she lived again under her grandmother's care—in a house filled with warmth, the memory of her late grandfather, and the small rituals of love that shaped her earliest days.

Mornings smelled of freshly fried parathas, sweetened milk, and the faint perfume of roses from the terrace garden. Sonia would walk across sun-warmed tiles, clutching her favorite blanket, and sit beside her Jhaai—green eyes wide with curiosity—watching winter light spill gold across the rooftops.

Together, they laughed over flour-covered hands, sticky fingers, and the mischievous joy of making pinni. Even when her parents could not fully understand her, her Jhaai always did—sensing her fears, her questions, and the unspoken longings of her heart.

Afternoons were for stories—of undivided India, of childhoods once lived differently, of heroes, courage, and quiet kindness. Her Jhaai's voice rose and fell like music, filling every corner of the home.

As the sun dipped into shades of copper and rose, Sonia would curl into her grandmother's lap, resting against a heart that loved her beyond measure.

"Be ethical. Speak your truth. Stand tall even when you stand alone," her Jhaai would say.

Those words etched themselves into Sonia's soul, quietly shaping her into someone brave and bold, though the world often taught her to hide that fire.

After six beautiful months in Delhi, Sonia returned to Mumbai to join preschool—but this time, her Jhaai came with her.

School, however, was a battlefield. Sonia struggled to express herself, to speak fluently, and to ask for what she needed. Teachers misunderstood her quiet intelligence; classmates overlooked her insight. Yet she remained responsible, sincere, and deeply aware of her duties—qualities that set her apart even when the world seemed unkind.

She learned early that the world could be cruel, manipulative, and unforgiving. Trust was fragile; betrayal came too often. Still, she remained steadfast—loyal, patient, and quietly resilient. Her mind was sharp, her words thoughtful, her heart unwavering. She loved deeply, questioned endlessly, and refused to surrender to despair.

After thirty-one years of unwavering love, the heart of her world—88 years old her Jhaai—left her.

The home that once held laughter, warmth, and safety now echoed in silence. The world outside, already harsh and unyielding, felt colder than ever. Sonia searched for love, for guidance, for the comfort she had always known—and found only betrayal, indifference, and heartbreak.

How does one survive when the anchor of life is gone?
How does one rise when the hands that held you steady are no longer there?
How does one find light in a world determined to extinguish it?

This is the story of what came next—of a heart that refused to surrender to despair, and of a journey that would shape Sonia in ways the world could never have imagined. A journey of courage, awakening, divine grace and truth waiting to be discovered.

And now… Sonia speaks.

From the next page, she will guide you, challenge you, make you laugh, make you cry, and take you into the heart of her world.

Listen closely.

For Sonia is no longer just a child nurtured by love—she is a voice, a fire, a story just beginning.

CHAPTER 01

Krishna Calling

Thursday, 20 February 2025 I Mumbai

"Didi, I hope you've reached the airport on time this time!"

TINGG!

A message lit up my screen—**Riya**, my cousin in Ludhiana, with her usual blend of concern and playful sarcasm.

If only she knew.

I pride myself on being punctual. Truly, I do. And yet, somehow, the universe conspires to turn every airport departure into a cinematic affair. It is a strange paradox: I build in ample buffer time—an entire hour, sometimes more—just to be safe. I have never missed a flight in my life. Never.

And yet… the drama. Oh, the drama.

From the outside, you would think I thrive on chaos. The way I dart around the house like a woman possessed, barking out last-minute reminders, dragging my younger brother into my urgency—it is enough to make anyone assume I am on the verge of catastrophe.

"She's definitely going to miss her flight today," a bystander might whisper, watching the frenzy unfold.

But not my siblings. They have seen this spectacle too many times to be fooled.

"She's Sonia Didi," they say with a knowing smile. "She will pull it off—she always does."

There was a day—unforgettable, almost cinematic—when I rang up Vistara's counter in Jaipur on my return from Khatu

Shyam Ji and asked them to delay the flight. Not requested—asked, as if I had the authority to reroute air traffic. I invented a last-minute emergency, delivered with such conviction you would think I was either a VIP or the secret owner of the airline.

And somehow, they listened.

I raced through the terminal like a woman on a mission—bag swinging, heart pounding—arriving just as the gate agent was preparing to close the doors. I did not walk onto that plane. I claimed it—panting, triumphant, and unapologetically late.

It has always been like this. Trains, flights, anything with a departure time—I flirt with the edge, dancing dangerously close to disaster, and yet somehow I always make it. Not out of luck, but sheer, inexplicable will.

The world may roll its eyes, but it waits for me just long enough. There is something oddly thrilling about these close calls, as though the universe watches me on the edge of disaster… only to step back at the last second and let me pass.

And mind you, I am only running from pillar to post at airports and train stations. In my professional life, I am the goddess of punctuality—so punctual I could schedule a meeting in my sleep and still show up five minutes early, coffee in hand.

Just as I finally allowed myself to breathe, the airport speakers crackled to life:

"Boarding for flight QP-1491 from Mumbai to Varanasi will commence in thirty minutes. Passengers are requested to remain seated."

I exhaled, a small victorious smile playing on my lips. I immediately called **Riya** and my brother, letting them know the storm had passed.

"I'm finally seated at the gate, relaxing."

They answered in unison.

"Shukar hai," they both said, followed by the familiar abrupt end of the call. No questions, no drama. They knew the drill.

It is strange—when you are racing through terminals with adrenaline as your co-pilot, basic needs like food or the bathroom feel irrelevant. But now, with time on my side, everything came rushing back. Hunger growled like a petulant child. Fatigue clung to my limbs.

I scanned the waiting area and found an empty seat tucked away in a quieter corner. I sank into it with a sigh, the cold metal frame grounding me. Tick. Tick. Tick. A rhythmic ticking reached my ears—deliberate, almost meditative. I turned slightly.

Beside me sat a woman of quiet grace, somewhere in her late thirties or early forties, applying chandan (sandalwood paste) and kumkum (sacred vermilion) with delicate precision. Her lips moved silently in chant, and in her hand, a small plastic device clicked with each repetition—a quiet heartbeat of devotion tucked inside circuitry. Her fingers moved with the steady rhythm of someone far removed from the clamor of boarding announcements and overpriced snacks.

It was a surreal juxtaposition—ancient prayer flowing through a modern shell, sacred time unfolding in the middle of a departure lounge.

I watched her for a moment, quietly intrigued. How easily some people carry their sanctity with them, I thought. A temple within their minds.

I, on the other hand, require space. Solitude. Silence. A physical boundary between the sacred and the mundane.

But my stomach had no such boundaries.

With a sigh, I stood to hunt down something to eat. As I turned, our eyes met. She paused mid-chant, and we shared a fleeting, wordless understanding—the kind strangers exchange in moments of quiet trust. I gestured toward my bags and gave her a polite nod, silently asking her to watch them. She returned the nod with serene assurance.

Without hesitation, I walked toward the food court, my mind already wrapped around the idea of comfort food. It had been a while since I allowed myself something indulgent, something soul-satisfying.

At the counter, I ordered a hot, cheesy veg burger and a molten chocolate brownie—extra rich, just the way I liked it. I double-checked that it was eggless. Something about traveling solo to a tirtha (pilgrimage site) made me extra cautious, as if purity extended all the way to pastry.

And as I waited, the aroma of food curling around me, I felt something shift—a strange but welcome stillness. As if this trip, already offbeat, was quietly preparing to change something deep within me.

I settled back into my seat, nearly finishing my burger, when I noticed a little girl—about six years old—watching me intently, eyes wide as I savored each bite. She glanced at her parents and quietly asked for a burger or a snack.

They gently said no.

"Not now, sweetheart. Once we're on the flight," they told her, handing over a toy to keep her busy.

If I had ever asked my parents for something like that, their reply would have been a chorus of:
"Such spoiled kids! Why can't you eat at home if we're traveling?"

It is the classic middle-class—or even upper-middle-class—parent dilemma, isn't it? The gentle refusals, the quick distractions, the unspoken rules about when and where you are allowed to indulge.

Watching that hopeful little face turn to her toy, I couldn't help but smile. Some things really do stay the same.

But it wasn't just contentment—I was swept away by a joy so intense it spilled over, unstoppable and raw. I felt weightless, drifting above the chaos of life, as if I had fallen in love all over again. I call it freshly baked love—that warm, radiant kind, still tender at its heart, alive with hope and endless possibility.

It is the flutter of restless butterflies deep in your stomach, the sudden catch in your breath, the way your heart races even when nothing extraordinary is happening. It is the quiet thrill of thinking about someone—just one person—so often that their smile becomes a secret soundtrack playing behind your every moment. It is the dizzying mix of vulnerability and exhilaration, the way every glance, every touch, feels electric and new.

Your eyes begin to see the world in vivid, impossible colors, as if painted just for you. It is a smile that refuses to fade, no matter what storms rage around you. Even when someone is angry or hurtful, you remain calm, anchored by a force far greater than yourself.

Because love is not just a feeling—it is a force. Quiet, fierce, and relentless. It breaks down walls, mends fractured pieces within, and carries you through the darkest nights. It gives you strength when you believe you have run out, softens the sharpest edges of your soul, and whispers that no matter what, you will endure, you will forgive, you will keep loving.

That freshly baked love—wild, untamed, and unyielding—reminds you that hope is real. It is the reason you open your heart again, the reason you risk pain, the reason you believe, deep down, that love will always find a way to conquer.

Alright, ladies and gentlemen, before you start weaving your own tales, before the assumptions settle in—let me be absolutely clear.

I am not in love.

Not with anyone else.

This is not about late-night texts or stolen glances across crowded rooms.

This is not about someone sweeping me off my feet.

No.

This feeling surging through me—this quiet fire—is not for another soul.

It is for mine.

For the first time in my life, I have turned inward and seen myself not as a collection of flaws to be fixed or parts to be hidden, but as a whole being—worthy, wild, and radiant.

I have chosen myself. Fiercely.

With the same tenderness I once reserved for others, I now hold my own heart.

With the same loyalty I once gave away too easily, I now stand by my own side.

This is not falling in love.

This is rising—rising into love. A love that is not soft or quiet, but elemental. A love that burns through shame, that silences the old voices telling me I am not enough. It feels like I have finally exhaled after years of holding my breath, like I have broken free from a cage I did not even know I was in.

I am falling into rhythm with my own breath, in love with the stretch of my skin, the curve of my thoughts, the storm and stillness of my soul. I feel liberated. This love does not wait to be invited—it breaks the door down. It is my revolution. It is my homecoming.

And after all the years spent begging for scraps of affection, I have become my own feast. Yes, after all this time, I have finally fallen in love—and this time, it is with myself.

LOVE.

Yes, love makes you do crazy things. Not the kind of love that is written in rom-com scripts or sung about in heartbreak ballads. I am talking about the kind of love that only you understand—

when the world looks at you like you have lost it, but deep down, you know you have finally found yourself.

When you love someone—or something—with all your being, you are willing to break every door that tries to keep you away. You walk the extra mile, climb the impossible, tune out the noise. Because when love calls, you show up. No matter what.

Today, I almost broke every heart that tried to stop me from going to Mahakumbh—a major Hindu spiritual gathering held every twelve years in India. I did not just go against opinions; I went against expectations, fears, and so-called wisdom. Every voice that tried to lecture me—giving me "gyan" (spiritual knowledge or advice) about how unsafe or unnecessary this trip was—became background noise to the only voice that mattered: my soul.

Are you kidding me? My soul had already decided. So who was I to ignore it?

I stopped explaining. I stopped convincing. I stopped sharing my plans altogether—even with the people I love the most. Yes, that includes my parents, especially my father, whom I adore with every fiber of my heart and soul.

But this… this was my journey. A journey I had to take alone. A calling I could not deny.

I did not want to hurt him. I did not want to make him worry. With him sitting all the way in the United States, the last thing I wanted was to burden him with concern about my whereabouts. Worrying him was not on my list—it was not even the last thing on it. It simply was not an option.

So I told him a version of the truth—softened at the edges. I said I was going with a group of friends, that they had VIP access, that some were from the Army, and it was all planned and secure. Just enough to let him breathe, not quite enough to let him in.

He did not protest. By now, he knew he could not control my choices—especially when it came to my spiritual journeys. He had seen enough of me to know that once my soul decided, I followed.

But still, with that quiet softness only a father carries, he said:

"Dekh le, Nona…" (Look, my child — affectionate nickname he uses for me)
"Mahakumbh (a major Hindu spiritual gathering) has become such a hype these days. Everyone is running like it is some trend. What is the need to go right now? If you can skip it, skip it, beta (child). We have taken all of you kids to Haridwar (a holy city in India) so many times. It is the same thing—baat toh ek hi hai (it is essentially the same thing). Apni safety pehle dekh (first take care of your safety)."

I kept quiet, trying to let the moment pass, hoping he would stop there. But then, after a pause, he added softly—like he already knew the answer:

"But knowing you… I know you have already made up your mind. You will go, no matter what I say. So just… be safe, please. And let me know if you want me to arrange anything for you."

I smiled and said, "Thank you, Daddy. I will be safe, I promise."

Then I gently changed the subject—and ended the call.

But the truth? It was beyond necessary. There was no other option. No negotiation. This was something I had to do. Something already written into the blueprint of my being.

He still does not know it was a solo trip. Maybe he will find out later—when I find my purpose in life.

Maybe then he will understand that when the soul calls, you do not ask for permission. You answer.

The Sibling Pact (Also Known As: "We Don't Snitch")

Honestly, my younger brother, Gaurav—Goru Bhai—knew better than to waste time trying to talk me out of things.

He did not bother with the usual "Are you sure this is safe?" or "Have you thought this through?" Instead, he gave me that classic wide-eyed look and said, in the most resigned voice ever:

"Didi, please… just be safe. And please, don't get lost."

I flashed him a grin, full Bollywood-hero style.

"Tu chal mere saath, toh I won't get lost." (If you come with me, I won't get lost.)

He immediately backed away, hands in the air like I had offered him a lifetime supply of trouble. Then came a dramatic bow, hands folded like he was standing before a temple idol.

"Mujhe maaf karo, yeh sab sirf aap hi kar sakte ho!" (Forgive me, only you can do all this!)

I was still laughing when he suddenly switched to interrogation mode.

"Wait—did you actually tell Daddy about this 'much-awaited solo trip'? What am I supposed to say if he asks? And did you tell Kake Didi?"

Kake Didi—Ruchi—my younger sister by just two years, yet carrying herself with the authority of a full-fledged elder sibling. Settled in Canada with her loving husband and two adorable children, Maya and Jai, she still somehow manages to keep tabs on me as if it were her unofficial side hustle.

"I have not told her," I said, very strategically. "And I might just… not."

Because with her, things do not stay contained—they sometimes travel.

But when I finally told her, she completely surprised me.

"Whaaat! Solo trip? That is amazing, Didi! Go, have fun—and take a holy dip for all of us!"

No overthinking. No cross-questioning. Just instant excitement and full support.

Honestly, I had a whole explanation ready. Completely wasted.

With Mom in Delhi and Daddy on a need-to-know basis, I stuck to my carefully edited version of events. But now—with my sister clearly on my side—I felt like I had already won half the battle.

Ah, there it was. The real sibling dilemma.

If you have grown up with siblings, you will know: Indian parents have a magical sixth sense that tells them when one child is up to something. But instead of asking the actual culprit, they interrogate the most nervous-looking sibling in the room. It is like emotional polygraph testing—with zero warning.

And in most families, the youngest one always slips up. They crack. They blurt things out. They accidentally confess to crimes they did not even commit.

But not in our house.

In our house, we are professionals.

We—me, Ruchi, and Gaurav—have an unspoken pact: no one snitches, no one breaks, no matter what.

So if our parents start grilling Goru Bhai, he just puts on his best confused face and says:
"I do not know… I don't know what is going on."

No eye contact. No extra words. Just confusion.
Translation - plausible deniability, level 100.

And the second he escapes the interrogation?
Phone call. Instant update.

"Oi, they are asking questions. Handle it. I repeat: HANDLE IT."

It is like a secret sibling spy network operating under high parental surveillance. And we? We are blessed. Not just because we are close, but because we trust each other with our lives—and also with secrets that could get us grounded for eternity.

We do not need passwords. We do not need meetings. We just know.

Because in this wild world of family drama and parental sneak attacks, there is only one rule that truly matters:

Siblings who do not snitch, stay rich… in freedom.

It was such a simple exchange—but honestly, one of my favorite moments.

When Goru Bhai looked at me and said:
"Jao, jeelo apni zindagi. Main sambhal lunga." (Go, live your life. I will handle it.)

It made me laugh at first. Classic filmy line. So over the top. So him.

But underneath the drama… there was love. There was trust. And more than anything, there was that quiet understanding that sometimes, no one else can walk the path for you—even if they want to, even if they would drop everything to go with you.

This one was mine to take.

And Kake and Goru Bhai, my younger siblings, understood that better than anyone else ever could.

I stopped telling people I was going to Mahakumbh. Not because I was hiding anything—but because I did not want to invite negative energy, doubts, or unsolicited opinions into something so sacred to me.

In my mind, I had already taken that holy dip a thousand times. I had imagined it, dreamed it, felt it in every corner of my being. This journey was not about planning—it was about fulfilling a vision my soul had already lived. All that was left now was to go there in the flesh and let the body catch up with the spirit.

When you truly, deeply want something—when your heart is in complete alignment and your intentions are pure—the universe somehow conspires to make it happen. And believe me, that is not just a line from an SRK movie. It is real. My truth. I have felt it time and again—moments when everything seems impossible, yet the path opens up, as if the universe softly whispers: "You are meant to be here."

The rest—the why, the how, and what followed—I will share when I talk about my time at the Mahakumbh. Because that is when everything truly began to shift.

Just as I finished the last bite of my burger, the woman beside me slowly opened her eyes, pausing her chant. She glanced over with a tentative smile carrying quiet warmth.

I returned it with a broad grin—showing all thirty-two teeth—and said, "Hi, I am Sonia. What is your name?"

She smiled shyly and replied, "Radhe Radhe! I am **Nidhi**."

"Hi! Are you traveling alone?" she asked gently, curiosity mixed with concern.

I smiled, slightly too proudly, and said, "YESSSSS."

Her eyes widened. "Kahan ja rahe ho?" (Where are you going?)

"Filhaal Varanasi, and then Kumbh—Mahakumbh!" I replied, excitement rising in my voice.

Her gaze sharpened. "Akele?" (Alone?)

My smile softened as I met her eyes. "Yes. Kya hua?" (Yes. What happened?)

She hesitated. "Aapko dar nahi lagta?" (Aren't you afraid?)

"Dar kaisa?" (Fear of what?) I replied.

"Kuch ho gaya toh?" (What if something happens?) she asked softly.

I shrugged. "Arre, kuch nahi hoga. My Krishna is protecting me."

That is when I noticed her smile—a quiet, knowing curve, like a shared secret.

In that moment, something connected between us—effortlessly, unexpectedly.

Strange, isn't it?

But let me tell you how this meeting unfolded.

She greeted me softly, "Radhe Radhe." I replied instinctively, "Hare Krishna."

For a moment, I wondered if I had done something wrong by not matching her greeting.
But I quickly stopped myself.

Shut up, Sonia. Do not embarrass yourself now.

She stood about five feet six inches tall, her broad shoulders giving her quiet strength that contrasted with her soft complexion.

Side-swept strands framed her face. Behind delicate glasses, her deep brown eyes held a flicker of vulnerability beneath composed stillness.

Each time she closed her eyes in prayer, faint lines appeared on her forehead—revealing the anxiety she carried silently about traveling alone.

She lived in Daman and was used to early-morning travel, when the world is still half-asleep in quiet shadows.

That morning, she had taken an early train to Mumbai and met a college friend for lunch in Borivali.

Now she was heading to Varanasi first, then Prayagraj, to meet her parents the next day.

I asked gently, "Why are you not traveling with your family?"

Her smile faded slightly, almost wistful, as if the question touched something delicate.

"I am married now," she said softly. "I live in Daman. My parents are in Pune—they will be traveling with my sister, brother-in-law, and the kids. I am going alone because they will join me later."

Her voice lowered. "Honestly, I get anxious traveling alone."

No drama. No complaint. Just honest acceptance of her fear.

But something about her—alone yet steady—stayed with me.

This was not just a journey. It was a leap of faith.

I said gently, "Why be scared? This is a sacred pilgrimage—a tirtha—and you are also getting time with yourself. Solo journeys reveal things we miss in noise and routine."

She gave a small smile and looked away, lost in thought.

I softened my tone again. "Is everything arranged? Your hotel in Varanasi? Tomorrow's travel?"

"Yes," she replied. "The hotel is booked, and the driver will pick me up in the morning. I will reach Prayagraj by noon."

Her words were calm—but her energy wasn't.

There was stillness in her.

Not peace.

But the quiet pause before something unknown.

I leaned in, curiosity edged with concern. "Then what's really on your mind?"

She hesitated—not out of reluctance, but as if she was choosing the right words to match the weight in her heart.

Before she answered, I asked lightly, "Do you work, or are you a homemaker?"

Her gaze met mine, steady and sure.

"I'm an astrologer, numerologist, and tarot card reader."

As I took a bite of my brownie, it caught in my throat. She noticed immediately and handed me water, gently rubbing my back. Concern softened her features. "Are you alright?"

I smiled, brushing it off but steady inside. "**Nidhi,** you're so spiritual and wise—why did you feel scared?"

Her voice dropped, almost secretive. "It's Uttar Pradesh. Traveling alone. Staying alone. That long drive to Prayagraj by myself. What if something goes wrong?"

There it was—fear, plain and raw. But more than that, vulnerability. The kind that comes from stepping into the unknown without a safety net.

She didn't need logic right then. She needed faith.

I met her eyes, calm and unwavering. "Nothing will happen to you. Trust me. Krishna walks with you. When He's by your side, what could possibly go wrong?"

That's when I noticed the delicate peacock feather tattoo on the inside of her left wrist—almost hidden, yet a quiet symbol of devotion.

I smiled gently and pointed.

"You carry His mark. And still you doubt? If people like us—who believe—start to lose faith, if we let fear drown out trust, even God might wonder, 'How can I help those who refuse to believe I am already here?'"

She was silent, but something in her shifted—the tension in her shoulders eased, her breath deepened, and her eyes found a new steadiness.

The silence between us turned sacred.

Then, without warning, she pulled me into a hug.

"Sonia," she whispered, her voice trembling with gratitude, "Krishna sent you to me. This is a sign. My journey will be blessed."

I hugged her back, a smile blooming across my face.

"Of course it will be," I said gently.

Then, with a playful glint in my eye, I added,
"He doesn't really have a choice now, does He?"

As our conversation unfolded, layers of each other's lives gently revealed themselves. With every word, we found new threads of connection, a shared humanity bridging the space between us.

Suddenly, an announcement broke the moment:
"All passengers, please be ready to board now."

We exchanged a glance, a quiet wish lingering in the air—for more time, more stories, more of this unexpected kinship. In unison, we murmured, "Pata nahi kab milenge." (We don't know when we will meet again.)

Though we sat side by side on the bus, it wasn't just physical proximity—it was a closeness of spirit. Before parting, we exchanged numbers.

She smiled softly and said, "Chalo phir, dekhte hain." (Alright then, let's see.)

I returned her smile warmly. "Yes, see you soon."

As we prepared to part ways, she suddenly turned and asked, "Sonia, what's your seat number?"

"18E," I replied.

She grinned and said, "I'm 18F."

We both erupted into joyful laughter, hugging each other tightly. In perfect unison, we exclaimed, "IT'S A SIGN!"

In that instant, I saw her confidence soar to a whole new height—the nervousness replaced by radiant assurance.

By now, we were so comfortable in each other's presence that every word was unfiltered and genuine. We spoke freely about our education, upbringing, culture, and careers. And, as if drawn by an unseen thread, our conversation gently circled back to our favorite subject—Krishna.

I've wanted to visit Vrindavan in Mathura for as long as I can remember. It's more than just a place to me—it's a deep longing, a promise I made to myself. I had nearly decided to make it my birthday trip in January 2025. But I want that first visit to be unforgettable—something that stays with me forever.

More than anything, I want to take my younger brother with me. He's not exactly eager, but this journey feels incomplete without him—my favorite person, my baby brother, "Goru Bhai." He means the world to me in ways words can't fully express.

There's so much about him I'll share with you later. For now, let's return to Krishna—because that's where our story truly begins.

Nidhi's face lit up, her eyes sparkling with a mixture of joy and reverence as she spoke of Vrindavan. A chill ran down my spine, goosebumps rising along my arms. My eyes widened, caught in a moment so electric it felt as if a sudden shock had passed through me.

I was so lost in the moment that the world around me began to blur—the hum of the aircraft, the shuffle of passengers, even time itself. It was only when the flight attendant leaned in, her voice soft but firm, asking us to fasten our seat belts, that reality briefly returned. We nodded, almost reluctantly, as if being pulled away from somewhere far more real than the present.

Because where we truly were… was with Him.

We spoke of Krishna not as a distant God seated on a pedestal, but as someone intimately woven into our lives—someone who lingered in ordinary moments, pulling up a chair at the dining table, smiling through our laughter, and standing silently beside us in our most fragile hours. He wasn't someone we prayed to—He was someone we lived with.

Nidhi's eyes shimmered with something I couldn't quite name as she reached for her phone. "I have to show you this," she said.

It was a video—simple, unpolished. But what it held was anything but ordinary.

There she was—barefoot, in Nidhivan.

The sacred grove seemed to breathe around her, wrapped in the golden hush of temple lamps and the distant echo of bhajans. She told me how she had met a family there, how she had begun dancing playfully with one of the young girls—just a moment of joy, nothing planned.

And then—something shifted.

The crowd faded. The noise dissolved. Even the little girl drifted away.

What remained… was her.

Alone.

And yet—not alone.

Her movements changed. They slowed, deepened—like something ancient had taken over. There was no audience now, no self-consciousness, no effort to be seen. It was as if she had stepped into a space where only devotion existed.

She wasn't dancing anymore.

She was answering a call.

Her limbs moved with a grace that didn't feel learned, but remembered. Each step, each turn, felt like a whisper offered to the divine. Her face—soft, luminous—held a kind of surrender that cannot be performed, only felt.

And in that moment, something within me stilled.

Because what I was hearing… what I was seeing through her words… did not feel like a story.

It felt like a return.

Radha, I thought.

Radha had found her way back to Nidhivan.

And if, in that sacred stillness, Krishna had stepped forward to meet her, no one would have questioned it—least of all me.

The crowd stood motionless, suspended between awe and disbelief. And then—applause. Not polite claps, not casual admiration. This was reverence—heavy and electric—

reverberating through the temple air, as if even the lamps themselves bowed in recognition.

Nidhi's voice fell to a whisper, trembling with wonder:

"It felt like He was really there."

The family she had danced with began to leave—smiles exchanged, hands folded, compliments murmured. **Nidhi** praised the young girl's effortless grace. A few photos were taken, hands joined in quiet prayer, and then silence lingered like incense in the warm night air.

In the intoxication of the moment, **Nidhi** had completely forgotten to ask for the video the girl had recorded—or to take down her contact details. The dance had swallowed them both, leaving only memory: vivid, untouchable, suspended in the glow of the temple lamps.

The next morning, as **Nidhi** sat quietly at breakfast, lost in thought, a familiar presence appeared.

It was her—the same girl.

Their eyes met, and in that instant, a quiet warmth passed between them—fleeting yet eternal, like the first light of dawn brushing against skin.

"Radhe Radhe," they greeted each other.

Nidhi didn't pause. She asked, her voice urgent with anticipation, "The video?"

The girl's reply was teasing, almost mischievous: "You won't get them."

Confusion and hurt rippled through **Nidhi,** but she tried again—softer this time, hope threading every word.

The girl sighed, calm and deliberate, and handed over her phone. "Here. You can see for yourself."

Nidhi scrolled.

Shadows. Blurred movements. The rhythm of her turns, the sway of her feet, even the golden glow of the lamps—all swallowed by darkness, as if Nidhivan itself had absorbed the moment into its sacred silence. The dance existed only in memory, in heartbeat and breath, untouchable by lens or screen.

A chill ran through me as **Nidhi** spoke, her voice barely above a whisper, trembling with awe. My skin prickled; every hair on my arms stood on end.

"Sonia… do you see?" she breathed, her hand brushing mine, eyes wide, luminous, searching mine for understanding.

I stared at her, unable to blink. Goosebumps rose like tiny lightning bolts across my skin.

"Are you serious?"

She nodded slowly—serene, certain—her smile quiet but unshakable.

"You'll understand when you go to Vrindavan."

And in that instant, I felt it—a subtle, insistent pull deep in my chest, a silent whisper threading through time and space.

Not a suggestion. Not a choice.

A calling.

The boy looked up at him with a serene smile, unbothered by the question. Without saying a word, he slid a golden bajuband—an ornate (armlet)—from his upper arm and placed it gently on the counter.

Then, without another glance, he turned and walked away.

Moments later, something strange struck the shopkeeper. He rushed out to call the boy back—but the street outside was empty. The boy had vanished, as if into thin air.

The next morning, the town buzzed with a strange announcement: the bajuband from Baanke Bihari's murti (idol) had gone missing during the night.

As soon as the shopkeeper heard it, his heart skipped a beat. The golden armlet… could it be?

He dropped everything and ran to the temple, clutching the bajuband in both hands. When he arrived, his eyes went straight to the murti—and sure enough, the right arm of Baanke Bihari was bare.

With trembling hands and tearful eyes, he handed the armlet to Prabhu Ji and told him everything.

"Mera jeevan safal ho gaya," he said, overwhelmed.
(My life has been fulfilled.)

"Baanke Bihari ne mujhe darshan diye."
(Baanke Bihari gave me divine vision.)

The bajuband was returned to its rightful place on the deity, but for the shopkeeper, something had changed forever. He had looked into the eyes of a stranger—and seen God.

For a fleeting moment, a skeptical thought crossed my mind—what if the shopkeeper had stolen the bajuband himself?

I turned to **Nidhi** and asked her, half-serious, half-curious. She didn't flinch. Instead, she looked at me with a calm, unwavering gaze and said, "People in Vrindavan don't steal. They're not God-fearing… they're God-loving."

She went on to explain how the shopkeeper was known in the community for his integrity, how Prabhu Ji clearly remembered forgetting to offer the milk and makhan that night, and how the appearance of that specific bajuband was too precise—too divine—to be dismissed as coincidence.

Then **Nidhi** smiled, a quiet reverence in her voice.

"Jahan chamatkar hai, wahan Krishna hai."
(Where there is a miracle, there is Krishna.)

And in that moment, I smiled with her.

Yes, I thought. Some things are not meant to be understood. Miracles and magic exist beyond logic—and that is where Krishna lives.

This holds true in life too:
"Maano toh Bhagwan, na maano toh patthar."
(Believe—and it is God. Don't believe—and it is just a stone.)

I've always found that line both simple and profound. Faith, after all, doesn't demand proof—it asks for presence.

And I'll be honest—I'm not what most would call "extremely religious."

Don't get me wrong. I visit temples, bow my head in reverence, light a diya when I feel grateful—or lost. I fast on certain days, chant a few aartis and shlokas. I grew up hearing, and have stood in long queues at holy places just like everyone else.

But I've never worn my spirituality on my sleeve.

I'm not the type who follows rituals with militant devotion or quotes scripture in daily conversation. Still, somewhere deep within me, there's a quiet belief. A knowing.

To me, faith isn't about how loudly you pray or how many rules you follow—it's about those silent moments when your heart surrenders without needing a reason.

It's in the goosebumps that rise when you hear a bhajan that stirs something deep inside. It's in the tears you can't explain when you stand before a deity and feel truly seen.

I may not be devout in the strictest sense. But I believe in grace. I believe that sometimes, something greater is at work—guiding, watching, showing up in small, impossible ways.

And perhaps… that's enough.

Does anyone else feel this?

There's a voice within us—not always loud, not always logical—but persistent. Whether it whispers in the mind, pulses in the heart, or tugs gently at the gut, it knows. It knows before we do. It sees what our eyes miss. It feels what logic tries to silence.

Over the years, I've come to recognize that voice as the voice of my soul.

It's taken time—years of second-guessing, of silencing it in favor of noise outside. But again and again, life has shown me that voice is never wrong. Not almost never. Never.

We're taught to trust facts, reason, and evidence. We're told to be practical, to weigh pros and cons, to think things through. And yet—how many times has your soul known the answer long before your mind catches up?

That quiet nudge. That unshakable feeling. That sudden knowing, without explanation.

I've stopped brushing it aside.

Because now I understand—when that inner voice speaks, it's not just intuition.

It's guidance.

A kind of divine compass that doesn't scream or argue—it simply knows.

And if we're brave enough to listen, it always, always leads us home.

That inner voice? It comes in many forms.

Sometimes it's a gut feeling.

Other times, raw instinct.

It could be wisdom carved from past mistakes or the quiet ache of unfulfilled desires.

It might rise after hitting the same wall a hundred times, or emerge from stillness after a long, exhausting struggle.

Now, no matter what the world says, no matter how loud the noise, I follow only that voice.

I don't waste time worrying about the how or the what.

I close my eyes, turn inward, and ask my soul where it wants me to go.

And often, it answers.

Sometimes that answer leads to life-changing choices.

And sometimes… it just leads me to pick up one too many things from H&M during the Black Friday sale. 😅
(What can I say? The soul has its own sense of humor too.)

I'll be diving deeper into the idea of the Soul's Calling in the chapters ahead—because trust me, it's way more than just a phrase. It's a way of living, choosing, and most importantly, listening.

Now, let me confess something.

I truly believe I'm one of the funniest girls on this planet.

Some of you might laugh along with me. Others might roll your eyes—and that's okay. I've made peace with both reactions.

Because at the end of the day, I write the way I live—heart wide open, with a touch of unfiltered simplicity.

It's the only way I know how to be.

And if, along the way, I make you smile or think a little deeper—or better yet, both—that's more than enough for me

Coming back to **Nidhi,** our conversation naturally drifted into the bittersweet terrain of life's highs and lows.

You know, the kind of talk that sounds like something everyone has had before, but when you're sitting next to someone who feels as deeply as you do, it becomes something else entirely. Something real.

We spoke about patience—not just as a virtue—but as a slow, silent battle fought every single day.

And perseverance? It's not a glorious, cinematic triumph.

Most days, it looks like crying in silence, failing in private, and still waking up the next morning to try again.
We laughed a little, sighed a lot, and shared those invisible scars—the ones that don't bleed but burn.

Then came that moment—you know the one—when a seemingly casual conversation suddenly hits a nerve.
We talked about how, despite our efforts, resilience, and endless capacity to hold it all together, we've still been misunderstood.
Misread. Misjudged.
That part lingered. Echoed long after our words faded.

Later, sitting alone, I caught myself wondering—how many times had I shown up with love, only to be met with silence?
How many times had I broken into pieces just to protect someone else's version of peace?

And yet—we rise.
Not because we're fearless, but because something inside refuses to give up.
A quiet promise we made to ourselves… or maybe one our soul made to the universe long ago.

Is there a book somewhere that defines all the rights and all the wrongs?
A manual that tells us what it truly means to be a perfect human?

What defines an impeccable mother?
A superhero father?
Or the purest love between siblings?
Are there any real rules for life?

Honestly… I don't know.

What I do know is this: perfection, as we imagine it, doesn't exist.
We aren't gods. We're not meant to be.
Even the scriptures—if you read between the lines—make that abundantly clear.

Take the Mahabharata, for instance. Even Krishna—my beloved Krishna, whom I love more deeply than anyone—wasn't perfect in the way humans define perfection.

He molded truths.
He strategized.
He bent the rules.

But he did it for dharma—for a higher truth.

So no, I'm not pointing fingers. Not even close.

In fact, I can't bring myself to question Him—ever.

But I can reflect.
And when my soul starts to speak, I've learned that my brain and heart sometimes struggle to keep up.
So please… hear me out.

Maybe we're not here to be flawless.
Maybe we're here to be real.

To be raw.
To be cracked open by life—and still keep going, still keep loving.
And if that's not perfection, then I don't know what is.

From my experience—of what we all loosely call "life"—one truth has become undeniably clear: every person carries a unique lens through which they see the world. These views are never random. They are shaped by a blend of internal experiences and external influences—our upbringing, culture, heartbreaks, triumphs, faith (or its absence), and the endless thoughts we don't always voice.

And the most fascinating part? These views aren't fixed. They evolve.

Sometimes slowly, over years of quiet reflection.
Sometimes suddenly, in a moment that changes everything.

A once-rigid atheist may begin lighting a lamp with trembling hands.
A deeply religious soul may walk away from rituals, seeking silence.
A spiritual seeker may lose themselves temporarily in the glitter of the material world.
A career-obsessed mind may one day crave nothing more than love and connection.

And that's the beauty of it—whether we realize it or not, we are all growing. Every interaction, every heartbreak, every uncomfortable truth, every gentle kindness shifts something inside us. Even when it's subtle. Even when we don't see it in the moment. We are, all of us, evolving.

That's what evolution really means—not just biological change, but emotional, spiritual, mental transformation.

We're not here to be finished products.
We're here to change. To shift. To become.

And maybe that's the true purpose of this journey—
Not to arrive, but to keep unfolding.

Lately, I've begun to realize that the deeper our spiritual understanding becomes, the lighter and more meaningful our journey ahead may be—perhaps even bringing us closer to moksha (liberation). We may build homes, earn wealth, and surround ourselves with comforts, but none of these things leave this world with us. What remains is not what we owned, but what we understood, felt, and awakened within ourselves.

I've come to believe that the soul carries forward only its inner growth—the wisdom, awareness, and spiritual understanding gathered through each lifetime. In many ways, we continue from where we left off.

Because of this, my heart has slowly shifted toward nurturing my inner self rather than only chasing material achievements. I'm not rejecting life or its pleasures, but I no longer want them to become the center of my existence. Whatever I gain or lose in this lifetime, I do not want to lose sight of what truly stays with the soul.

Suddenly, the conversation shifted—effortlessly—to our favorite bhajans. It wasn't planned; it just flowed, as most soulful things do. And before we knew it, we were humming the same lines together in perfect rhythm:

"Pakad lo haath Banwari…
Nahi toh doob jaayenge.
Humara kuch na jaayega,
Tumhari laaj jaayegi."

("Hold my hand, O Banwari (Krishna)…
Otherwise, we will drown.
We will lose nothing,
But your honor will be at stake.")

We looked at each other and burst into soft laughter—the kind that comes from deep comfort and shared faith. A few passengers turned to smile at us, not out of annoyance, but with quiet appreciation. It felt like, for a moment, the entire space around us had softened.

Without even realizing it, I leaned my head gently on her shoulder. The bhajan still echoed in my mind like a lullaby. Wrapped in faith, warmth, and a peace beyond words, I drifted off to sleep.

"The flight is about to land. Please open your window shades," the attendant announced.

We woke almost in sync and smiled at each other—still drowsy, yet strangely refreshed. It felt as if we had rested in faith rather than fatigue.

After collecting our bags, we shared a cab into the heart of Varanasi. On the way, she asked, "What's the name of your hotel?"

"Live Free Hostel," I replied with a half-laugh. "Everything else was out of budget—I wanted to stay close to the ghats."

Without hesitation, she said, "Come stay with me."

I smiled, assuming she was joking, and declined. But she insisted softly, "I have a car and driver booked for 9 a.m. tomorrow to Prayagraj. Come with me."

Still unsure, I replied gently, "It wouldn't feel right."

She met my eyes. "Don't think about money. It's an SUV—there's space. You won't pay anything. You'll be more comfortable, and we'll get more time together."

I fell silent. Not from confusion, but from being moved. A stranger from a flight was offering not just space, but trust. It didn't feel transactional—it felt like a soul connection. And I knew, somewhere deep within, that Krishna had woven this meeting.

I finally said, "Your kindness overwhelms me. But I am safe in my solitude. My stay is confirmed, and my ticket for the evening train is booked."

Inside me, a quiet conviction had already taken shape—a promise to follow the path I had chosen, even when easier ones appeared.

Had I been stranded, I would have taken her offer as grace. But everything was already in place. To change course now would feel like breaking a silent agreement with myself.

This was not pride or stubbornness, but reverence for the journey itself.

A voice within me said clearly:

"Sonia, there is a reason you chose this path. Trust it."

It is easy to be pulled toward comfort and distraction. But I was meant for something else—to follow my inner calling, even when it is misunderstood. When the world turns left, I turn right.

My path is not easy, but it is mine. And I want to live in a way that lets me meet myself with respect in the mirror.

Nidhi's offer was kind and practical—especially in a crowded place like Mahakumbh. But I am not just a woman navigating safety. I am someone learning to stand fully in her own strength. Others may call it recklessness; I call it clarity.

I'm grateful I trusted my path, because it brought me here.

I embraced discomfort—the crowded train, the humble hostel, walking alone through the ghats—and slowly began to feel free in my own company.

In short, I was falling in love with myself.

Nidhi is a beautiful soul, and perhaps things would have been different had I accepted her offer. But this was my choice—the harder, quieter, truer path. Like a diamond shaped under pressure, it was meant to refine me.

She smiled as she left. "If you change your mind, you know where to find me." I smiled back, grateful but firm.

At her stop, she hugged me. "You came to me like Krishna when I was nervous. Be safe."

As she left, I felt it again—not a voice, but a presence. Krishna's call, woven into silence.

Vrindavan has never been just a place for me; it has lived like a quiet longing within me. I have waited to go there not alone, but with my younger brother, Goru Bhai—my constant companion in this journey of becoming.

I don't know when that path will open. But I know this: when it does, I will not hesitate. I will go.

Because Krishna's call never arrives early or late.

It arrives exactly when it must.

And when it does, everything else falls silent.

This is not the end. It is the beginning of being called.

CHAPTER 02

Shamshan Se Shiv
Part I: Manikarnika, The Burning Ghat

It was 11:30 at night, yet the streets still glowed, and the ghats lay open—silent, ancient, and alive. I knew the morning would bring its own chaos: waves of pilgrims, blaring horns, the crush of footsteps echoing through narrow lanes. I wanted to reach the Kashi Vishwanath Temple before all that.

But tradition stood in the way.

They say you don't walk into Shiva's sanctum without first facing the gatekeeper—Kaal Bhairav, the Kotwal of Kashi. Not just a ritual, but a warning. Fierce, dark, and watchful, he guards the city itself. Some call him the punisher of those who act without dharma; others, the protector of seekers who walk the razor's edge between worlds.

I checked the time and saw that the Kaal Bhairav temple had shut at 10:30 p.m. I couldn't make it on time. It wouldn't reopen until 5:30 a.m. I stood still, unsure for a moment.

Then I let go.

If the door was closed, perhaps it was meant to be. I chose to surrender—not to circumstance, but to something larger. If I were meant to stand before Bhairav, I would. And if not, then perhaps Shiva would still see me, wherever I came from. I decided I would walk toward Vishwanath Ji anyway, and if Kaal Bhairav came along the way, I'd stop. I didn't need a perfect sequence. I needed presence.

Before arriving in Varanasi, I had made myself a quiet promise: with only twenty hours in this overwhelming city, I would stay grounded. No chasing checklists. I would follow tradition where

I could, but trust my instincts when I couldn't. My safety and intuition would be my compass; the sacred would follow.

And yet, something about Bhairav lingered. Not as a missed stop, but as a challenge left unresolved. He is the one who strips you bare before you meet Shiva—not through fire or storm, but through a single, unblinking gaze. To stand before him is to stand before your own fear, ego, and illusion. Perhaps that's why they say his blessing must come first. He doesn't let you meet Shiva with baggage.

Maybe that's what this night was for.

As I stepped out of the e-rickshaw one kilometer away from my hostel, adjusting my sling bag and shawl against the night chill, my eyes caught a Pandit ji nearby. He was quietly helping someone arrange their travel. On an impulse, I approached him and asked softly, "Pandit ji, do you have any connections at the Kashi Vishwanath Temple? Is there a way to get a VIP pass, something to skip the long queues?"

I know what you might be thinking—after coming all this way, why seek a shortcut?

But here's the truth: if there's a way to navigate the chaos without losing the essence of the experience, why not take it? My love for the Divine wasn't measured in waiting hours, but in the quiet truth of my heart when I stood before Him. I wasn't chasing privilege. I was simply seeking presence—one undistracted, sacred moment with my God.

He looked at me for a moment—at my curious eyes, my accent, the way I scanned the street—and smiled knowingly. I clearly didn't belong here, at least not in the geographical sense.

"Aap UP ya MP se toh nahi lagti," he said gently.
(You don't seem to be from UP or MP.)

I returned his smile. "I'm Sonia."

He folded his hands in a half-namaste and said, "Pandit Rohit Pandey. I serve at the Kanchi Kamakoti Peetham Temple, near Hanuman Ghat; it's dedicated to Lord Shiva."

There was a warmth about him—genuine, grounded. Perhaps he sensed my sincerity, or maybe this city was weaving these moments like sacred threads. He told me he knew someone whose father served at Kashi Vishwanath itself. "Let me try to connect you," he said, already dialing the number.

The call went unanswered.

After a pause, he suggested I either visit the temple early the next morning or late at night, mentioning that the gates remain open until 12:30 a.m. As we spoke, he brought up the possibility of arranging quicker access—an informal "VIP entry." Of course, there was an additional cost. We discussed it with ease, and I eventually negotiated it down to ₹500.

In my mind, this wasn't about privilege—it was about practicality. I wasn't rushing the experience; I was just navigating it wisely. Time is precious, and in moments like these, it feels right to use it well.

We began walking slowly toward Dashashwamedh Ghat, the heart of Kashi pulsating around us with a strange, ancient rhythm. The ghats were alive even at this hour—lamps flickering, chants echoing, time itself feeling suspended. As we walked, an old longing stirred within me—my unfulfilled desire to visit

Manikarnika Ghat from my previous trip. It had stayed with me like a whisper in the dark, and now, it rose again with quiet urgency.

Just then, a familiar sound cut through the night—"Mera Bhola Hai Bhandari..."

The bhajan rang out from a phone nearby, and I smiled as I realized it was Pandit Rohit's ringtone. Somehow, it felt perfectly timed, as if Shiva himself had nudged the universe to remind me: You are on the right path.

He answered the call—it was Shubham, the boy he had mentioned earlier, the son of a pandit at the Kashi Vishwanath Temple. Rohit ji assured me that Shubham would come to meet me within 30 to 45 minutes and assist me with the temple visit.

Pandit ji struck me as different—unlike the usual pandits one often encounters. There was an unmistakable calmness about him, a quiet confidence that immediately put me at ease. The moment I approached, he looked at me kindly and said,

"Devi ji, aap fikar mat kijiye, aapke darshan ho hi jaayenge."
(Don't worry, Devi ji, you will surely have your darshan.)

He must have been in his fifties, with a lean frame and a medium complexion. A light beard framed his face, and his hair was tied back in a modest ponytail—a simple yet distinctive look that somehow suited the depth in his eyes. There was something about his presence that felt both reassuring and profoundly sincere.

He asked me if this was my first visit to Kashi. I smiled and said, "Second time. Last time I came with my family, but this time the crowd feels never-ending."

Then he asked about my husband. My mind raced for a moment—saying that I was married, that this wasn't my first pilgrimage, would make me seem older, more mature, and safer in his eyes. Yes, whatever is meant to happen will happen, I thought, but if I can make him believe I'm married, all the better.

So I replied, "Actually, we were supposed to come together, but he's preparing for exams. The dates clashed with our travel plans, so I had to come alone on behalf of both of us. He's arranged my stay and travel, and I have relatives in Prayagraj." I just made all of this up because it felt safe.

I felt a quiet satisfaction at my timing—how spontaneously the moment had unfolded in my favor.

I told him, "Last time, I wanted to visit Manikarnika, but we couldn't make it."

He smiled gently. "Until Shubham calls you back, if you have time, would you mind accompanying me?" I asked.

"Bilkul, chaliye."
(Of course, let's go.)

"Bas aap mujhe pehle apna phone charging pe rakhne dijiye."
(Just let me first put my phone on charge.)

He stayed close to the ghats, the soft glow of oil lamps flickering nearby, casting long shadows. We began walking toward his place. The lanes were dimly lit and unusually quiet—empty except for the distant call of a temple bell, lending the air a mysterious stillness.

"Chai?" I asked, spotting a chaiwala tucked away at the corner of the road.

He smiled, a warmth in his eyes. "Kyon nahi, Devi ji?"
(Why not, Devi ji?)

"Do cutting, please," I said, as the chaiwala busied himself with steaming kettles.

"Are you from Mumbai?" Pandit ji asked, watching me closely.

"Yes," I replied. "How did you know?"

He chuckled softly. "Cutting chai is a Mumbai thing—you don't find it anywhere else."

We shared a quiet laugh and soon found ourselves savoring the strong, hot kulhad chai. The winter chill in the air made it taste even better—earthy, comforting, familiar.

Out of habit, I pulled my shawl over my head, just like the women back home in Punjab

I was dressed simply, exactly the way I loved. A soft, peachish-pink mul cotton kameez, loose and knee-length; my plain salwar gathered softly at my ankles, the quiet counterpart to the delicate pattern above. Instead of a dupatta (a long traditional scarf worn with South Asian clothing), I had draped a warm peach-gray shawl around me—light, but enough to keep the cold at bay.

On my left wrist, my trusted tan-brown Fossil watch with a clean white dial; on my right, my kada (a rigid metal bracelet worn as a symbol of faith)—silent, solid, unwavering. A small red bindi (a decorative mark worn on the forehead in Indian culture) sat centered between my brows like a quiet declaration of identity. My hair was braided in a traditional khajuri choti (a long, tightly braided hairstyle), slightly loose but tidy, and around my neck, a delicate gold chain held a tiny Krishna (Lord Krishna, a major Hindu deity) pendant that rested against my skin like a blessing.

No makeup—just me, as I am. And I love it that way.

Slung across my shoulder was a small black H&M sling bag (a compact cross-body bag from the brand H&M), packed not with clutter, but essentials: my Aadhaar card (Indian national identity document), some cash and a few crisp notes, sunglasses, headphones coiled in a corner, a charger, wet wipes, a tiny pair of scissors, and the lone key to the luggage I'd left safely back at the hostel.

On my feet were plain tan-brown Punjabi juttis (traditional embroidered flat footwear from Punjab, India), simple and comfortable enough to walk as much as I wished.

He then asked, "You don't mind if I have a paan?"

"Please, go ahead," I said.

"Do cutting chai, please," I said.
(""Two servings of cutting chai (small half-glass portions of Indian street tea), please," I said.)

We paid the chaiwala (a tea seller in India) and resumed walking through the winding lanes—just a turn or two away from the ghats (riverfront steps leading to the river Ganga). The scent of the river hung in the air, mingling with faint traces of incense (aromatic substance burned in rituals) and damp stone. Through the gaps between the old buildings, I could glimpse the ghats running parallel to us, flickering with the soft glow of distant diyas (oil lamps used in Hindu rituals).

"Didi! Badi Didi!" ("Sister! Elder sister!") he suddenly called out, his voice warm but firm, echoing through the hushed alley.

I turned to him, curious. "Is this the temple? Do you live here?"

He nodded, a slight smile playing on his lips. "Haan, bas yahi ke paas. Woh meri badi behen hain." ("Yes, just nearby. She is my elder sister.")

"And I'm the poojari (temple priest responsible for performing rituals and worship) here."

There was something humble in the way he said it—no pride, just quiet commitment.

"With the rush of tourists these days, I barely get a few hours of sleep," he added, adjusting the cloth on his shoulder. "Subah ki aarti 5:30 baje shuru hoti hai, chahe neend ho ya na ho." ("The morning prayer ritual begins at 5:30 a.m., whether I have slept or not.")

His voice held no complaint, just a kind of surrender—the kind that comes from years of living with the rhythm of devotion, chaos, and faith.

He handed his phone to his sister to put it on charge, then turned to me and said, "Shubham ka number apne phone mein save kar lo, just in case." ("Save Shubham's number on your phone, just in case.")

Then, with a spark in his eyes, he said, "Main tumhe real Kashi dikhaata hoon." ("I will show you the real Kashi.")

I did—though not without caution. My steps were curious but calculated. I stayed alert, scanning the lanes, reading the energy, and noting every possible exit. After all, what if I got kidnapped?

(Not that it would end well for them. The moment they laid eyes on me, they'd regret it—because once pushed, I can bring hell on earth. Plus, I'm talkative. Imagine trying to kidnap someone who won't stop asking questions and talking your ear off. They'd be begging for mercy by day one. Still, female instincts kicked in, uninvited and dramatic, somewhere between self-preservation and pure Bollywood flair.)

We entered a quiet ghat, and just as I was soaking in the surroundings, I stopped dead in my tracks.

Before me stood a temple—tilted, almost unnaturally, leaning to one side like it had been caught mid-fall and then frozen in time.

"That's Ratneshwar Mahadev (a form of Lord Shiva worshipped in Varanasi)," he said, noticing my gaze. "One of the most mysterious temples in Kashi (ancient sacred name of Varanasi)—tilted at exactly 9 degrees."

"Why is it tilted like that?" I asked, stepping closer, unable to look away.

He smiled faintly, as if he'd been asked that a thousand times. "No one knows for sure. Some say it was built by a servant of Raja Man Singh (a Rajput noble of the Mughal era), who named it after his mother, Ratna Bai. It is believed she once said she had done more for Lord Shiva than even her own son—and that arrogance led to the temple leaning in defiance."

I raised an eyebrow. "Divine ego-check?"

"Something like that," he chuckled. "Others say it's just the result of weak foundations and the waterlogged ground of the ghat (riverfront steps leading to the river). But in Kashi, even science folds its hands before faith."

The temple stood partially submerged during the monsoons (seasonal heavy rainfall period in India), he told me, and yet never fully collapsed. "It leans—but never falls. Like the city itself."

I stared at the tilted shikhara (temple spire or tower), half in awe, half in disbelief. A temple that bowed but didn't break—maybe that's what Kashi does to everything it touches.

And slowly, we began walking toward the next ghat.

Anyone who's truly walked the soul of Kashi knows—it's not just a city, it's a pilgrimage of ghats. There are eighty-four of them, strung along the Ganga (Ganges River, considered sacred in Hinduism) like a garland of time—each carrying centuries of breath, prayer, death, and rebirth. Their names appear just as you arrive, painted or carved onto the ancient stone, as if each one is quietly introducing itself before swallowing you whole.

The ground grew slick beneath my feet—wet, uneven, and cold. The cries of dogs echoed somewhere in the distance, low and long, not unlike mourning. A sudden, almost suffocating warmth hit the air—not from the sun, but something else. Something closer.

Then came the smell. Thick. Pungent. Human. It clung to the throat. It clung to the soul.

The path narrowed. It was crowded, but strangely quiet. Lit with a golden glow that didn't comfort, only revealed. Wooden and bamboo logs (long, dry wooden and bamboo pieces used for cremation) were stacked around us—tall, leaning, dry. They looked fragile, almost threatening, like a single shift would send them crashing down in a blaze of fire and fate.

And then I heard it.

"Ram Naam Satya Hai..." ("The name of Ram is the ultimate truth...") "Ram Naam Satya Hai..."

A voice. Then another. Then many—monotone, heavy, emotionless. Like a chant carved from habit, not heart.

I froze. My chest tightened.

We had entered Manikarnika Ghat (a sacred cremation ground in Varanasi, India, believed to grant liberation from the cycle of rebirth).

The ghat where death never sleeps.
The ghat where flames never die.
The ghat where night never falls—because fire is always burning.

The ground here breathes smoke. It devours everything that touches it. Someone was being cremated just a few feet away. Another body had arrived—wrapped in white, carried by relatives who wore no tears, only duty.

All around me were piles of wood—measured, sorted, sold by weight. Death, like everything else in this country, had a rate card.

They say that if you're cremated here, your soul escapes the cycle of birth and death—Moksha (liberation from the cycle of rebirth in Hindu belief). Liberation. Freedom. An end.

And people want that. They come here to die. They wait here to die. Some are left here, half-alive, half-dead, wrapped in cloth and silence, staring at the sky, waiting for release.

I stood there, frozen in the middle of it all—surrounded by ash, smoke, cracked silence, and the weight of a thousand goodbyes. My eyes scanned everything—the flickering fires, the faces of the mourners, the indifference of the logs, the dust on the priests' feet.

I tried to absorb it. Tried to stay strong. But the truth hit harder than I expected:

This was the end of every story.

Unfiltered. Undecorated. Final.

And still, it was sacred.

All I could see was fire and unbearable warmth surrounding me. People moved with heavy silence, carrying lifeless bodies wrapped in white cloth. One after another, the bodies were laid upon the pyres, and in moments—almost impossibly fast—they turned to ashes, disappearing into smoke that curled upward and vanished into the sky.

"Devi ji! Devi ji! Kya aap thik hain?" ("Lady! Lady! Are you okay?") his voice was low but urgent.

I nodded faintly, my voice barely a whisper. "Yes."

He looked at me with concern. "Chaliye yahan se. Aap theek nahi lag rahi hain. Main aapko dusra ghat dikhaata hoon." ("Let's get out of here. You don't look well. I will show you another ghat.")

I tried to follow him, but as we moved toward the shore, my eyes caught sight of something that stopped me cold.

There, lying side by side, were five or six bodies wrapped head to toe in orange Banarasi cloth (traditional silk fabric from Varanasi, India). Multiple garlands adorned their heads and torsos, but the faces—hidden beneath the layers—left me unable to tell if they were male or female.

I couldn't take another step. I froze.

Pandit ji gently held my hand. "Beta, chalo yahan se." ("Child, let's go from here.")

I wanted to walk away with him, but something inside me refused to move. Clutching his hand tighter, I whispered, "Can we stay here a little longer?"

My eyes burned red, tears threatening to spill. He stared at me, disbelief flickering across his face.

With a heavy breath, I finally broke, my voice trembling. "Pandit ji... please stay with me. Take me back to where the 'Daar Sanskar' is happening." ("Priest... please stay with me. Take me back to where the cremation rituals are happening.")

He understood—I was overwhelmed, caught between wanting to run and the need to witness.

"Mere saath chaliye," he said softly, "aur jaise hi aapko uncomfortable lage, hum chale jaayenge. Vaada." ("Follow me, and the moment you feel uncomfortable, we will leave. Promise.")

I nodded, my heart pounding.

There were two more floors above, like rooftops overlooking the ghats, where the Daar Sanskar (funeral cremation rituals performed in Hindu tradition) rituals were taking place. Pandit ji led me up the stairs, his steps steady and calm.

As we passed by, I caught sight of a Shiva (Hindu deity known as the destroyer and transformer) temple, its ancient walls worn but sacred. At its heart stood a massive Shivling (an abstract representation of Lord Shiva), dark and glistening under the flickering light of a giant jyoti diya (sacred oil lamp flame used in worship). From that single flame, every pyre below seemed to draw its first spark, as if the fire itself was a living thread connecting life and death.

Around us, vendors moved quietly, selling tea, water, flowers, cloth, ghee (clarified butter used in Hindu rituals)—everything needed for the cremation rites. The air was thick with the mingling scents of smoke, incense, and burning wood.

We reached the second floor, and I stopped dead in my tracks.

Around 15 or 16 bodies were being cremated simultaneously.

Flames roared beneath wooden pyres (wooden structures used for Hindu cremation rituals), swallowing one body after another. The moment the last ember turned to ash, water was poured over the remains, and the next was brought forward—unceasing, relentless.

There wasn't even a space to stand.

I turned to Pandit ji, my voice barely more than a whisper, trembling with something I couldn't quite name.

"Kya hum kahin aur khade ho sakte hain? Yeh jagah… yeh unke liye nahi hai. Unhe shanti milni chahiye—aakhri, pavitra vidaai. Par hum, zinda log… hum unhe marne bhi nahi dete. Hum unki aatma ko rok lete hain, unhe Moksha (liberation from the cycle of rebirth in Hindu belief) aur khamoshi dono se door kar dete hain."
("Can we stand somewhere else? This place… it is not for them. They deserve peace—a final, sacred farewell. But we, the living… we do not even let them die properly. We trap their souls, denying them liberation and silence.")

He didn't speak. Only a slow, heavy nod.

We moved to another rooftop, an open terrace far from the smoldering pyres below. From here, the Ganga (Ganges River, considered sacred in Hinduism) stretched out like a dark, endless ribbon, flowing silently past the chaos. Down beneath us, the Daar Sanskar (Hindu cremation rituals performed after death) raged on. Across the way, larger bodies were engulfed by towering flames—fire licking at the sky, hungry and merciless.

We saw everything.

The endless, brutal dance of fire and flesh and spirit—twisting and writhing beneath the open sky, raw and relentless.

A crowd had gathered—tourists and locals alike—phones raised high, indifferent eyes capturing every flicker of flame, every agonized breath, every whispered prayer. I did not raise my phone. To do so felt like a sacrilege, a violation of the sacred, fragile thread between life and death.

Faces surrounded me—faces twisted with grief, curiosity, numbness. Each soul there was caught in their own struggle, their own story.

Some filmed without pause, converting grief into clicks and views. Others spoke casually into phones, as if this hellscape were just another tourist stop, a checkbox on a weary itinerary.

Groups huddled together, some bowed in silent reverence, others wiped tears they dared not show. Quiet sobs broke the heavy air—tears for the last glimpse of a face, the last fading sound of a voice now gone forever.

In the electric tension between grief and spectacle, sorrow and indifference, the ghats whispered their ancient, brutal truth:

Death touches everyone differently—but here, it's impossible to look away.

I stood there, watching it all unfold with quiet intensity. My eyes blurred with unshed tears. My heartbeat slowed to something barely audible. My palms were cold, yet slick with moisture—trembling with a strange, sacred awe.

I was frozen—unable to move, unable to speak. It felt as though something had lodged deep in my throat, choking me silently.

In that suspended moment, a wave of nostalgia (a deep emotional longing for the past) crashed over me, pulling me back through time—to memories I hadn't expected to revisit here, in the shadow of fire and finality.

I lost my grandmother on February 8, 2019, at exactly 9:20 p.m. Since that day, not a single moment passes that she doesn't cross my mind. Today, here amidst the flames and smoke, I felt her presence again—clear and overwhelming.

It was as if I was losing her all over again. The pain, sharp and raw, gripped me with an intensity that nearly broke me. But I didn't flinch. I wanted to stay, to absorb every bit of this moment, to live through this pain rather than escape it.

Something inside me screamed, shouting over the silence: Sonia, this is life. What you're witnessing is not death—this is the undeniable truth, the raw reality of existence.

Pandit ji's voice gently interrupted my thoughts. "Beta, do you want some water?" ("Child, do you want some water?")

I shook my head.

"Beta, pani pi lo," ("Child, drink some water,") he insisted—only the second time he had called me Beta (a Hindi term of affection meaning child; used for someone younger or cared for).

Reluctantly, I took a few sips, then splashed cold water over my face and head.

The sudden chill brought a strange relief, a fleeting lightness that settled over me like a quiet breath.

And just when I thought I had seen the worst life could show me today, I saw them.

A group of men emerged, barefoot, their skin smeared in ash (sacred ash used in Hindu rituals, especially associated with Lord Shiva), like remnants of a forgotten ritual. They wore little more than rags—their bones jutting out, ribs visible, their eyes hollow yet eerily calm. They looked like they belonged more to the dead than to the living. In their hands, they carried long chimtas (large metal tongs used in cremation grounds to handle burning wood and remains), not as tools—but as weapons, or extensions of some ancient, silent duty.

They moved without flinching. No fear. No reverence. Just... detachment. As if death had long stopped meaning anything to them.

I turned to Pandit ji, terror tightening in my chest. My eyes pleaded for an answer—or at least an explanation.

But he simply looked at me and said,

"Himmat hai toh dekho... warna ankhein band kar lo."
("If you have courage, look... otherwise close your eyes.")

There was no pity in his voice. No softness. Just a quiet dare.

And I didn't close my eyes.

I should have.

But something inside me—some cracked, stubborn part—whispered: Face it. Don't look away.

And so I watched.

One of the men stepped into the fire-lit chaos, his silhouette flickering between shadow and flame. He approached a burning pyre, the body on it half-consumed—bones exposed, skin curling like burned paper.

Then, without a word or pause, he reached in with the chimtas (metal fire tongs used in cremation grounds) and lifted a half-burned piece of human flesh from the fire.

Not wood.

Not ash.

Flesh.

He held it for a moment, inspecting it like it was nothing more than a charred offering. Then he turned and walked away, disappearing into the night.

The world tilted.

I couldn't breathe. My legs buckled. The sky, the flames, the smoke—it all blurred into one choking, suffocating darkness.

A thick wave of nausea surged up my throat. I fumbled for my bottle, forced a few gulps of water down—just enough to stop myself from collapsing or vomiting.

Just enough to stay standing. Barely.

I turned to Pandit ji, my voice fractured.

"Let's go. Please… I've seen enough for tonight."

He didn't move. He didn't panic. He just stood there, still and grounded, as if this nightmare was as normal to him as morning tea.

"Paanch minute aur. Bas thoda sa sambhal lo khud ko, phir chalte hain," (Five more minutes,, just calm yourself down and then lets go) he said gently, like he was talking to a child on the verge of tears.

He tried to shift the air—to distract me.

"Mumbai mein kahaan se ho?" (Where are you from Mumbai)

No answer.

Punjabi ho?" ("Are you Punjabi?") Still nothing.

It wasn't silence. It was a shock. A kind of numbness that buries itself in your bones when you've seen too much too quickly. Not because I was ignoring him—I simply couldn't respond. Words had abandoned me. Language didn't belong in this place.

I was suspended somewhere between time and breath, between fire and silence—a place where nothing made sense and yet, everything suddenly did. The weight of what I had just witnessed clung to me like smoke—thick, heavy, inescapable.

And then, Pandit ji spoke again. Softer this time. His voice no longer carried the tone of a guide, but that of something more intimate—a father, perhaps, or a witness who had long made peace with grief.

"Devi ji… yeh toh zindagi ka niyam hai. Jo aata hai, usse ek na ek din jaana hi padta hai."

("Child… this is the rule of life. Whoever comes, one day must go.")

A simple sentence.

Ancient. Final.

No poetry. No comfort. Just… truth.

And somehow, it hit harder than the flames I had just seen devour a body. Because this wasn't just about death. This was about what's left behind. About what never comes back. It wasn't a funeral anymore. It wasn't a ritual. It wasn't even horror. It was reality, stripped bare—unadorned, unkind, and terrifying.

There, in the heart of the ghats (steps and riverfronts along the Ganges used for rituals and daily life), I finally understood:

Death doesn't arrive like a thief in the night.

It waits, patiently, in plain sight.

And one by one, it takes everyone we love, everything we cling to—until all that's left is smoke, memory, and silence.

"Pandit ji," I said, my voice barely steady, "will you please be honest with me? What exactly did I just witness?"

He looked at me with calm, knowing eyes, as if expecting the question. "Aghori babas," he began slowly, "are a sect of Shaiva (followers of Lord Shiva in his ascetic form) ascetics who live on the edges of society, mostly here in Varanasi (Varanasi, Uttar Pradesh, India), especially near the Manikarnika Ghat (a major cremation ground along the Ganges River)—the heart of the cremation grounds."

I swallowed hard, still haunted by the image of that man reaching into the fire.

"But why? Why would someone do what I just saw?" My voice was barely a whisper, trembling between disbelief and something darker: fear.

Pandit ji's expression softened, like a father trying to explain something heavy to a child. "They follow Lord Shiva, in his fierce form as 'Bhairava' (a fierce manifestation of Lord Shiva associated with destruction and transformation)—the destroyer, the transformer. The Aghoris live outside society's rules. They deliberately embrace what most fear—death, corpses, ashes… even flesh."

I felt a chill crawl up my spine. "But eating human flesh?" I asked, voice catching.

He nodded slowly. "It's not like what people think. They don't kill. They take only what is already dead, bodies abandoned and unclaimed."

I stared at him, searching his face for judgment or horror, but found only calm understanding.

"Why?" I asked, my heart pounding. "What drives someone to do that?"

He took a breath. "To break the illusion."

"The illusion?"

"Yes. They believe there is no pure or impure, no sacred or profane. No difference between what we love and what we fear.

To them, the flesh is just matter. The body, a cage of bones. Eating from a dead body, even once, is a way to shatter every fear and taboo society has imposed."

A wave of nausea hit me hard. My stomach twisted, and I nearly vomited on the spot.

The world spun wildly. Legs weak, vision blurred—I was dizzy, sick to my core.

The urge to throw up clawed at me, suffocating. I wanted to scream, to escape this body. But most of all, I wanted to erase what I'd just seen—wipe that memory from my mind forever.

"Most people run from death," he continued gently. "Aghoris sit with it. They meditate beside corpses, smear ashes on their skin. They don't do it to shock anyone—they do it to free themselves from the illusion that this world is clean, safe, or permanent."

I looked away, eyes stinging. The fire flickered behind us, but the weight of his words felt heavier than any flame.

"So it's not cannibalism, then?" I whispered.

He shook his head. "Not in the way you think. They never harm. They never kill. They take only what is already gone. For them, it's not about hunger. It's about truth. And truth," he paused, eyes fixed on the glowing embers, "is always ugly before it sets you free."

Suddenly, from somewhere nearby, a phone's speaker came alive with a haunting melody—the voice singing clear and raw in the quiet night:

"Mat kar maaya ko ahankaar,
Mat kar kaaya ko abhimaan,
Kaaya gaar se kaachee…"

The refrain repeated, folding over itself like a prayer, or a warning.

"Ho kaaya gaar se kaachee,
Jaise os ra motee,
Jhonka pavan ka lag jaae,
Jhapaka pavan ka lag jaae,
Kaaya dhool ho jaasee,
Kaaya teree dhool ho jaasee…"

The lyrics lingered in the air, a tender reminder of the fragility of the body—how it is as fleeting as dew on a leaf, as delicate as dust carried away by the wind.

The flames crackled nearby, devouring flesh and bone without mercy, and yet the song made the night feel almost sacred, a silent teaching whispered through time.

Pandit ji's voice broke the moment, calm and steady:
"Devi ji, yeh Kashi ka sach hai—yahaan sab kuch chhodna sikhata hai. Guroor, ahankaar, moh—sab mitti ki tarah gir jaate hain. Yeh sharir naazuk hai, anitya hai, bas hawa mein udti dhool jaisa hai."
("Child, this is the truth of Kashi—everything here teaches letting go. Pride, ego, attachment—all fall like dust. The body is fragile, impermanent, like dust in the wind.")

The song's refrain echoed inside me, stirring a strange peace amidst the overwhelming darkness.

I whispered to Pandit ji, "Meri daadi kehti thi, 'Na kar ahankaar, sab mitti mein mil jaana hai.'"

("My grandmother used to say, 'Do not be proud, everything will turn into dust.'")

He nodded gently and asked, "Chalein, Devi ji?"
("Shall we go, dear?")

We began walking toward the other ghats, passing silently by the shore where the bodies lay lined up in quiet procession. Words felt inadequate; I simply followed him in reverent silence.

This walk was unlike any other. Though I wasn't alone physically, a strange solitude enveloped me. Pandit ji walked a few steps ahead, offering me space—a subtle gesture of respect—yet frequently glanced back, ensuring I was still with him.

Around us, life carried on. Families waited in quiet groups, sharing soft conversations. Friends laughed and captured memories in pictures. The ghats were brightly illuminated, the glow so vivid that it belied the late hour—half past one in the morning. Nearby, Aghori babas (a sect of ascetics associated with extreme Shaiva practices, often found in Varanasi) lay asleep, curled beneath blankets or sheltered in humble tents they had erected.

Though surrounded by warmth and light, a profound emptiness gripped me. A hollow void stretched inside, vast and unyielding.

My hands were icy, my breath shallow. I clutched my shawl tighter, seeking comfort from a cold that seemed to seep from within.

I was numb—unable to sense my heartbeat or the rhythm of my breathing.

In those hours, something within me irrevocably shifted. It felt as though my soul had slipped free, leaving behind only an empty shell.

I followed Pandit ji like a ghost, head bowed, footsteps barely touching the ancient stones beneath me.

Life moved all around—laughter, chatter, joy—yet none of it penetrated the barrier I felt inside.

Then I stopped.

I gazed at the Ganga (Ganges River, considered sacred in Hindu belief) flowing beneath the moon's silver light, and a disquieting thought settled over me: I don't belong here. What is the purpose of this life?

Though I am blessed beyond measure, with everything one could desire, a silent question echoed deep within—am I truly living, or merely dying piece by piece?

Had I, perhaps, already died?

The sensation was indescribable, shaking me to my core.

I felt weightless yet lost in the vastness of my own existence.

What had just transpired?

Surrounded by countless souls, I was engulfed by an overwhelming loneliness.

All I could hear was the echo of my footsteps—steady, solitary—resounding through the night.

And nothing else.

In an instant, everything inside me shifted. It was as if a veil had lifted, and suddenly, the faces of my ancestors appeared before my eyes—one after another, clear and vivid like they were standing right in front of me. Alongside them came memories of all the people I had lost in my life, as well as those who were still alive but had drifted away, no longer part of my world.

I was swept back into nostalgia, transported through time to the years I spent with my late grandmother. I could see her so clearly—at peace, glowing softly with a pure white light that seemed to wrap around her like a gentle halo. The light felt warm and protective, as if it were a visible sign of her presence beyond this world.

She smiled at me with quiet assurance and whispered, "Khush reh." ("Stay happy.")

In that moment, I felt an overwhelming sense of comfort, as if she was embracing me, holding me close despite the years and distance. The warmth of her presence settled deep within me, stirring something I hadn't realized I'd been missing.

"Devi ji! Devi ji! Jaldi chaliye, chal kar ghar se phone le lete hain," ("Dear, dear! Come quickly, let's go and pick up the phone from home,") Pandit ji's voice broke through the silence—soft but urgent.

"Ji, Pandit ji," ("Yes, Pandit ji,") I answered, my pace quickening almost without thinking.

He must have sensed the sudden change in my energy, the way my whole being shifted in those moments. Without a word, he understood that something profound had just passed through me.

Pandit ji called out to the tea vendor again, "Do kulhad chai," ("Two clay cups of tea") and handed me a steaming cup of tea. I cupped the kulhad carefully in my hands, hiding it within the folds of my shawl to keep warm.

Just then, his sister—Badi Didi (elder sister)—came out and handed him the phone.

We began walking toward the ghats. Shubham was supposed to meet Pandit ji there.

I glanced at my watch and said, "It's almost 2 a.m. Won't the temple be closed by now?"

Pandit ji smiled gently and said, "I suggest you come back at 5 a.m. for the morning aarti (Hindu ritual of worship involving light and devotion). It's a different experience altogether."

I stayed silent for a moment, unsure.

He continued, "Let Shubham arrive first, and then we'll decide. If you feel tired, you can visit in the afternoon. Don't worry, you won't have to wait in the long seven- to eight-hour lines. But there will still be a wait—maybe one or two hours. So, be patient."

We sat down outside the corridor, the cool night air wrapping around us. Pandit ji looked at me and said softly,

"Yeh sab moh maya hai, Sonia. Hum itne saalon se mandir mein pooja kar rahe hain, par jab akhri samay aata hai, toh paisa, property, yahan tak ki apna naam bhi sab bekaar lagne lagta hai. Us waqt keval ek cheez keemti hoti hai—shanti aur moksh. Shanti ke saath is duniya se chale jaana."

(This is all illusion, Sonia. We have been worshipping in temples for so many years, but when the final moment arrives, money, property, even one's own name—all of it becomes meaningless. At that time, only one thing is valuable—peace and liberation. To leave this world in peace.)

He was gently coaxing me to speak. His eyes were calm and steady. He didn't rush me.

And then, finally, the words broke through like water through a cracked dam. I met his gaze, tears welling up, and whispered:

"Then why, Pandit ji… why can't we shed our egos?"

My voice trembled, but I couldn't stop now. The flood had begun.

"Why do we hold onto the deepest wounds—the ones carved by those we once called family?

Why do siblings rip each other apart over property?

Why do husbands and wives turn love into power, and marriage into war?

Why are young girls robbed of their innocence before they even understand what it means?

Why are the elderly left to fade alone, discarded like withered leaves?

Why is everyone chasing money and status like it's salvation—and no one chasing peace or love?

Why does no one hunger for love anymore?"

I wasn't asking him. I was asking the sky, the river, the gods—whoever was still listening.

Pandit ji sat in silence, absorbing every word.

Then, gently, he spoke.

"Devi ji," he said softly, "as long as the heart beats, it is difficult to break free from moha—the web of desire, illusion, and attachment. Property, power, pain… the world is intoxicated by it. But true living—real living—only a few ever understand."

A lump rose in my throat.

"I know," I whispered. "This is all maya—illusion. And deep down, most people know it too. But facing that truth… that is the fiercest battle. We want to believe we are invincible, eternal. So we hold on to illusion—because truth burns."

Pandit ji nodded slowly, as if carrying centuries of silence.

I exhaled deeply.

"Life is simple," I said. "But ego muddies it. Greed blinds us. We have strayed from our own souls—chasing shadows, forgetting light."

Below us, the Ganga flowed—ancient, indifferent—silvered by moonlight.

But within me, something stirred.

"The soul wasn't meant for this noise," I continued."It did not come here to drown in roles, labels, and duties we barely understand."

"It came with a purpose—to love without fear, to heal through presence, to awaken others gently—not through force, to break karmic cycles passed down like silent burdens."

Every soul is born with a sacred intent. But we are placed into illusion, forgetting why we came.

The deeper we fall into worldly entanglements, the further our purpose drifts.

So the soul returns—lifetime after lifetime—until it remembers.

Sometimes the path is karmic, shaped by discipline and integrity. Sometimes it is revolutionary—to lead, teach, create, or serve. But always, it is about growth—a return to truth.

I felt the weight of it—not just mine, but ancestral. Unspoken traumas. Inherited patterns. Most of us don't even know we carry them. We simply repeat them and call it fate.

"But instead of rising," I said, "we shrink. Into fear. Into conformity. Into identities crafted by others. We wear masks for so long, we forget what's underneath."

Pandit ji remained silent—a witness, unmoved.

And then something shifted in me.

Not just grief—something older.

A remembering.

We are not here to repeat pain. We are here to rise through it. "We weren't born to carry generational wounds forever," I said quietly.

"Not to live in cycles of guilt, shame, anger, or fear. We are here to alchemize that pain—to end what was never ours to begin with."

Tears gathered, but there was no sadness—only truth.

"We are here to find freedom. Not just from death, but from everything that keeps us from truly living—craving, clinging, and constant striving. Moksha is not the end. It is a return—to peace, in life, not just after it."

I paused, breathing deeply.

"We did not come here to own or conquer. We came to remember. To forgive. To become. To bring light into places where generations only knew darkness."

The knowing rose in me—not from thought, but from something deeper.

"Each of us has a sacred assignment. Sometimes it is to hold space for another's healing. Sometimes to speak truth when silence feels safer. Sometimes to break chains of violence, silence, and fear—so no one after us has to carry them."

Pandit ji nodded gently.

"But we forget," I said.

"The world is loud. It tells us who to be, what to want, what success should look like. And under all that noise, we lose our own voice."

I looked up at the sky—dark and endless.

"But the voice within," I whispered, "it never leaves. It waits. It taps at our ribs. It keeps asking us to remember who we were before the world told us who to be."

And in that stillness, I finally understood—

not everything that breaks you is meant to destroy you.

Some things break you open.

Not to leave you empty—

but to let the light in.

हर हर
महादेव
ROYAL
ENFIELD

CHAPTER 02

Shamshan Se Shiv

Part II: Royal Enfield

Pandit ji and I were waiting.

I leaned casually against a parked Royal Enfield—matte black, solid, quiet. Something about it pulled my attention. On its chrome tank, etched in bold, were two words: "AK 47."

The name struck me—sharp, jarring, a little too loud.

I glanced at it again, half-thinking it might belong to Shubham—the boy I had only heard of until now. But something didn't sit right.

The longer I stood there, the colder the metal felt against my back. There was a strange weight to it. A silence that didn't feel peaceful.

My instincts, quiet but firm, whispered: This isn't his.

Or maybe… I hoped it wasn't.

Broooom. Wroooom.

The sound split the silence.

Across the road, beneath a flickering streetlamp, stood a lone figure. Helmet on. Hands steady on the handlebars.

The engine of his black Royal Enfield Bullet 350 growled low and deep—like a living beast holding its breath.

It was Shubham.

And in that moment, I knew: Not everything that looks familiar truly belongs. Some things carry echoes from another story. And some meetings are written long before they ever happen.

I was here—alone—on this quiet pilgrimage of sorts. Seeking connection. Searching for self

And in this space of stillness, every small detail carved itself into my senses:
The hum of the engine. The glint of iron logos. The way I gently steadied myself.

I was paying attention—fully present.
Open to signs. Receptive to symbols. Anchored in energy that could guide or protect me.

I was careful.
But I was present.

And with Shubham there now, the ride ahead… didn't feel quite so uncertain anymore.

"Devi ji se milo… Sonia hain, Bombay se—Kumbh ke liye aayi hain."
("Meet Devi ji… This is Sonia, from Bombay—she has come for the Kumbh.")

"Hi Didi," Shubham greeted, his voice nearly swallowed by the growl of the engine.

Broooom. Wroooom. Broooom.

That bike was definitely louder than he was.

Pandit ji raised a hand and gestured for him to kill the engine.

Shubham smiled, cut it off, and said again—this time with more warmth:
"Hi Didi. Welcome to Banaras."

Something in the way he said it made me pause.

For a moment, I saw Goru Bhai—my little brother.
That same innocence. That same soft reverence.

No one in this world comes close to the bond I share with Goru.
It's not love. It's magic—pure, sacred, soul-level magic.

And yet, in that moment, the way "Didi" rolled off Shubham's tongue—so effortlessly, so naturally—
It melted something in me.
Just a little.

My woman's instinct—sharp, ancestral, holy—stood alert like a flame.
I wasn't judging, but I was reading the energy. Feeling the moment.
Measuring it not with logic, but with intuition.

And as always, I chose to trust my gut.
Mindful. Open. But rooted.

That's the only way I've learned to walk through this world.
And tonight, Banaras was no different.

Pandit ji instructed Shubham to circle around and meet us on the other side of the ghats—just outside the sacred corridors of the Kashi Vishwanath Temple.

Shubham nodded, started his bike with a familiar broooom, and vanished into the winding lane.

Pandit ji and I began walking slowly toward the temple.
The air was still, heavy with the silence of the hour.
Only the occasional rustle of the river breeze or a distant chant broke through the night.

We reached the temple before Shubham and sat quietly on the steps, overlooking Ganga ji.

Nearby, families moved through their own sacred rhythms—some grieving quietly, some whispering stories or prayers, some simply staring into the water, as though it might answer something left unspoken.

After a while, I stood abruptly and turned to him.

"Pandit ji… I don't think I can enter the temple in these clothes," I said, adjusting the shawl draped around my shoulders.

He looked up at me, slightly puzzled.

"Kyon? Shawl mein bhi thand lag rahi hai kya?"
(Why? Are you still feeling cold even with the shawl?)

I shook my head.

"It's not that. We just came from the shamshaan… and we were there for quite a while.
As per tradition, we shouldn't enter a temple without purifying ourselves first."

He nodded slowly, understanding dawning in his gentle eyes.

Then, with a soft smile, he said,
"Iska hal bhi hai."
(There is a solution for that too.)

He paused, looked directly at me, and asked,
"Devi ji, kya aap mandir Brahma Muhurat mein darshan karna chahti hain?"
(Devi ji, would you like to visit the temple during Brahma Muhurat?)

My heart stilled.

Something ancient stirred within me—something soul-deep.

"Yes," I replied without hesitation.

What could be more auspicious than that?
A visit to Shiva's temple… during Brahma Muhurat?

"Bas phir," Pandit ji smiled gently, "tum Shiv ke darshan Brahma Muhurat mein hi karogi."
(Then it's settled—you will have Shiva's darshan during Brahma Muhurat itself.)

I looked at him, hesitation flickering in my eyes.

"But how? I haven't bathed, and I can't enter the temple like this..."

Without missing a beat, he replied,
"Chalo, aao mere saath."
(Come, come with me.)

We walked in silence toward the ghat, the stillness of early dawn enfolding us like a soft shawl.

The city lay asleep, yet Ganga ji flowed endlessly—whispering ancient secrets to the waking sky.

When we reached the river's edge, he turned and asked quietly,
"May I sprinkle some water on you?"

I nodded without a word.

He cupped the sacred water in his hands, dipped them gently into the river, and from a respectful distance, let the cool drops fall softly onto my head.

Then, with calm reverence, he guided me to wash my hands, face, and feet in the holy river's embrace.

And something changed.

Within seconds, I felt a profound shift—not just a cleansing of the body, but a quiet awakening of the spirit.

As if a heavy weight had lifted.
As if Ganga ji herself had reached deep inside, soothing a restlessness I hadn't realized ran so deep.

Pandit ji watched me carefully and asked,
"You feel better?"

I nodded again, a small smile breaking through.

"Much better."

He smiled knowingly.

"After visiting a shamshaan, cleansing isn't just tradition—it's an energetic necessity. The vibrations from the cremation grounds linger, especially when emotions run deep and raw. A full bath is ideal, yes, but when that's not possible, Gangajal is enough. She is the purifier of all—the eternal mother who asks for nothing and yet gives everything."

In that quiet moment, I understood—it was never just water.

It was surrender.
It was grace.
It was a gentle reminder that no matter how heavy the night, the path back to light is always open.

"Broooom… Wroooom… Broooom…"

The engine's roar echoed through the silent lanes as Shubham appeared, skidding his Royal Enfield to a halt beside us.

With a hint of irritation, he said,
"Kab se dhoond raha tha aap logon ko… Corridor ke paas ho? Aur phone kyun nahi utha rahe the?"
(I've been searching for you both for so long… Were you near the corridor? And why weren't you answering the phone?)

Pandit ji smiled calmly, completely unfazed.

"Mera kaam ho gaya," he said with quiet satisfaction. "Ab tum Devi ji ko mandir le jaakar Shiv ke darshan karwaoge."
(My work here is done. Now you will take Devi ji to the temple for Shiva's darshan.)

I looked at him, unsure.

"Can't you come with us?"

He shook his head, the soft saffron of his shawl fluttering in the breeze.

"Nahi beta. Yeh mera kaam nahi hai. Tumhari Manikarnika aur Shiv Mandir ki ichha aur jazba ne mujhe aapke saath chalne par majboor kiya. Ab teen baj chuke hain… mujhe ghar jaana hai, thoda rest lena hai. Subah ki aarti ke liye taiyari bhi karni hai."
(No, beta. This is not my role. Your desire and determination to visit Manikarnika and the Shiv Mandir compelled me to walk this path with you. It's already three in the morning now… I need to go home, get some rest, and prepare for the morning aarti.)

He turned, ready to leave.

I hesitated, then softly called out,
"Pandit ji… ruk jaiye."
(Pandit ji… please wait.)

He stopped and glanced back. I stepped closer, my heart full and my eyes heavier than I realized.

"Thank you," I whispered. "For guiding me through what I couldn't have found alone. For helping me feel safe in a city that overwhelms yet awakens at the same time."

He smiled—a timeless, gentle smile—and almost to himself, began to hum,
"Pata nahi kis roop mein aakar Narayan mil jaayenge…"
(Who knows in what form Narayan may come to meet us…)

The tune drifted through the cold morning air, as if Ganga ji herself were listening.

I took out a small amount of money and offered it with both hands.

"Please… accept this as Gurudakshina."

He hesitated, then nodded, accepting it with grace.

And just like that, without a word of farewell or dramatic goodbye,
Pandit ji melted into the misty darkness of Kashi—
a guardian who came, fulfilled his purpose, and quietly returned to wherever such souls belong.

"Didi, you want to walk around? Anything specific you'd like to see?" Shubham asked casually.

I nodded. "Okay," I said half-heartedly.

Truth be told, I felt low.

I had just emotionally parted from **Nidhi**—a stranger who had felt like family within minutes—and before I could process it, I had to let go of Pandit ji too.

And now, this young joker was going to take me to the temple?

Yes, "Joker." Not disrespectfully—just that early-20s vibe. High on confidence, low on maturity. That wild mix of adrenaline, bikes, gym selfies, late-night rides, and blaring music. His world felt galaxies away from mine.

Nidhi and Pandit ji had touched my soul somehow—matching my pace, my thoughts. They slowed me down, yet nudged something forward inside me.

And now… this boy?

What could he possibly teach me about devotion or depth? How could he lead me to Shiva?

But then I reminded myself—do I even have a choice? No.

The divine often moves in mysterious ways. Maybe this "joker" was also chosen—handpicked by the universe to play his part.

I took a deep breath, adjusted my shawl, and whispered:
"Sonia, just follow the path. Trust yourself. And above all—trust God."

We started walking. Honestly, it felt like a drag.

An awkward silence stretched between us. We were like two poles, so far apart. His energy felt too young, too restless. I doubted we'd find common ground.

Trying to break the silence, I asked, "How long till the temple opens?"

"About an hour and a half, maybe two," he replied.

Reading my boredom, he added, "Didi, if you're getting bored… I can show you Varanasi on the bike."

I hesitated, unsure where this ride might take me. But the part of me that had surrendered to this journey's flow nodded yes.

"Okay, let's go."

And just like that, I chose to trust him—and follow his lead.

"SHUBHAMMM! Slow down!" I screamed, my voice snatched mid-air by the freezing 3:30 a.m. wind.

"Arey Didi! Chill! Don't be scared—just enjoy the ride!" he yelled back, grinning like a madman, as the Royal Enfield roared through the ghost-town gallis of Banaras.

Enjoy the ride? At 3:30 in the morning?

With temple bells still echoing from the last aarti, dogs howling like backup singers, and me clutching this thundering beast like I was strapped to karma itself?

His riding skills surprised me.
Not because he was some pro racer—this wasn't MotoGP.
But the way he took those sharp turns, slammed the brakes without warning, and whipped through the narrow gallis like we were in a low-budget action movie... it made my heart race and my soul ready to exit my body.

(Not in a romantic way. More like, "O God, this is it, isn't it?")

At one point, I thought:
Amazing. I survived the chaos of Manikarnika, had a spiritual awakening, didn't get lost—or trampled—at the Kumbh (which, let's be honest, would've earned me serious karmic brownie points and maybe early access to Moksha). And now? Now I'm going to die on the back of a Royal Enfield. In the middle of Banaras. With a stranger named Shubham.

If I died, the family group chat would explode.
And don't even get me started on what Daddy would do to Goru Bhai when he found out.

Daddy would burn Goru Bhai's driving license with camphor.
The poor guy would be grounded so hard that his next seven lives would be on lockdown.
No phone, no outings, no oxygen.

I could already see the headlines:
"Mumbai woman goes searching for Shiva, meets Shubham… and ends up with a cracked skull instead of cosmic insight."

Blockbuster stuff.

Honestly, if I had to go, I was hoping for something more… epic.
Like disappearing into thin air mid-aarti. Or levitating into the Ganges during meditation.

Not flying off the back of a roaring Enfield with a Banarasi joker who probably thinks helmets are a government conspiracy.

We zipped past sleeping cows, abandoned cycle rickshaws, flickering tube lights, and a sadhu casually brushing his teeth with a neem stick. The Bullet backfired once so loudly, I'm pretty sure it woke up Shiva.

And there was Shubham—dodging potholes, dead ends, and divine retribution—like he was born on two wheels and raised by traffic cones.

"Brake, Shubham, BRAKE—!"

We missed a paan stall by an inch.
A dog barked like we'd insulted its ancestors.
I mentally made peace with all eighty-four lakh yonis.

At one point, he shouted, "Shortcut!"
I screamed, "That's not a shortcut, that's a drain!"

Too late. We flew through a gap that barely qualified as legal architecture.

If you've ever been to Varanasi, you'd know exactly what I mean.
The lanes are ridiculously narrow—barely enough room for two people to walk side by side, let alone a roaring Bullet weaving through the chaos.

Add to that the madness:
Two-wheelers parked like they own the place, garbage bags tossed like afterthoughts, khats (manjis) scattered around like public benches nobody asked for.

It's definitely not a city made for speed.
But somehow, Shubham made it work.
He zipped through those alleys like he had the entire city's map hardwired into his brain.

Now, I'm no stranger to bikes—but I've always been uneasy.
Because, unlike cars, bikes are just you and the open air.

No seatbelts, no steel cage.
Just wind, speed, and a whole lot of trust.

And then… something shifted.
I stopped overthinking.
I let go—just a little—and tried to be fully in the moment.

I felt the cold breeze kiss my face and tangle softly in my hair. There was a strange stillness that wrapped around my body. A quiet joy blooming within. In the chaos of sharp turns and narrow lanes, I found my calm.

I wasn't just a passenger on that bike—
I was a bird.
Flying high.
Weightless.
Fearless.

That wind, that speed, that silence between the streets—
They weren't just sensations.
They were reminders.

That this is my moment.
This is my journey.
This is my life.

And for the first time in a long time—
I wasn't chasing anything.
I wasn't pleasing anyone.
I wasn't proving a point.

I was simply being.
Alive.
Independent.
Rooted in the now.

Maybe it was the thrill.
Yes, I've always loved speed—rollercoasters, races, that heart-in-the-throat adrenaline rush.

But this ride?

It wasn't about excitement.
It was about stillness in motion.
Calm within chaos.
Peace at full speed.
And that… I can't even put it into words. But I felt it—with every cell in my body.

Eventually, the bike screeched to a halt near a new ghat—one I hadn't seen before. Shubham turned around, positively glowing with pride.

"See? Told you! Smooth ride."

I couldn't move. My hair looked like it had lived through fourteen past lives. My soul had ascended, panicked, come back, and now just sat quietly inside me—a little stunned, but still intact.

But beneath the chaos and exhaustion, something had shifted. I felt… liberated. I felt… alive. Not the loud, firework kind of alive. But the quiet, steady kind. Like something deep within me had exhaled—finally. Like I had stopped carrying the weight of questions I didn't need answered. Like I had peeled off a layer of fear I didn't even know I was wearing.

It wasn't about adrenaline. It wasn't about the bike or the speed or even the madness of Banaras at 3:30 a.m.

It was about letting go—truly letting go—even if just for a moment.
Letting the wind untangle the knots in my mind.

Letting the night wrap around me like a soft shawl.
Letting myself feel the now.

And in that moment, I wasn't thinking about where I had come from, or where I was going.
I wasn't worrying about who I had to be, or who I had failed to become.

I was just… here.
Whole.
Free.
Unapologetically, unmistakably alive.

The ghat had a large "Namaste" carved at the entrance—two folded hands in devotion, as if welcoming every soul with quiet warmth and reverence.
But the gates were shut.

It was around 4 a.m., and entry was clearly closed to visitors.

From where I stood, I could still see the other side—glowing softly under amber lights. The steps, the still water, the hush of dawn beginning to stretch across the river…

It looked untouched.
Peaceful.
Empty in the most magical way.

The kind of place that didn't need words.
The kind of moment that begged to be felt—not posted.

"Madam ji, kahan chalein?"

A voice broke the stillness.
A security guard approached us from behind, his footsteps slow, steady, not rushed—like someone who knows the city isn't going anywhere.

He looked tired but alert. Calm but clear.

Shubham, ever the smooth talker, jumped in immediately:
"Sir, bas ek minute… kuch pictures lene hain, phir nikal jaayenge."

But the guard—he was unwavering.
Firm in his tone, polite in his words, and completely unmoved.
No was a no.

And honestly? I respected that.

4 a.m. Chilling cold. Maha Shivratri week.
And here was this man—standing guard over something sacred.
Not for money. Not for show.
But because he believed in the place he was protecting.

I stood quietly, observing this unexpected tug of war—a dialogue that felt like a scene straight out of a play.

On one side: a security guard in his late 50s.
Decent build. A woolen sweater over his uniform.
A thin stick in one hand and a cutting chai in the other—the ultimate combination of authority and warmth.

On the other: Shubham.
Young. Full of life.
Nike sneakers. Smartwatch. Leather jacket.
Helmet in one hand, and (figuratively) a law degree in the other.

With a priest for a father and a well-off background, he was confident, persistent… and definitely not used to being told no.

It was hilarious and fascinating—these two men, from completely different worlds, negotiating with full passion and conviction.

When neither could convince the other, they both turned to me—as if I were some kind of High Court judge, expected to issue a final verdict.

I smiled.
The moment was absurd… and oddly heartwarming.

The guard said,

Madam ji, aap toh samajhdar lagti hain. Aaj kal ke bachche zid kar lete hain. Aap hi samjhaiye."
(Madam, you seem sensible. These days youngsters can be quite stubborn. You please make them understand.)

Shubham chimed in quickly,
"Didi, inko bolo—sirf ek baar aapko dikha kar chale jaayenge."
(Didi, please tell him—we'll just show you once and then leave.)

I looked at both of them and said playfully,
"Sir, aap bhi chaliye na saath… I'll take a quick photo, and we'll leave."
(Sir, you also come along… I'll take a quick photo and we'll leave.)

The guard shook his head, holding his ground.
"Madam, main duty pe hoon. 6 baje ke baad aa jaaiye, main khud aapko sab dikhaunga."
(Madam, I am on duty. Come after 6 o'clock, I will personally show you everything.)

Shubham's face fell—his confidence dimmed just a little.
He mumbled something under his breath, disappointed.

Then said quietly,
"Chalo, Didi… Mandir ki taraf chalte hain."
(Let's go, Didi… let's head towards the temple.)

I smiled.
"Chalo…"
(Let's go…)

And we turned to leave.

But something about this moment stayed with me.
Because sometimes, the detours… the dead ends…
they are part of the divine path, too.

I didn't know it yet,
but this little interruption—this almost-comical standoff—had its own purpose.

As we walked away, I turned back with a smile and called out,
"Lage raho, sir. You're doing a great job."
(Keep it up, sir. You're doing a great job.)

He returned a big, genuine smile.
"Phir milenge, Madam ji."
(We'll meet again, Madam.)

We started walking toward the temple, only to find the corridor packed with people—shoulder to shoulder—and still an hour-long wait ahead.

Shubham turned to me and asked,
"Fuel bharwa lein kya? Warna baad mein phas jaayenge."
(Shall we get fuel filled? Otherwise we'll get stuck later.)

It made sense, so I nodded.

We rode out in search of fuel—tried two, maybe three petrol pumps.
But they were either shut or eerily unattended.

Empty booths. Flickering lights. Silence.

And then, without missing a beat, Shubham hit the throttle—full power—and suddenly, we were no longer in familiar territory.

The alleys blurred into wider roads, and the roads into unknown lanes.

I looked around.
I didn't recognize this part of the city.
Not even slightly.

A quiet wave of nervousness began to build.
That old feeling—the one that whispers worst-case scenarios in the back of your mind—started to creep in.

For a moment, I even considered sharing my live location with my brother.
Just in case.

Then I realized:
He'd be fast asleep.
And even if something did go wrong, he wouldn't know until morning.

I glanced down at the little Krishna pendant around my neck.
Felt its familiar weight.

My talisman.

I've always believed He's with me—quietly watching, gently guiding.
I know… maybe it's just psychological.

Maybe it's just a story I tell myself to stay calm.
But in moments like this—when fear grips the edges of my mind—it's that little story that saves me.

Because sometimes, faith is the only map we have when nothing else makes sense.

I've never hurt a soul—not even a mosquito.
I've lived simply, tried to help where I could, and tried to be kind.
And in doing so, I've trusted in the quiet balance of karma.

My belief is simple:
Do good, and goodness will walk with you.
Be kind, and kindness will shield you.
Stay humble, and life will lift you when you fall.

Even in the middle of an unfamiliar street, on the back of a near-empty bike, with no fuel and no plan—
I chose to trust.

Trust in my karma.
Trust in the path.
Trust in Krishna.

Because fear may speak loudly—but faith doesn't need to shout.

The Leap of Faith: What If Things Go Right?

If something is truly meant for you, it will arrive—not through force or fear, but through quiet divine timing.

So why do we overthink ourselves into paralysis?
Why is our first instinct to ask:
"What if things go wrong?"

But here's the shift that changed everything for me:
"What if things go right?"

What if the unknown isn't danger, but direction?

What if the universe isn't punishing you—but positioning you for something better, deeper, and more aligned?

A leap of faith isn't about reckless risk or blind belief.
It's about sacred trust.
The kind that whispers, "You don't have to see the whole path.
Just take the next step."

Because let's be honest—overthinking has never made us safer.
It's only kept us stuck in fear, rehearsing tragedies that haven't happened.

And yet, we rarely pause to imagine one beautiful outcome.

Life isn't meant to be figured out entirely.
It's meant to be felt, trusted, and lived.

You won't always get clarity before the decision.
You may not have proof that you'll be okay.
But you'll have a pull—a quiet nudge that says, "Go anyway."

That's faith.
It's not the absence of fear, but the choice to move through it.

Every turning point in your life probably began with something that didn't make perfect sense—a risk, a yes, a moment when your soul moved faster than your logic.

And yes, you might fall.
But you also might rise.
You might land exactly where you're meant to—in a way only grace could design.

So now, when fear speaks, I ask:
"What if this isn't rejection, but redirection?"
"What if this no is making space for a better yes?"
"What if fear is the final test before a breakthrough?"

Because the truth is: The universe doesn't ask for perfection. It asks for presence. And for participation—even when your knees are shaking.

So leap.

Try. Begin. Trust.

Not because you're sure of the outcome—

But because you're done living half-heartedly. You were meant to ride into the unknown with wind on your face and the Divine by your side. To release the need for control…And let life show you just how right things can go.

I was reminded of this during a wild ride through Banaras at 4 a.m.

Lost. Cold. Low on fuel.

And yet—I trusted. I clutched my Krishna pendant and surrendered.

In that moment, I wasn't just riding a bike. I was riding with faith.

With life.

With something greater than fear.

As Krishna says in the Bhagavad Gita:

"Sarva-dharman parityajya mamekam sara?am vraja…

Aham tvam sarva-papebhyo mok?ayi?yami ma sucah."

("Abandon all dharmas and surrender unto Me alone.

I will liberate you from all sins. Do not fear.") (Bhagavad Gita 18.66)

And that—that is the true leap of faith.

To trust that even when the road is unclear…

The Divine already knows the way.

What's the Worst That Could Happen?

If we live in constant fear of failure, we'll never achieve anything worth remembering.
We'll never start that journey.
Never take that leap.
Never breathe life into the wild, burning dream inside us.

We often ask, "What if I fail?"
But here's a better question:
"What if I don't?"

What's the worst that could truly happen?
No, not heartbreak or financial loss. Not rejection, job loss, or faded beauty.
I'm talking about the one inevitable truth we all fear, yet refuse to name—
Death.

Death—the final page in every story.
It doesn't discriminate.
It doesn't care about your money, status, skincare routine, or degrees.
It comes for everyone—young or old, healthy or sick, ready or not.

And since death is certain—a chapter already written—why are we wasting our prologue living in fear?
You don't escape death by playing small.
You only lose life before it ends.

We're so afraid of dying that we forget to live.
But let me ask you this—
What's more tragic: dying once at the end of your life, or dying a thousand silent deaths over the years by shrinking, suppressing, settling?

I've lived those quiet deaths.

Each time I abandoned a dream because someone said it was "too much."
Each time I dimmed my light for someone else's comfort.
Each time I stayed in a place, a job, or a relationship that suffocated my soul.

No more.

If I had just one day to live, I would choose to spend it fully awake,
with people who see me, love me, and lift me.
Doing things that make my heart beat louder than my fears.
Speaking my truth. Living my truth.

Not for approval. Not for applause.
But for peace.

The Antidote to Fear is Action

There is no magic pill for courage.
No external force that will hand you strength on a silver platter.
The only way to defeat fear… is to face it.
Not recklessly. But bravely.
With intention. With faith.

So if you're stuck—afraid to take that job, book that ticket, start over, speak up—
remember this:

The only thing standing between you and the life you crave… is fear.
But fear is just a story.
A shadow.
A test.

And sometimes, all it takes is one decision. One yes. One act of rebellion against the voice that says "you can't."

Even if the odds are stacked against you—try anyway.

Even if failure feels inevitable—take the leap.
Because what if it works?
What if that risk you're so afraid to take… becomes the very thing that sets your soul on fire?

People may laugh when you fall.
But they'll clap when you rise.
They'll say you were lucky.
But you'll know it was faith, persistence, and a refusal to quit.

This Dream Is Yours

If your soul keeps returning to a dream, don't abandon it.
No matter how slow the progress, how ridiculous it sounds,
how long it takes, or how lonely it feels.

This dream is yours. It was planted in you for a reason.
It doesn't need to make sense to anyone else.
It just needs to set your soul on fire.

And if fear still whispers, "But what if it all goes wrong?"
tell it calmly—
"Even death doesn't scare me anymore."

Because when you've made peace with the worst…
you become unstoppable.

And I truly believe with every cell in my body:
You are not here to keep the world happy.
That's not your job.

Your only sacred duty is to honor your joy, protect your peace,
and live a life that feels true—not just impressive.
When you are happy, grounded, and whole, you uplift everyone
around you.
You radiate light.

You carry the weight of others without losing your center.
Let the world follow later.
Start with you.
Choose yourself.
Not out of selfishness, but out of clarity.
Because when you choose yourself, you choose life.

So the next time fear visits, remember this:
"What's the worst that could happen?"
Death? I'm not afraid anymore.
I'm already living—and that's more than most can say.

"In short, I'd just say—Zindagi lambi nahi, badi honi chahiye."
(Life need not be long, but it must be meaningful.)
—From the film Anand

But no matter how much I grow in life—no matter how strong, courageous, or successful I become—I can't get over one fear. Cockroaches.

OMG. That's my one and only fear.

I'm the kind of person who wouldn't flinch at taking a bullet in a war.
I'd dive into a river to save a stranger—even though I don't know how to swim.
If there's a fire? I'm probably the one running into the flames to pull someone out.
Haunted jungle at midnight? As long as there's network and 100% battery, I'm in.

I've survived messy heartbreaks.
Sat in silence while my heart screamed—and still smiled when someone asked, "Are you okay?"
Told the truth in a room full of liars—stayed standing, even when my voice shook.
Handled emergencies like a pro, then quietly broke down when no one was watching.

Accidentally walked into a men's washroom in London while escorting my little brother—didn't blink.

Got lost in Moscow on a family vacation—no money, no phone, didn't know the language—still found my family.

Unshaken. Unbothered. Unstoppable.

But a cockroach?
Crawling. Flying. Breathing.

I will scream like I'm being murdered.
Sprint. Panic. Climb a chair like it's a life raft. Possibly die of a heart attack mid-jump.

Because nope. I'm not dealing with that demon insect.
Because of some battles?
Even I'm not ready to fight.

I know, I know. I'm different.
And that's exactly why I'm special.

Main sach mein apni favorite hoon :)

I can be funny and sad at the same time.
Ambitious and lazy at the same time.
Deeply in love, yet ready to fight like a warrior—all at the same time.
I can be ethically correct—and still get things done my way.

This?
This is all me.
No filters. No edits. No apologies.

And trust me—you'll get to know more in the coming chapters.

Anyway, back to Shubham.
I was on a high—wind in my hair, soul dancing in freedom, and a boy named Shubham riding us through the sleepy streets of Varanasi. Life felt like a scene straight out of a movie.

But then we pulled into a dimly lit petrol pump on the outskirts—the kind of place that instantly makes your brain whisper, "This is how crime documentaries begin."

Naturally, I felt a flutter of nervousness.
"It's okay," I told myself, clutching my sling bag a little tighter.
"I have a pair of scissors."

Yes—scissors. That was my grand self-defense plan.
If things went south, I wasn't going down without at least a snip of resistance.

Trying to stay calm, I started quietly chanting Krishna's name—the way Draupadi did in her moment of total surrender. She didn't fight, she didn't plead—she just called out to Him with complete faith. And He showed up.

So in that moment, I thought… maybe He'll show up for me, too?

And in my head, He didn't just appear. No, no—
He made an entry.

Just like Akshay Kumar as Krishna in Oh My God—
Gliding in on a sleek, peacock-blue motorbike, light literally following Him like a celestial spotlight.

Dressed in that crisp white low-neck shirt, casually unbuttoned at the collar—just enough to reveal a sculpted chest (because clearly, Bhagwan doesn't skip gym day).
Smart beige pants, luminous skin, that radiant smile, and an effortless charm that silently said, "Relax. I've got this."

And of course—spinning the bike key around his index finger like it's the Sudarshan Chakra. Because… He is Krishna.

I imagined myself standing there, frozen—wide, tearful eyes, the biggest, most overwhelmed smile stretching across my face.
Hands folded instinctively, heart pounding with something between awe and relief.
All drama, all devotion.

"Krishna... you came."

But let's be real—
He'd probably pull up, park the bike with a perfect cinematic skid, raise an eyebrow, and say:

"Sonia... main Bhagwan hoon, assistant nahi.
Itni spontaneous trips, random strangers, aur Netflix-level plot twists—
Even I need a Google Calendar invite just to schedule your rescue!
Chamatkaar karne ka kaam hai mera... par thoda notice toh do!"

("It's my job to perform miracles... but at least give me a little notice!)

And honestly? He'd be right.

Still, in that half-nervous, half-exhilarated moment, one thing became crystal clear to me:
I've always protected the people I love like a warrior. No second thoughts, no hesitation.

And now, I'm deeply in love with the most important person in my life—ME.

So I asked myself:
If I can stand up for others without fear... shouldn't every cell in my body rise up to protect me too?

HELL YES.

With that thought, I smiled, let go of the fear, and chose to trust myself.

And—giving credit where it's due—I chose to trust Shubham too.

Because sometimes, the moment you stop waiting for divine rescues and start backing your own intuition?
That's when the real magic begins.

And somewhere between the chaos of narrow lanes, midnight fears, and unexpected detours, I realized this wasn't just a journey through Banaras—it was a journey through myself. Nothing was fully in control, yet everything was unfolding as it should. Faith, I understood, is not certainty but surrender—the courage to keep moving anyway. As dawn touched the ghats, one truth became clear: I was not lost. I was being led

CHAPTER 02

Shamshan Se Shiv

Part III: Shiv Shakti

Wroom. Wroom. Wroom.

He took sharp turns with reckless ease, weaving through narrow streets like he knew every inch of this city. And just as suddenly as it all began, he hit the brakes—right outside BHU.

Yes, Banaras Hindu University.

It was 4 a.m.

Still recovering from the whirlwind ride, I tapped his shoulder, mildly annoyed.
"Why here?" I asked, trying to mask my irritation.

He glanced at his watch.
"We've got forty-five minutes before the temple opens. Thought I'd show you around the campus."

My voice rose, half in disbelief, half in protest.
"Are you serious? Right now?"

Without missing a beat, he replied,
"If you haven't seen BHU, have you even seen Banaras?"

I didn't have a real choice, so I agreed—somewhat begrudgingly. But as we started walking, my mood and energy began to shift.

The campus was sprawling, quiet, and almost meditative. I couldn't see everything, but there was a calm beauty in the chaos. Tree-lined roads snaked between faculty buildings, each space with its own rhythm. Cafeterias buzzed quietly in corners, their scent mingling with the crisp February air.

Somewhere between the crimson-bricked academic halls and the cool, shaded courtyards, a fleeting memory stirred—the vibrant energy of PUC (Punjab Agricultural University College of Agriculture, Ludhiana) surged back into my mind, transporting me to that unforgettable night, December 31, 2024, in Ludhiana, when I had once surrendered myself to the pulsating beats and roaring crowd of Diljit's grand finale. The electrifying atmosphere, the sea of exhilarated faces, the infectious rhythm—it all flooded back like a sudden rush of wind.

A few steps further, the ambience shifted subtly. It reminded me of Syntel's campus in Pune, which I had explored with a friend back in 2007–08—that unique blend of disciplined structure and spontaneous creativity. The quiet hum of focused ambition mingled with the gentle murmur of everyday life—familiar, yet distant, like a half-remembered dream.

Who could have imagined that, here in the heart of Banaras, under the stillness of the pre-dawn sky, fragments of my past would quietly resurface? This unplanned detour was far more than a mere way to pass the time. It became a gentle revelation—a reminder that sometimes, the places we stumble upon without intention leave the deepest impressions, embedding themselves in our story long after we've left their shadows behind.

After winding through narrow, dimly lit lanes and feeling the hushed pulse of the campus around us, he finally slowed and stopped the bike right outside a temple. I looked up, a flicker of curiosity sparking in my chest.

"What temple is this?" I asked, my voice barely above a whisper.

He turned, eyes gleaming with a quiet pride.
"Didi, this temple is open to everyone, but very few know it's

here—hidden deep within BHU's grounds, like a secret waiting to be discovered."

He cut the engine and gestured for me to get off. Together, we stepped forward, drawn toward the temple's graceful, towering gates.

But as we approached, a strange stillness settled over me—
not the kind that comforts, but one that unsettles. My breath caught. I stopped and murmured,
"Actually… I'm feeling a little uneasy."

He halted beside me and looked down with gentle understanding. His eyes held no judgment, only calm acceptance.

"It's okay," he said softly. "Go ahead inside, at your own pace. When you're ready, I'll be waiting to take you to the Kashi temple."

I hesitated, the weight of something unspoken pressing on my heart. Summoning a trembling breath, I finally confessed,
"You know… maybe it's not the right moment for me to go in."

His eyes widened, surprise flickering across his face. Until now, I had been eager, even insistent, about seeing the temple. Now, without warning, I was stepping back—retreating from a path I'd so confidently chosen.

He studied me quietly, as if my sudden retreat had paused the rhythm of our journey—as though I'd touched on something deeper than either of us could explain.

And in that delicate pause, the hidden temple stood silently behind us, guarding its secrets—a quiet sanctuary in the heart of Banaras, waiting for those ready to see its magic.

It's not my fault. All my life, I've witnessed a pattern unfold around me—rituals followed blindly, traditions passed down without question or reason. When you grow up watching your elders, your family, your community perform certain rites, you start to imitate them, almost instinctively, without pausing to understand why. I'm not saying that following traditions is wrong. On the contrary, many are rooted deeply in wisdom, designed for specific times and circumstances. But when those circumstances change, shouldn't we learn to adapt? To embrace change with grace rather than resist it?

In my heart and mind, I was still wrapped in the same old clothes I wore when I visited Manikarnika. Visiting Manikarnika was never wrong, and coming to this temple was no mistake either. Yet somehow, I found myself trapped in self-reproach—blaming myself for not changing sooner, chastising myself for not planning better, endlessly spiraling into negative thoughts about my purest intentions. And that, I realized, was the real mistake.

Imagine doubting your own intentions—forget what the world might say, because honestly, their opinions barely touch me. But the real question gnaws at me: why am I not trusting myself? Why do I question my own love, my devotion, my passion for the temple? Why do I cast shadows of doubt over my own actions when all I sought was sincerity and faith?

In a low, hesitant voice, I turned to Shubham and said,
"Listen… I'm still in the same clothes I wore earlier. I don't think it's right. A temple is sacred—a place to worship Lord Shiva. I should've changed before coming here."

Even as I spoke, guilt clawed at me. It wasn't about superstition—it was something deeper. A quiet voice within whispered that I had crossed an invisible line. I braced myself for agreement, a nod, a silent judgment.

But what came instead shook me.

Shubham looked at me—not with confusion, not with rebuke, but with a kind of calm clarity I wasn't prepared for. And then he said, almost in a whisper,

"Didi… Shiva toh shamshaan mein hote hain. Hum log hi hain jo unhe mandir mein dhoondte hain."
(Didi, Shiva resides in the cremation ground. It is we who search for Him in temples.)

I froze.

For a full minute, I couldn't move. I couldn't speak. His words didn't just land—they struck, reverberating through something ancient and rigid within me.

This boy—whom I had quietly doubted and half-dismissed, unsure whether he could even keep up with the depth of my thoughts—had, in a single sentence, unraveled something far greater than understanding. He had pierced through conditioning, bypassed the layers of inherited guilt and silent shame, and reached the core of what devotion truly mean

There was nothing performative in his words. No pretense. Just truth—raw and effortless.

And I… I stood there, disarmed. All the spiritual pride I thought I carried dissolved in that moment. His perspective wasn't just broader—it was boundless.

In that single moment, everything I thought I knew about purity, ritual, and rightness shifted. And this boy, whom I thought might not even match my wavelength, had crossed over into something far beyond it—into silence, into stillness, into Shiva himself.

His words didn't just offer comfort—they felt like a message straight from the divine. A quiet nudge from Shiva himself. It was as though, in that moment, the universe held up a mirror to my thoughts and gently asked, "Why are you being so harsh on yourself?"

His response didn't just ease my discomfort—it cracked something open inside me.

Here I was—educated, wise, self-aware. Someone who had lived enough, learned enough. Someone older than Shubham by more than just a few years. And yet, despite everything I believed I had grown into, I had just fallen into the trap of doubting my own intentions, questioning my own purity, silently accusing myself of something my heart knew was innocent and unplanned.

If someone like me could spiral into such unnecessary guilt, what must others go through? No wonder society, drenched in unbending traditions and fearful righteousness, is quick to raise fingers—not out of wisdom, but out of habit.

I looked at him again—this boy I had underestimated—and before I could say anything, he smiled and said,

"Chaliye, I'll join you."

And just like that, he walked with me into the temple—no hesitation, no judgment, just quiet companionship.

That moment stayed with me—not because I entered the temple, but because I entered it after shedding the weight of shame I never should have been carrying in the first place.

It was 4 a.m.
The air was cool and still, touched by the faintest hint of morning. The sky outside remained dark, but the temple within seemed to hold its own light—a soft, unwavering glow that rose not from lamps, but from the space itself.

A kind of still, sacred illumination that needed no source.

I entered quietly, my footsteps echoing gently against the pure white marble beneath me—polished, seamless, and cool to the touch. It felt as if the marble had been poured from silence itself, holding within it the weight of a thousand whispered prayers.

The temple unfolded before me—vast, but not overwhelming. It opened into a wide corridor lined with evenly spaced pillars of white stone, each carved with subtle simplicity. There were no excessive embellishments, no loud ornamentation—only a clean, minimal grace that gave the space an eternal, almost otherworldly quality. It was modern in structure, yet ancient in soul.

This corridor led into a larger sanctum hall, where high ceilings dissolved into soft shadows above. The openness invited the eye to wander, yet every gaze inevitably returned to the center—to the Shivling, resting under a circular canopy, glowing in soft contrast to its pale surroundings.

The Shivling itself was immense—black stone, smooth and endless in its curve, encircled at the base by a silver yoni, polished to a mirror-like sheen. It stood still and powerful, like a cosmic anchor suspended in absolute stillness.

Not a symbol. Not an idol.
A presence.

The air around it felt different—charged, yet not heavy. Alive, yet profoundly quiet. It was a stillness that made me aware of my heartbeat, one that silenced thought without effort.

Above, the dome-shaped ceiling carried the softest echoes—not jarring, but sacred, as though the temple amplified intention itself rather than sound. Even the birds outside had not yet begun their morning chorus.

Inside, only three people sat scattered far apart, each in their own quiet orbit. There was an unspoken understanding that this space was not meant to be filled, but respected. It was not emptiness—it was presence in its purest form.

The poojaris moved with quiet care, draping garlands, arranging offerings, and preparing for the Mangala Aarti. One of them looked up, caught my eye, and smiled—not as a priest, but as a witness. As if he could sense that something within me had already begun to shift; that I had not come here seeking answers, only peace.

And in that moment—standing within this vast stillness, carrying both doubt and release—I could almost hear Diljit Dosanjh's voice rising like a prayer through the silence:

"Tere bina nahi koi mera, oh Shiva…"

It wasn't imagination. It felt cosmic. A divine echo meeting me exactly where I stood.

Being a die-hard Diljit fan, my love for his music goes far beyond his electrifying Punjabi party anthems. What truly anchors me are his devotional songs—raw, heartfelt, and pulsing with soul. I haven't just listened to them—I've memorized them, lived with them, let them move through me.

I've carefully curated a playlist of all his spiritual tracks and named it Devotional Music by Diljit—my personal sacred space in sound. At the top sits "Shivaya"—intense, reverent, a thunderous offering to the divine. Then there's "Aar Nanak Paar Nanak," which feels like a soft embrace from the universe on days when the world feels too loud.

And believe me, whenever the weight of life begins to press too heavily on my chest—whenever I feel even the slightest crack forming in my spirit—I step into a cold shower, close my eyes, and press play. Within minutes, the water, the rhythm, the voice—all of it—washes me clean. Not just physically, but emotionally and spiritually. I emerge not just refreshed, but reawakened, as if I've been stitched back together by sound and surrender.

In that moment outside the temple, as doubt gently dissolved and deeper truths began to unfold, Diljit's voice became more than just melody—it became a bridge. A soft invocation. A sacred reminder that Shiva isn't bound by ritual, space, or time. He is not just worshipped—He is felt. He does not always arrive with thunder, but sometimes in the hush of a song, the hum of a familiar voice, or the stillness between two heartbeats.

Returning to "Shivaya," the song no longer felt like just music. It was a mantra echoing from the deepest corners of my being—as if it had been composed for this very moment. I instinctively reached for my headphones, longing to hear that divine resonance once more. But the signal vanished, and the world grew still. No music. No noise. Only silence.

And in that sacred silence, I heard Him clearer than ever.

It was as if Shiva whispered gently: "Don't search outside—go inward." This was not a moment for devices or distractions. It was a moment for surrender.

So I closed my eyes, breathed deeply, and let the temple's energy move through me—invisible yet undeniable. A current of stillness and power, humming through the air, vibrating in the soles of my feet, pulsing with the rhythm of something eternal.

And within that silence, the song rose—not through speakers, but from memory, from within me.

"Koi toh raasta dikhaiye mujhe, haath pakad ke samjhaiye mujhe…"
A cry for guidance. A raw plea for the Divine to hold my hand and walk me out of the fog.
"Oh tere bina nahi koi mera, o Shiva… tu hi suraj tu hi andhera."
The truth revealed—that there is no me without Him. No light or shadow, no joy or sorrow. He is the sun. He is the darkness. He is everything in between.

The temple dissolved into something more—not just stone and silence, but a living, breathing sanctum where devotion hung in the air like incense. The boundaries between form and formless blurred.
Shiva was here.
Not on a distant mountaintop. Not hidden in texts or rituals. But here—in the rustle of leaves, in the rhythm of my breath, in the tears that quietly traced my cheeks.

And again, the sacred refrain rose from within:
"Yeh jungle bhi tum hi Shiva, yeh jharna bhi tum hi Shiva...
Tum hi toh ho pita mere, tum hi toh meri maa ho Shiva."
(You are the forest, the waterfall… You are my father. You are my mother.)

In that moment, I no longer felt separate. I was not a devotee standing before the Divine—I was part of Him. He was the pulse in my veins, the silence in my stillness, the breath beneath all existence.

And then something miraculous happened—the kind of magic that cannot be seen, only felt.

The stone beneath me was cold, yet grounding—ancient, worn smooth by centuries of prayer. A faint trail of incense curled through the still air, dissolving into the open sky. Somewhere in the distance, a temple bell rang once and faded, leaving behind a silence more alive than sound.

I sat cross-legged on the floor of the Shiva temple at BHU, palms resting gently on my knees. The world around me dissolved—no footsteps, no whispers, only the quiet hum of breath, the flicker of flame, and the presence of something far greater than myself.

And then, without effort, peace arrived.

Not as a wave, not as a revelation—but as a soft, steady presence.
Like the echo of Om settling into the marrow of my bones.
Like a truth I had always known, but forgotten how to feel.

I became both empty and full at once.
Empty—because all the noise, regret, guilt, and weight of the past slipped away.

Full—because I had never felt more alive, more present, more whole.

Tears gathered quietly in my eyes—not from sadness, but from recognition. A remembering.
They were not just mine; they belonged to every version of me that had waited for this return.

We often chase peace as if it lives in the future—after success, healing, or answers. But here, in the quiet gaze of the Shiva lingam, I understood: peace is not achieved. It is allowed.

Desire never sleeps. It shifts, reshapes, always asking for more. But peace asks for nothing.

I realized that we often mistake peace for comfort, success, or external fulfillment. We imagine it hiding in achievements, relationships, or validation. But peace is not a destination—it is a return.

Not loud. Not flashy. Not fleeting.
But quiet. Steady. Already within.

This is what I came to understand—not through effort, but through stillness. Not through answers, but through surrender.

And once I stopped grasping, peace arrived—gently, completely, like breath.

The Quiet Power of Peace

Peace does not roar. It enters like breath—unnoticed at first—until suddenly, everything inside you becomes still. Not numb. Not empty. But awake in a way no achievement can offer.

You do not need the right setting, the right people, or a perfect version of yourself. Sometimes peace arrives the moment you stop running.

When you stop grasping for meaning and simply allow yourself to be—not happy, not sad, just here—something shifts. You become enough.

In that stillness, the soul speaks—not in words, but in deep, silent knowing.

We spend years chasing significance—careers, relationships, applause—forgetting that the voice we were searching for was always within us.

Life will break you. It will scatter your plans and strip away what was never truly yours. But those cracks are not endings—they are openings through which light and truth enter.

Those who accept this invitation—who sit with themselves even in discomfort—become something else entirely. They become unshakable.

They walk the world with a quiet fire.
No longer needing approval.
No longer fearing solitude.
They are rooted. Aligned. Free.

This is the quiet power of peace:

It does not make you louder—it makes you clear.
It does not make you invincible—it makes you whole.
It does not harden you—it softens you into truth.

It brings you home—not to a place, but to yourself.
It teaches you to walk through chaos with steady feet.

That silence can be strength.
That letting go is wisdom, not weakness.

Peace is not passive.
It is presence without pressure.
It is power under control.
It is knowing who you are, even when the world forgets.

In a world that glorifies noise and speed, peace is the most radical act of all.

It means you no longer perform to be loved.
You no longer run to keep up.
You no longer shrink to fit.

You simply are—and that is enough.

And once you taste this kind of peace, you stop searching for it outside. You start protecting it within.

It becomes your compass, your fuel, your quiet fire.
And from that fire, you begin to live—not by fear or force—but by truth.

I didn't hear any divine voice echo through the temple.
No thunder. No miracles. Just silence—sacred, still, and complete.
And in that silence, something inside me shifted.
Not everything changed. But I did.
I was no longer chasing peace.
I was living it.

It was just past 4 a.m.
The world outside still lay in the womb of night, but inside the temple, time had already shifted.

The air felt charged—not with electricity, but with the quiet hum of the divine. A kind of sacred stillness that didn't belong to this world.

I slipped into a corner and sat, almost disappearing into the marble. Everything was white—the floor, the pillars, the soft early light—like the temple had been carved from a single block of silence. Even my thoughts felt distant, as if they had been asked to wait outside.

Then, without warning, a voice gently broke through the hush.
"Beta ji, yahan aana," a priest called out.

I rose and walked toward him, my heart calm but alert. He handed me a small vessel—holy water infused with the scent of flowers and something ancient. I sprinkled it over myself as instructed, and then he did the same, placing a few sacred drops on my head.

In that moment, something shifted.
I wasn't just receiving water—I was receiving permission.
Permission to enter a space beyond logic, beyond fear.
Permission to return.

Nearby, the other priests prepared the Chandan tilak. They moved with the kind of reverence that only comes from deep knowing—like every gesture was in sync with an unseen universe.

First, they adorned the Shivling—silver and black, resting like a cosmic axis in the heart of the sanctum. Then, to my surprise, they turned to me.

I was first.

I bowed slightly as the priest stepped forward. Without a word, I whispered:
"Hare Krishna… Bhool chuk maaf karna…"

As the cool sandalwood paste touched my forehead, it felt like being branded with something holy. But instead of burning, it healed.

A current surged through me—not external, but from deep within. As if my soul was passing through colors… from shadow to blue to white. As if my inner world was being rinsed clean.

And then the mantra rose, unbidden but certain:
"Om Namah Shivaya… Om Namah Shivaya…"

Each repetition echoed inside my chest like a bell struck softly, endlessly. The moment was brief, but eternal.

I could feel it—something in me had been touched, or claimed, by the Divine.
I hadn't just walked into a temple.
I had stepped into the hands of God.

It was 4:30 a.m. The rituals were beginning to shift, and I slowly made my way outside. I spotted Shubham waiting and rushed toward him, thinking I might be running late. But before I could reach him, an old woman passed by and stopped.

"Beti," she said, her voice steady with quiet authority,
"Aarti ka samay ho gaya hai. Bahut kismat se yahan ki aarti mein rehne ka saubhagya milta hai. Train ya flight nahi hai toh aarti karke jao."

(Its time for the aarti. You are fortunate to witness it here. If you don't have a train or flight to catch, attend the aarti and then leave.)

I smiled politely. But her words lingered in me like incense

Then Shubham said simply,
"Didi, if you want to attend the aarti… attend it here. At Kashi Vishwanath, there's no guarantee. It's all luck."

That hit differently.

This boy, whom I had underestimated, had unknowingly given me the clearest wisdom of the morning.

He was right.

Both temples are sacred.
Both bear the name of Vishwanath, the Lord of the Universe.
Both are in Kashi.
Both begin aarti at Brahma Muhurat.

But here—this one called to me.
This one opened its arms.
This was not the temple I had planned for, but it was the temple that had chosen me.

And suddenly, I saw the choice clearly:

One temple might allow me to witness the aarti.
But in this one, I could be part of it.

There, I might stand behind barriers, distant from the sanctum.
Here, I had already received blessings with my own hands.

Faith is not always about grandeur. Sometimes, it is about the invitation you did not expect—but feel in your bones.

So I turned to Shubham and said,
"I'll stay. I'll attend the aarti here."

He smiled. "I'll be outside. Call me if you need anything."

As he walked away, I realized something that made me smile in disbelief—I had completely forgotten to bring any offerings. No flowers. No milk. Not even a diya.

"This is my punishment," I told myself.

But a quiet voice within gently corrected me:
No—this is your lesson.

As I re-entered the temple, the same old woman noticed me and smiled, as if she had been waiting.
"Bahut accha kiya jo tum ruk gayi," she said.
"Shiva ne tumhe khud bulaya hai."
(You did very well by staying. Shiva Himself has called you here.)

And just like that, the entire space shifted.

It was now 4:45 a.m.

The white marble beneath my feet seemed to pulse with energy. Devotees began arriving in a quiet, reverent stream, as though drawn by an invisible thread.

Women in vibrant sarees, adorned with sindoor, alta, bangles, and payal, entered with graceful precision. Some were barefoot, others carried brass plates of offerings. Their movements felt timeless—like a ritual not learned in this life alone, but carried through many lifetimes.

And I stood there in awe.

Not as a visitor.
But as someone who had been called.
Who had been claimed.

The temple no longer felt like stone.
It felt alive—breathing through every chant, every footstep, every drop of sandalwood.

I knew then, without a trace of doubt:

This was not just a morning ritual.
This was a meeting with the Divine.
And somehow, I was right on time.

The Surge of Devotion

By now, around eight to ten devotees had gathered, and I couldn't help but be awed by the depth of reverence in their eyes. It felt as though I had stepped into a world where time slowed down and everything became rooted in faith. Most of them appeared to be in their sixties—some retired, others in the autumn of their lives—while a few younger devotees in their thirties were equally absorbed in devotion.

They arrived with offerings that spoke only of gratitude and surrender—fruits, mithai, milk, curd, and even kalash. Some carried black til, honey, and bay leaves. The simplicity of these offerings was profound. It was never about wealth or status, but about the purity of giving.

I sat quietly, taking it all in, watching each devotee absorbed in prayer. Their faces glowed with tranquility, each one lost in their own connection with the Divine. No one was rushing. No one was restless. There was only stillness and serenity everywhere.

Some wore shawls like mine, while others, wrapped in socks and sweaters, braved the chill of the early morning with hearts warmed by devotion. And there I was, sitting among them—feeling suddenly small, even guilty of my own forgetfulness.

How had I missed the most essential thing—my offerings? I had been so focused on reaching the temple, securing a place for the aarti, and seeing Lord Shiva, that I had forgotten the essence of it all: the act of giving. A wave of guilt washed over me.

But I refused to be consumed by regret. Instead, I chose to honor the moment. I quietly offered water from the kalash as my humble offering. It was small, but it felt sincere. And in that act, something within me softened. I felt connected, even if only in the smallest way.

Then the aarti began, and the energy in the air shifted.

Three devotees played the damru, its sound deep and resonant—like the rhythm of the universe itself. In the background, a music system subtly amplified the beat, blending with the natural sound and creating an atmosphere that felt both ancient and otherworldly.

The aarti was not just a ritual; it was a song of the soul. The air was thick with devotion, and my heart swelled. It felt as though I was being bathed in pure peace. The vibrations of the damru, the chanting, the energy of the devotees—it was all deeply healing.

Time dissolved. Forty minutes passed in what felt like moments. When I opened my eyes, I saw the vastness of the temple—not just in size, but in presence. It felt alive, breathing in rhythm with the Divine.

The priests moved with steady reverence, bathing Lord Shiva in sacred waters, milk, curd, and honey—each drop a prayer. Then they applied chandan and offered flowers, mostly white, like countless prayers in bloom.

After the Shiva aarti, we were led toward the other deities within the temple complex. The space was vast, with multiple shrines dedicated to various gods and goddesses. Though I had begun in the Shiva sanctum, each space we entered carried its own distinct energy—different, yet equally powerful.

It felt as though we were part of something larger, moving together behind the priest, who led us with quiet authority. Seven jyots—large lit diyas—illuminated the path, followed by devotees playing the damru and the steady ringing of bells. We walked in silence, completely surrendered to the moment.

Then the same woman who had earlier urged me to stay stepped forward. Without a word, she took my hand and gently led me upward toward the upper level of the temple.

I followed her as if in a trance. When we reached the top, I found myself before something I had never imagined.

It felt like crossing into another realm—one I did not know existed, and was not sure I was ready for. Yet I stood there, certain that I had been guided by something far greater than myself.

In that moment, I realized the temple had given me something beyond expectation. I had come seeking darshan, but I had received something far more profound—a sense of belonging in this exact moment.

Before me stood a colossal statue of Shiva—majestic, commanding, and alive. Draped in a flowing leopard-print garment, His form glowed in a deep celestial blue, as though infused with the cosmos itself. In His left hand, He held the trishul and damru—symbols of creation and destruction, rhythm and power. Serpents coiled around His neck, alive with silent energy, while a crescent moon rested gently in His matted hair, glowing like a distant star.

I stood breathless, completely entranced. The aarti around me faded into the background. I barely registered anything except Him.

The woman gently urged me forward to bow and receive prasad. Overwhelmed with awe and gratitude, I remained still for a moment before she firmly guided me ahead, asking the priest to offer me prasad—two pieces of tender coconut and half a ripe banana.

I lifted the prasad to my eyes in reverence before tasting it slowly, as if absorbing its meaning. Almost immediately, she tugged my hand again, urging me forward with gentle urgency.

It felt as though she was carrying me on invisible wings—both playful and nurturing. In that moment, two strangers were bound not by words or identity, but by devotion alone. She held me like a mother would her child, guiding me into prayer with a sincerity I had never experienced before.

Once our prayers concluded, we descended the steps together. Now, each devotee was invited to present their offerings to the Divine. Most carried five sacred items—a tradition steeped in symbolism: milk for purity, curd for nourishment, flowers for beauty and devotion, water for cleansing, and honey for sweetness and healing.

I searched for water but found none. Accepting my circumstances, I resolved to offer only my love, respect, and a few humble coins.

The same kind woman called out warmly, "Beti, idhar aao!" (Daughter, come here!). Without hesitation, I went to her, moved by her warmth.

Within moments, she filled a kalash with milk, curd, water, and honey, encouraging me to blend the sacred liquids together in harmonious unity. She then pressed white flowers and fragrant bay leaves into my palms, placing a banana gently atop them. "Yeh sab apni taraf se chadha do, pooja achhi tarah karo," (Offer all of this from your side and perform the puja properly) she instructed softly.

Heart brimming with devotion, I stepped into the small queue, offering everything with reverent hands while chanting "Om Namah Shivaya." The atmosphere shimmered with an almost palpable sacredness. It felt as if time itself had slowed, and the very air hummed with divine grace. The experience was nothing short of magical—a sublime dance of soul, ritual, and the infinite.

Returning the kalash to her, I asked if I might wash it and bring it back. She smiled, eyes twinkling, and replied, "Pooja hi toh ki hai, jootha thodi ho gaya hai." (It was only used for worship; it hasn't become impure.) Bowing deeply, I sought her blessings.

She sat humbly on the floor, her saree modestly covering her feet, and I touched them gently in gratitude. Her blessing resonated deeply: "Hamesha khush raho aur bahut tarakki karo." (Always stay happy and achieve great success.) I was struck by its modern grace—not limited to tradition, but extending toward happiness, freedom, and success for all women.

All the while, my phone buzzed insistently—Shubham was surely waiting outside, quietly gathering flowers and leaves.

I hurried out and found him by his bike. "Didi, be quick. The queue at Kashi Vishwanath is already long," he urged. Smiling gently, I replied, "Let's leave it for another day. If it's meant to be, it will happen. For now, I am deeply grateful for this blessing here." I thanked him and settled on the bike.

He hesitated for a moment, then steered toward the Kashi Vishwanath Temple. From afar, we saw endless lines of devotees, restless and anxious, waiting for a glimpse of Shiva. We exchanged a knowing glance—an unspoken decision to step away from the rush.

In my heart, I had already received the purest blessing.

Within that sacred space, something within me quietly shifted. Shiva was no longer just a statue of stone and form—He became the eternal pulse beneath the chaos of my mind, the fierce yet tender compassion within destruction, the infinite stillness that renews everything.

Shiva asked for no grand spectacle, only presence—a raw, honest surrender.

And in that surrender, I found a peace so deep and unshakable that it seemed to reach the very core of my being and rearrange it. A gentle yet powerful fire ignited within me, lighting the path ahead with steady clarity.

This pilgrimage was far more than a journey. It was a calling—a return to something sacred within myself, long buried beneath noise and chaos.

As I stepped away from the temple, holding the warmth of blessings close, I knew—deep in my bones—that the dance of

Shiva had already begun within me. A sacred rhythm, eternal and unbreakable, alive in every breath.

"Chalo phir Ganga kinare… sunset dikhata hoon," (Let's go to the banks of the Ganga… I'll show you the sunset) Shubham said confidently.

I gave him a mock-serious look.

"Abhi… aur sunset?" (Now… sunset?)

We both burst into laughter.

"Slip of the tongue ho gaya, Didi—sunrise!" (It was a slip of the tongue, Didi—sunrise!) he said, laughing and rubbing the back of his head.

And with that little comedy of errors, we set off toward Assi Ghat—chasing the promise of a sunrise I had only imagined and dreamed of.

I was buzzing with excitement. Everyone had said the sunrise here was spectacular—almost surreal—and I wasn't going to miss it for the world.

In my mind, I had pictured myself in a small boat, floating across the Ganga as the golden sun painted the sky. But every time I mentioned a boat ride, Shubham would shake his head and say, "Too expensive."

Practicality: 1, my Bollywood moment: 0.

So instead, we settled on the steps of Assi Ghat, wrapped in silence and fading stars. The night hadn't fully given up yet—a faint crescent moon still clung stubbornly to the sky. I kept glancing eastward, waiting for dawn.

A few families were already there—teenagers and young adults recording reels, fully immersed in their own worlds. Watching them was unexpectedly entertaining while waiting for time to pass.

Just then, I spotted a kulhad chai stall. Without hesitation, I ordered two cups. The first sip hit like poetry.

Meanwhile, Shubham seemed increasingly restless—fidgeting, pacing slightly, glancing at the sky as if he could will the sun to rise faster.

"Mandir kab jaana hai, Didi?" he finally asked. ("When do we go to the temple, Didi?")

I smiled, took a slow sip of chai, and said, "Not now. This moment is enough. I've already received Shiva's blessings. Let's just be here now."

Then I pulled out my Banaras food bucket list and began reading it like sacred scripture: "Ram Chaat Bhandaar, Blue Lassi, Laxmi Chaiwala, Kashi Chaat Bhandaar, Gauri Shankar Kachori, Neelu Kachori…"

He looked at me, half shocked, half amused. "Didi, itni bhookh lag gayi?" (Didi, are you that hungry?)

"Not yet," I smiled, "but I plan to eat like I've been fasting for a week."

He tried to tempt me—cold coffee, pizza, cafés.

I shook my head. "No. Only local food. Only Banaras."

Then he said with quiet certainty, "Main le jaunga, Didi, don't worry." (I will take you, Didi, don't worry.)

And somehow, I believed him.

It wasn't just words. It felt like trust arriving in human form.

In that moment, I didn't feel like someone searching anymore. I felt carried—by the city, by timing, by something unseen that had already decided the path for me.

We watched life unfold around us—strangers passing like fleeting chapters, laughter spilling into the air, people performing their ordinary moments like they were unaware they were part of something sacred. And we just observed. Quietly. Like children witnessing a world they were still learning to understand.

Even the idea of rush began to dissolve.

I went down to the boatmen, memorized their rates, and was even offered a free ride—but I declined. Something in me refused to exchange this silence for spectacle. The ghat itself felt like enough.

And then, without warning, the world softened.

The darkness loosened its grip.

The sky began to change—grey dissolving into lilac, lilac melting into gold. The Ganga didn't reflect it; she became it. As if she had been waiting the entire night just to be touched by light again.

The sun rose slowly, deliberately—like truth arriving after silence.

And on the other side, the moon still lingered… unwilling to leave, as if witnessing the same miracle from afar.

I captured them together in a single frame—but even the best lens could not hold what my soul was witnessing.

It wasn't a sunrise.

It was a surrender between night and day.

A quiet handover of time itself.

I stepped closer to the river, pulled my shawl over my head, cupped the cold Ganga in my palms, and offered it to the rising sun.

No rituals. No instructions. No seeking.

Only presence.

Gratitude.

Surrender.

And something inside me went still in a way it never had before.

I sat back on the steps, letting silence enter me completely—not around me, but within me.

Everything I had seen until then—Manikarnika's fire, Shiva's stillness, the chaos of devotion, and now this golden awakening—were no longer separate moments.

They were one unfolding truth.

Kashi was no longer a place.

It was a mirror.

A mirror that does not show who you want to be… but who you are when everything else falls away.

And as I finally stood up from the steps of Assi Ghat, something within me bowed—not out of religion, but recognition.

I had begun my journey in the silence of the shamshan (cremation ground)—where endings lose their fear, and illusions fall without effort.

From there, I had been drawn toward Shiva—not as belief, but as presence itself… vast, still, unshakable… dissolving everything I thought I was.

And now, I stood before the Ganga—not as a seeker, not as a visitor, but as something quieter than both.

Something complete.

Shamshan se Shiv… Shiv se Ganga.

Ash to awareness… silence to flow… ending to eternity.

And as the river moved forward—unceasing, untouched, carrying everything yet holding nothing—I understood, with a stillness deeper than thought:

I was no longer walking through the journey.

The journey was walking through me.

CHAPTER 03

Fate in a Hostel Room – Meeting with Imaan

Thursday, February 20, 2025 | Varanasi

After dropping **Nidhi** at her hotel, I reached my hostel.
I stepped into the hostel with a quiet knot tightening in my stomach.
Budget stay. Bunk beds. First time.
The kind of place you book when the city leaves you no choice.

Varanasi had decided to test both my patience and my wallet—everything was either sold out or priced as if enlightenment came complimentary with the room. For someone who just needed a bed to crash on, it felt almost offensive. My flight tickets had already done enough damage, so this was me—adjusting, adapting, choosing practical over perfect.

There were separate sections for men and women, which should have been comforting. It was… to an extent. But labels don't tell you who you'll actually be sharing space with.

Strangers are unpredictable.
They could be kind. They could be chaotic. They could be the kind who set alarms at 5 a.m. and sleep through them like it's a personal talent.

And I was about to spend a night among them.

But then again—it was just one night.

I was traveling alone. And I've never been high-maintenance. I like a clean space, yes—but I don't crumble without air-conditioning or luxury toiletries lined up like a hotel ad. I don't travel to be pampered. I travel to experience.

If comfort shows up, great. If not, I'll survive. I always do.

I'm simple like that.
Simple enough to walk alone through unfamiliar streets—rain pouring, sun blazing, doesn't matter. Simple enough to get by on bread and water if the day demands it. I'll ask for directions without ego when I'm lost, and I'll take a train over a flight even when I can afford the latter—because sometimes the journey feels more honest than the destination.

But simplicity is often misunderstood.

It isn't softness.

Because beneath it, there's something else. Something sharper.

I am simple—but I am not naïve.
I am calm—but always aware.
I adjust—but never at the cost of my boundaries.
And when something feels off, I don't ignore it.
I pay attention.

So yes, I walked into that hostel—slightly nervous, quietly observant, taking it all in.

Because sometimes, the real story doesn't begin with where you go…
It begins with who you might end up sharing a room with.

I stepped into the hostel, whispering Krishna's name and deliberately planting my right foot first.

Does anyone else do this—consciously put their right foot forward when they really want things to work out? I do it everywhere. Entering the office at 8:30 a.m., stepping into an important meeting, walking into dance class, or even coming home after a day that could have crushed a lesser soul. Temples?

Naturally. My favorite shopping spots? Of course—because yes, choosing the right things matters just as much.

There's something quietly reassuring about it. A small ritual that says, I mean business. Or at least, I'm pretending I do.

So, right foot first, Krishna on my lips, I entered the hostel with what I'd call fake confidence. Fake, because this wasn't my first time in a hostel with bunk beds, and I had no real clue how it would all play out. But this confidence wasn't for the concierge. It was for me—my shield, my armor, my way of telling myself I could handle whatever might happen that night.

The hostel had a small, unassuming concierge desk, and the guy behind it… well, he was cute. Just cute—nothing more, nothing less. I'm speaking with full transparency here; no hidden agendas.

He took my details, confirmed my online payment, and delivered the essentials: the café closes at 10 p.m., so I'd have to manage my own meals. The room was shared. Here's a key for your luggage, the geyser and AC are working—switch them on yourself—and here's the Wi-Fi password. Simple, precise, functional.

Two boys from the United Kingdom and a girl from France were waiting on the sofa, quietly observing as I finished my questions. Their curiosity didn't bother me. I had bigger things on my mind: survival, observation, and mental notes for what awaited me upstairs.

The third floor revealed itself slowly, like a scene in a suspense movie. A huge living area led into another space, opening to a large room with six bunk beds stacked two high and a spacious washroom off to the side. The split AC hummed quietly, the geyser was ready, and each bunk had a shelf below to lock up luggage, a fluffy mattress, soft pillows, crisp white sheets, and even little curtains for privacy.

I paused. For ₹950 plus taxes a night, I hadn't expected this. It was shared—but immaculate, airy, positive. The staff was friendly, the layout thoughtful, the vibe… comforting and cinematic.

And then there was the balcony. A small perch overlooking the café below, a tree strung with lights, the concierge desk glowing softly like a lighthouse. Cozy, safe, and strangely thrilling—a tiny stage for the night in Varanasi to unfold.

For a budget hostel, this was unexpectedly perfect: charming, reassuring, and carrying just enough unpredictability to make it memorable.

The moment I stepped into the room, my eyes instinctively scanned the space around me. It was spacious and surprisingly neat, with the beds arranged along the edges of the walls in an L-shape, leaving the center of the room wide, open, and almost empty.

To my left stood a neatly made set of bunk beds, untouched and waiting. In front were two more sets—four beds in total. At the far end was an attached common bathroom, clean and well-kept.

Only then did I notice a young woman lying on one of the beds, stretched on her stomach with headphones on, completely absorbed in her own world.

She looked up.

Her eyes caught me first—big, round, dark brown, quietly observant. There was something composed about her, almost self-contained. Neatly shaped eyebrows framed her face, her skin clear and glowing under the soft light. Long, thick hair fell effortlessly around her shoulders. She wore a simple white ganji and khaki pants, but carried the outfit with an ease that made it stand out. There was a quiet strength in her posture—I could tell she worked out. And the small nose ring added just the right hint of edge.

"Hi," she said. "I'm **Imaan.**"

"I'm Sonia," I replied, leaning forward to shake her hand.

I walked in, set my suitcase aside, and shook her hand. She stepped out of the bunk almost immediately, and we exchanged introductions.

"Are you the only one here?" I asked.

She smiled. "Yes… and now you."

She was from Canada, traveling solo across India for three months. Her maternal roots traced back to Gujarat, and she had already explored a significant part of the country on her own.

"Dinner?" I asked.

"I ate earlier."

"Alright, I'll freshen up, grab something to eat, and then catch up with you," I said, sliding my luggage into the lower bunk before locking it.

Just as I was about to leave, she looked up and asked, "Are you Indian?"

I smiled. "Yes—born in Delhi, raised in Mumbai. I'm here for the Mahakumbh."

Her face lit up instantly. "No way, I'm going there too! I just booked a hostel."

"Really? When are you leaving?"

"Tomorrow evening."

I paused for a moment before asking, almost instinctively, "The 7:30 train from Varanasi?"

Her eyes widened in disbelief.

I laughed softly. "Same train."

For a moment, we both just stood there, grinning—caught in the surprise of it. Butterflies, excitement, a strange sense of familiarity. A coincidence too perfect to ignore.

We quickly aligned—different compartments, but we'd head to the station together.

I nodded, smiling. "Let me grab dinner. I'll see you in a bit."

And just like that, the unfamiliar room didn't feel so unfamiliar anymore.

Even in a modest hostel room, I realized, sparks of adventure could ignite in the most unexpected ways.

I freshened up, carefully stowed my dupatta, and wrapped a pale pink-peach shawl around my shoulders. My tan-brown juttis clicked softly against the floor as I left my handbag on the bed, taking only cash, my phone, and the bunk key.

Stepping out into the night, I let myself wander, the quiet thrill of independence settling in. About 200 meters down the lane, a small dhaba beckoned, promising Dal Baati Churma—the kind of Rajasthani comfort food that felt like a reward after a long day. My stomach grumbled in agreement.

But first, practicality tugged at the back of my mind: what if the hostel locked its doors at a certain hour? I retraced my steps to the reception. The same cute guy was still there, and I caught myself smiling at his calm efficiency.

"You can come and go whenever you like," he said, almost conspiratorially. "The main entrance is locked, but just call us, and we'll open it. No curfews. No restrictions. A free and independent place."

He leaned slightly closer, as if sharing a secret. "We have cameras in the main corridor and outside the rooms—but don't worry, they won't stop you from wandering the streets late into the night. Just give us a call."

I chuckled softly to myself. Safe, yes. Independent, yes. Slightly thrilling too—there was a delicious irony in being trusted to roam freely under the watchful eye of discreet cameras. A hostel that offered freedom with a dash of surveillance—that was tonight's perfect balance.

I was famished. The thought of Dal Baati Churma made it irresistible, quickening my pace without me even realizing it. As I approached the dhaba, a small tea stall—kulhad chai served in clay cups—caught my eye. I stopped, ordered a steaming cup, and took a deep, satisfying sip.

It had been almost two weeks since I last had tea on this trip. Two weeks ago, I had suffered severe acid reflux and had just recovered. Tea had always been my constant companion—four to five cups a day, chai pe charcha with friends, a comforting ritual whether alone or with people I loved. Upset? Ginger tea. Family outing? Tea, mandatory. Client meeting? Tea, naturally. Summer, winter—no matter the season, tea was my anchor.

But for two weeks, I had gone cold turkey. No matter how much I craved it, I couldn't risk another flare-up.

Yet here I was, in Kashi—the city where even the air tastes of ritual, incense, and possibility. I cradled the small clay cup, letting its warmth seep into my fingers, climb into my palms, and spread quietly through me. The winter air nipped at my cheeks, while the rising steam felt like a comforting little cloud.

A slow sip. Warmth rolled down my throat, spreading through my chest, a whispered promise in every swallow. Subtle bitterness, faint sweetness, the earthy scent of the kulhad—all of it grounded me, pulling me fully into the moment. I exhaled, shoulders dropping, chest expanding, breathing freely, feeling the world soften around me.

Each sip was a ritual: a pause, a surrender, a small celebration. Steam brushed my face, cold air kissed my nose, and for the first time in weeks, I felt untethered—a tiny flame of contentment flickering in the chaos of travel.

This tea wasn't just tea. It was a landing, a gentle exhale, a moment of victory. One stop completed in Varanasi, two more to go. I let the city seep in, feeling quietly, beautifully alive.

There's a special magic in a garam kulhad chai with strangers, in a different city, on a crisp evening. I had my moment. This—this is what I call living. 😊

And then, with a full heart, I stepped into the restaurant.

It was cozy and welcoming—warm in the glow of lamps and candles, yet pleasantly crisp from the evening air outside. The moment I stepped in, I asked what was on offer.

"Variety of Dal Baati thalis—definitely a must-try," they said, with a hint of a practiced pitch. I smiled, amused rather than annoyed, and let myself soak in the warmth of the place.

I ordered the thali and stepped out onto the veranda overlooking the ghats of Kashi, where the Ganga flowed silently below, reflecting the soft shimmer of lanterns and candlelight. Wooden manjis and charpais were scattered invitingly, each bathed in the golden glow, offering the perfect perch for a quiet meal.

The thali arrived like a treasure. Three types of perfectly roasted baati, golden and crisp. Smoky, earthy baingan bharta—made uniquely in mustard oil, deep and punchy. Cool, creamy raita balanced the spices. Rich, aromatic ghee glistened invitingly. Moong dal halwa, fragrant and comforting, promised the sweetness of winter evenings. A small pan held a medley of chutneys, pickles, and papads, each bite a little surprise.

Sitting cross-legged on the manji, I took a bite of baati, letting the crunch and warmth fill me. The smoky baingan, the silky raita, the sweet halwa—all danced together on my palate. The river murmured below, the candlelight flickered across the veranda, and the crisp night air kissed my cheeks.

For a few magical moments, time slowed. I wasn't just traveling; I was fully alive—savoring every flavor, every warmth, every breath of Varanasi.

As I savored the last bites of the thali, my mind drifted. I closed my eyes for a moment and let myself be carried away in thought—imagining the holy plunge at the Mahakumbh, the river brimming with pilgrims, the sacred waters embracing hundreds of thousands of souls in devotion and surrender. My heart thumped at the thought; the sheer scale, the devotion, the energy—it was almost too much to hold all at once.

I leaned back on the manji, letting the warmth of the veranda and the gentle glow of the lamps surround me. I let out a slow, deliberate sigh, a breath that seemed to release weeks of anticipation, travel, and longing. Finally, I was here. Finally, the place my soul had whispered about—perhaps planned a lifetime ago—was real beneath my feet.

Just one more day, I reminded myself. One more day and I would be a part of the Mahakumbh, immersed in something far greater than myself. The thought sent tiny shivers down my spine, goosebumps rising like tiny prayers on my arms. This wasn't just a pilgrimage or a travel plan—it was a calling, a rare alignment of time, place, and purpose.

I let the river below, the flickering candles, the soft night air, and the quiet hum of the ghats seep into me. In that moment, I felt suspended between the ordinary and the divine. Every step of this journey—the right foot forward at the hostel, the wandering streets, the comforting tea, the first taste of Dal Baati Churma—had led me here, to this exact pause, this exact breath.

I allowed myself to simply be—present, awed, and ready. Ready for the river, ready for the crowd, ready for the sacred chaos that awaited. My soul had arrived. I was home, for now, in Kashi, and the Mahakumbh was just a heartbeat away.

महाकुंभ
प्रयागराज
2025
॥ हर हर गंगे ॥
सनातन धर्म की जय

CHAPTER 04

Mahakumbh 2025: The Holy Dip

It was February 14, 2025—Valentine's Day.
No, I don't particularly believe in the commercial drama around it. But I do believe in love. Deeply. I'm a rom-com kind of person, with an old soul—quite a dangerous combination, if you think about it.

Because when I love, I really love. Whether it's a partner, a pet, a place, or even life itself—I'm either all in or completely out. There's no halfway, no gray area, no casual middle ground.

And no, that doesn't mean I lose myself or forget my responsibilities. It just means that when I choose something—or someone—I choose it with my whole heart.

I know all these "days" are mostly just a marketing gimmick—come on, we all know it.

But still… the girl inside me, the one who believes in spreading love, light, and happiness, refuses to ignore a reason to celebrate.

Because honestly, zindagi badi sakht hai (life is very harsh). It will hand you a thousand reasons to feel low, to break, to pause. But happiness? That… you have to go out and find for yourself.

And lately, this has become my philosophy—one that's working almost too well to be true.

Jo bhi darwaza dikhe khushi ka… bina soche, bas chal do (whichever door of happiness you see… without thinking, just walk into it).
Don't overthink it. Don't question it. Just walk in. Grab it. Hold on to it.

Kahin se bhi, kaise bhi—choti choti khushiyan dhoond kar le aao (from anywhere, in any way—find small joys and bring them).

Whether it's sipping kulhad wali chai (tea in an earthen cup) on a random evening…
or watching an old Kishore Kumar movie and getting lost in nostalgia…
or simply dressing up for no reason and stepping out like the world is your stage—

Jo bhi jaisi bhi khushi mile… bas use cheen lo (whatever happiness you get… just seize it).

Because at the end of the day—
Jeena isi ka naam hai (this is what living is).

So I knew no one was asking me out.

I didn't have any "prospects," and even if someone was interested, they probably wouldn't have the courage to ask me out anyway. Let's just say… my aura doesn't exactly scream approachable.

And my little Goru Bhai? Oh, he might pull off a surprise birthday plan—but a Valentine's flower? Highly unlikely. Let's not get carried away.

So during lunch that day, I decided—enough.

Let me get the perfect Valentine's gift for the woman I admire, love, respect, and fiercely believe in.

Yes. Me.

Within fifteen minutes—fifteen—I had cracked it.

Prayagraj.

Now, figuring that out wasn't cute or romantic. It was chaos. Demand was insane, prices were borderline criminal, and every option felt like it came with a plot twist. But somehow, through the madness, my travel agent came through.

And just like that—I was on cloud nine.

Five days.

In five days, I would begin something I couldn't even fully explain.

Mumbai to Kashi—flight.
One-night halt.
Then the 7:30 p.m. train to Prayagraj.
Arrival at 1 a.m.
At night. Alone.

Scary? Slightly.
Avoidable? Not even an option.

This was the only route I could get my hands on—and I took it without blinking.

Because for the past month, this plan had been made and canceled so many times, I had lost count. Mostly because I was depending on other people.

Not this time.

I even asked my house help, "Didi (sister), I'll pay for everything—just come with me." Not because I was scared of traveling alone, but because I had one very practical concern—who holds my stuff when I take the holy dip?

That was it. That was my biggest problem in life. Not safety. Not fear. Luggage management.

And if that didn't work? Oh, I had plans.

I would leave my bag at the station.
Hand it over to the station master like he was my long-lost chacha (uncle).
Or worst case—abandon it.

It's just a bag.

Phone? I'd tie it to myself in something waterproof and walk straight into the river like I had done this my entire life.

Because at this point, there was no question of if.
Only how.

I wasn't waiting for another alignment, another plan, another person, or another lifetime.

This wasn't a trip. This was… something else.
Something deeper. Older.

As if my soul had already taken that dip a million times… and now it was just waiting for my body to catch up.

I had already informed my reporting manager weeks ago—
"The day I get my tickets, I'm disappearing for three to four days."

No drama. No permission-seeking energy. Just a statement.

Because no bond, no responsibility, no logic could hold me back this time.

It felt bigger than all of that.

Almost like this was the reason I was here.

As if I had taken birth for this one moment—to stand at the edge of something sacred… and step in.

Yes, I had fallen sick a week before. Badly.

But I waited. I healed. I let my body recover—because I knew this journey wasn't casual. It demanded presence. It demanded surrender.

And when the time came—
I was ready.

Ready to go alone.
Ready to take the risk.
Ready to lose control.
Ready to feel something I couldn't name.

Even if it meant chaos.
Even if it meant fear.

And in some strange, dramatic corner of my mind—even if it meant dying there…
I was okay with it.

Because what bigger deal than that?

Mahakumbh.
Moksh (liberation).

And honestly…
I had never been more sure of anything in my life.

So technically, the Mahakumbh became my Valentine's Day gift to myself—and quite honestly, it was the most meaningful gift I could have chosen.

Because let's be real—flowers wilt, chocolates disappear, and expectations… well, they expire faster than both. This, though? This felt permanent.

I've always believed that a lot in life is already written—certain paths waiting quietly for us, certain experiences that feel less like choices and more like… inevitabilities.

But then, just to keep things interesting, we're handed a dangerous little weapon—free will.

And like any powerful thing, it can work both ways. It can build you, or it can beautifully derail you. Depends entirely on how you choose to use it.

Still, no matter how much we try to outsmart it, destiny has its own way of circling back. Because somewhere, beneath all the noise, our soul is constantly communicating—nudging, whispering, sometimes even pushing us toward what we truly need.

The irony? We do hear it.
But most of the time, we conveniently ignore it.

It gets buried under deadlines, distractions, social noise, and the very convincing illusion that we're "too busy" to listen.

Which is probably why people keep talking about yoga, meditation, solitude—all those things we casually postpone. Not because they're trendy, but because they force you to sit with yourself… and suddenly, the noise fades.

And that voice? It gets louder. Clearer. Slightly impossible to ignore.

It was always there. It never left.
We just weren't paying attention.

And the moment you do—really listen—something shifts. Life doesn't necessarily become easier, but it starts to make sense.

It feels intentional. Almost like you're no longer resisting the current, but moving with it.

There's a quiet alignment. A strange calm. A sense that you're exactly where you're supposed to be—even if it looks chaotic from the outside.

And maybe that's what this was for me.

Not just a trip. Not just a plan.

But something my soul had already decided…
and I was finally brave—or mad—enough to follow.

Back in 2019, when my grandmother passed away, the Ardh Kumbh Mela was happening in Prayagraj. And for reasons I couldn't fully explain even to myself, I wanted to go. Deeply.

We were even considering performing her asthi visarjan (immersion of ashes) there, letting her final rites merge with the sacred rivers at the confluence. But elders in the family guided us otherwise, reminding us of tradition—our ancestors had always done it in Haridwar, and perhaps, we should too.

And just like that, the first tiny seed was planted—the seed of a desire to visit Kumbh.

I didn't know then that this tiny seed—the desire to witness Kumbh—would quietly grow over the years, nudging me, whispering, waiting for the perfect moment to demand my attention.

Then January 13 arrived—the first day of Mahakumbh. It was also Lohri. I saw posts and videos of Sonali Ji, Diljit Dosanjh's manager, along with her family, celebrating, bathing in the sacred waters. Their images flashed in my mind again and again, like a gentle nudge, inspiring me, reminding me that this was day one of something monumental. I tried to quit the thought, to let it go… but it kept coming back, insistent, persistent, impossible to ignore.

After that, the news started everywhere. Headlines, posts, videos: the biggest Kumbh Mela in 144 years.

And that number—144—hit me like a cosmic punch. A hundred and forty-four years. More than a lifetime. Longer than I could even imagine. The Mahakumbh isn't just another festival. It's not just a pilgrimage. It's once in multiple lifetimes. The rivers meet, the stars align, and millions of souls gather, drawn by a spiritual current that's older than any history book. It's the confluence of faith, devotion, and cosmic timing—a celebration where time itself seems to bend, and the air vibrates with centuries of collective prayers.

I got hooked. Obsessively.

I couldn't stop imagining it—the Triveni Sangam thronged with millions, saffron-clad saints floating through the crowd, devotees braving the cold waters at dawn, the holy dips, the rituals, the chants echoing like an ancient heartbeat. People from across the globe, spiritual leaders, celebrities, the who's who of every imaginable field… all converging in a city that was pulsing with sacred energy. And then me. Not there.

I knew my family wouldn't accompany me. I certainly wouldn't get official permission. And yet, the thought of missing it felt unbearable. I tried—truly tried—to push it out of my mind. But the harder I tried, the louder the pull became.

The more I tried to ignore it, the stronger the pull. I didn't know why I wanted to go. I didn't know what was calling me, what purpose was pulling me there, why the obsession felt like a low hum in my bones I couldn't shake.

All I knew was—I had to go. And it felt impossible. A dream, maybe even one that could never come true.

Then the universe, as if growing impatient, started shouting.

Distant relatives, friends, colleagues… almost everyone around me seemed to be going, talking, sharing stories of their visits. Everywhere I looked, the Mahakumbh was happening, and I was not there.

It felt less like a coincidence and more like a cosmic jolt—an urgent whisper turned into a roar.

Wake up. Smell the coffee. Stop waiting.

And that's when I realized… this was no ordinary travel itch. This was the Mahakumbh. The 144-year Mahakumbh. A rare alignment of rivers, stars, and human devotion that happens once in more than a century. To miss it would be like closing your eyes in the middle of history. Something deeper was pulling me, insisting I pay attention.

On February 1, I reconnected with an old friend from my Taj Santacruz days back in 2016—Ashish. And as if the universe enjoys a bit of casual mischief, he mentioned he was planning to go to the Mahakumbh. His family had been before, and he might go again.

The moment I heard it, I practically shot up from my chair. I blurted into the phone, "I'm coming with you! Please, please take me along. I don't have anyone to go with—not that I'm scared, but... You know UP (Uttar Pradesh), right? I don't exactly know what I'll be signing up for!"

He laughed, naturally, the way people do when they don't yet realize they've just become your travel coordinator. He said the plan was still uncertain, and dates weren't fixed. I didn't care.

"Just give me a couple of days' notice," I insisted. "I'll apply for leave immediately. I can even club it with the weekend. We are going. Don't overthink it."

And just like that, I had unofficially inserted myself into a plan that didn't exist yet.

What followed was a strange ritual of hope and mild delusion. Every two to three days, I called him again—partly to stay updated, partly to make sure I hadn't imagined the entire conversation in some overenthusiastic moment.

Slowly, the plan started to take shape. February 15. Fixed. Final. I was ready to book my tickets. In my head, I was already halfway to Prayagraj, emotionally unpacked and spiritually halfway enlightened.

And then—February 11 arrived.

Ashish called. His voice had that careful, diplomatic tone people use right before they gently demolish your plans.

"It's looking difficult... I'm not even sure I'll go anymore."

I froze. The carefully constructed plan I had been obsessing over for weeks felt like it was crumbling. Anger, frustration, and disbelief collided inside me—I was furious at life, furious at him, furious at myself for ever thinking I could rely on anyone. My heart pounded, my mind raced, and a storm of "what ifs" threatened to drown me.

By February 13, I couldn't eat, sleep, or think of anything else. Every moment, every thought, every heartbeat was consumed by the Mahakumbh. I went over every scenario, every route, every timing—a million mental rehearsals of how I could make this happen. The obsession had become a ritual, a pulse that refused to quiet down.

I closed my eyes, pressed my palms together, and whispered to Krishna, "You decide. If I'm meant to go, make a way for me."

And then, as if the universe had been listening all along, Valentine's Day arrived—February 14. Out of nowhere, the tickets were booked. Just like that. All the thinking, planning, obsessing, waiting… done. The moment of hesitation was over. It was action time.

I was ready. Alone, determined, relentless. My heart thrummed with a mixture of fear, excitement, and a sacred sense of purpose. The Mahakumbh was calling—and finally, I was answering.

February 21, 2025:
I got back to the hostel after spending the entire night at Manikarnika, visiting the Shiva temple at BHU, experiencing the sunrise, and exploring the variety of chaats.

At around 11:30 a.m., the room was quiet—**Imaan** wasn't there.

I messaged her, and almost instantly, my phone buzzed.

"Hey Sonia, I'll be back by 4 p.m. Just stepped out to explore the city. The train is on time—I checked."

I smiled, reading her message. Even in her absence, there was a strange reassurance—like the plan was still intact, quietly moving forward.

I plugged my phone in and sat down for a second—and that's when it hit me. I was exhausted. Not just tired—zombie-level exhausted. The kind where your body gives up before your mind can even process it. I felt like I could collapse at any moment.

But priorities.

Shower first. Survival later.

Because clearly, I had been operating like some kind of overambitious superwoman. I had to see the ghats at night, experience the Shiva Aarti at dawn, catch the sunrise, and then—very importantly—sample every possible breakfast category Varanasi had to offer. Savories, chaat, chai, lassi, puri-chole… as if I was preparing for my last meal before the Amrit Snan.

There was a genuine concern—what if I fall asleep and don't wake up in time?

So, naturally, I did what any responsible adult would do. I messaged Goru Bhai: "Please wake me up at 4 p.m. anyhow."

Reinforcements in place, I crashed.

And just like that—lights out.

Next thing I knew, it was 4 p.m. The alarm was blaring. I woke up, slightly disoriented, staring at my phone… and of course, no call from my brother.

Even when I'm in another city, with a train to catch, my track record remains untouched—left to my own last-minute chaos.

I stepped out for a quick visit to Kaal Bhairav Temple (Kaal Bhairav Temple) — something I had missed earlier and didn't want to leave undone.

But the moment I reached, reality hit. The temple was overflowing with people. It was one of those moments where you have to make a choice—darshan or departure. And with a train to catch, I knew I couldn't risk it.

So I stood at the entrance itself.

I removed my footwear, pulled my dupatta over my head, folded my hands, and bowed down from where I was. My eyes were tired, my body drained—but my heart was full. Full of hope, devotion, and surrender. I closed my eyes and quietly asked for forgiveness—for anything I may have done knowingly or unknowingly.

And then… something unexpected happened.

An elderly couple walked out of the temple and paused right in front of me. The woman gently placed her hand on my shoulder; the man rested his hand on my head.

"Beta (child), can you help us cross the road?" they asked softly. "And this prasad is for you—please have it."

For a moment, I didn't know what to say. It felt… surreal.

Their car was waiting across the street, the driver casually sipping kulhad chai (tea in an earthen cup). I held their hands—both of them—and carefully helped them cross. It felt simple, but strangely meaningful.

Once we reached, they turned to me again, blessed me, and said,

"Khush raho, beta… kya naam bataya tumne?" (Stay happy, child… what did you say your name was?)

"Ji, Sonia," I replied.

They smiled warmly. "Badi acchi parvarish di hai tumhare bado ne tumhe." (Your elders have raised you very well.)

And just like that… my eyes filled up.

Because in that moment, they reminded me of my Jhaai (grandmother). The warmth, the affection, the way they spoke—it felt like something had come full circle. Like I hadn't missed the darshan after all… it had come to me, in a different form.

With a quiet smile and a full heart, I made my way back to the hostel.

Shubham kept calling, insisting, "Didi (sister), ek baar mil lo na… chaat khila deta hoon!" (Sister, please meet me once… I'll treat you to chaat!)

Under any other circumstance, I would have happily said yes. But my body had other plans. The nausea had kicked in, and the stomach pain—after almost two weeks—was back.

I guess this was inevitable. The amount of chaat I had attacked that morning, especially right after recovering… not my smartest decision.

So, for once, I chose restraint over temptation—and headed back, knowing the journey ahead still demanded more from me.

And then suddenly—it was 6 p.m.

Chaos. Absolute chaos.

Imaan and I stood there, phones in hand, frantically trying to figure out how to get from the hostel to Varanasi railway station. Every auto we approached refused without a second thought. Every app we opened failed us miserably. No cabs. No rides. Nothing.

In my head, the spiral had already begun. Of course. I knew I'd mess this up.

This train was my only shot at reaching Prayagraj—and here I was, leaving barely two hours before, with almost no buffer.

We exchanged glances—half hopeful, half on the verge of panic.

"Any luck?" she asked.

"Still trying…" I replied, my voice quieter than I liked.

And right on cue, guilt made its dramatic entry. I should have planned better. I know my history with last-minute travel. But no—I had spent time at the café, casually chatting with strangers about the Mahakumbh, sipping tea, eating Maggi… even while my stomach was clearly filing complaints.

Excellent decision-making. Truly.

And as if things weren't dramatic enough, every horror story I had heard began replaying—how even boarding the train from Varanasi could feel like a survival test. Last week of the Mahakumbh. Everyone is heading to Prayagraj.

Perfect timing.

Just when panic was about to peak, one of the hostel staff noticed us struggling—and almost magically arranged a ride.

Relief hit so fast, it almost felt suspicious.

Imaan had her seat in a different compartment, but I didn't even entertain that possibility.

"Come with me," I said. "We'll manage. We'll share the seat, request someone—something will work out."

And then, as if the universe decided to switch genres entirely, everything shifted.

The train wasn't overcrowded. No chaos. No pushing. No dramatic entry scenes. Almost… calm. Unusually calm.

There was even an empty seat from an RAC cancellation. We quietly took it, fully prepared to negotiate later.

When the TC arrived, he glanced at us and said, almost casually, "You both already have reservations. This seat got canceled at the last minute—you can sit together."

No questions. No extra charges. Just… allowed.

He even smiled and wished us luck for our first holy dip.

Imaan and I exchanged a look—half disbelief, half silent gratitude.

Somewhere between settling in and the train finding its rhythm, I turned to her and said, "Cancel your hostel booking. Stay with me at the ashram."

She looked at me, surprised.

"They've promised me a secluded corner. It's inside the Kumbh… barely 500 meters from the Sangam," I added.

That did it. She agreed.

Suddenly, the plan felt bigger. Realer. We even decided—we'd take the holy dip between 4 a.m. and 7 a.m. I wanted Brahma Muhurat, and I had to witness the sunrise.

And then, somewhere between Varanasi and Prayagraj, in those quiet, moving hours—the distance between us just… disappeared.

What started as small talk unfolded into something far more effortless. We spoke about everything—our upbringing, cultures, families, and what had brought us here. She had come all the way from Canada for a three-month exploration and had already seen more of India than most Indians I know. Her roots traced back to Gujarat, and there was a quiet strength about her—calm, composed, yet deeply aware. The way she carried herself, handled her luggage, moved with ease—it all spoke of discipline, of someone who had figured herself out in her own way.

And without even realizing it, we opened up. Fully.

We exchanged pictures of our families, spoke about pets like they were people, laughed about the chaos of our lives, shared ambitions, fears, work stories, music, food, and shopping—nothing was off-limits. No filters. No hesitation.

There's something disarming about strangers.

You can say things you wouldn't dare say out loud otherwise. Even your most awkward, vulnerable, or ridiculous moments—without the fear of being judged or misunderstood. And somehow, that honesty makes the connection purer. Simpler. Real.

In those few hours, we didn't just pass time—we understood each other.

What began as a coincidence started to feel like an alignment. Like we were meant to cross paths for this exact moment, this exact journey.

And somewhere between shared laughter and quiet pauses, we made a silent, certain pact—
We would take the dip together.

It was 1 a.m.

The train was running late by almost two hours. The ashram expected us at 1, but now it seemed like 3 a.m. would be the earliest we'd arrive.

My phone wouldn't stop buzzing. Messages from the ashram—Where are you? Are you safe? Did you cancel? They wanted answers I didn't have. Not yet.

But somehow, just knowing **Imaan** was beside me gave me a flicker of confidence. We'll figure it out, I told myself, clinging to that tiny lifeline.

Then my body decided to stage a rebellion.

I rushed to the train washroom, my stomach twisting in ominous premonition. Dizziness hit, a wave of nausea following close behind. My head spun, my limbs felt like lead. Perfect timing, right? The one day I had willed into existence for months, the day I had fought for, planned for, visualized every step of… and now this.

We had Limca. I took a cautious sip, trying to steady my churning insides.

"I've got this," **Imaan** said calmly, her voice steady and grounded. "Don't stress. Health first. Everything else comes later."

Her composure was contagious. I tried to absorb it, to swallow the panic along with the fizzy drink.

Inside, though, my mind was a maelstrom.

Really, Universe? Today? After all of this?

I had battled with logistics, chased every last-minute possibility, navigated chaos, and now, just hours before the holy dip, my body was staging a coup. I could almost hear it whispering: You think you can have it all? Think again.

And somewhere between nausea and exhaustion, I felt it—a fleeting, irrational thought. Nazar lag gayi kya? (Was I jinxed?)

But **Imaan** didn't let me drown in my spiraling thoughts. She stayed calm, quietly holding the chaos at bay. Her presence was like an anchor in the storm.

Finally, after what felt like an eternity, we arrived.

Prayagraj.

Even with my head throbbing and stomach protesting, I couldn't stop smiling. From the train window, the letters jumped at us—प्रयागराज (Prayagraj).

We looked at each other, eyes wide, a mix of disbelief, exhilaration, and childish joy lighting up our faces.

"We made it," we whispered in unison, almost reverent.

And then, the city hit us.

The streets outside were alive—lit up, pulsating with energy. Crowds surged like rivers of humanity, voices overlapping in chants, songs, and laughter, the scent of incense and street food weaving through it all. Every corner seemed to hum with devotion, mischief, and anticipation.

It didn't just feel like arriving somewhere.

It announced itself.

This was the Mahakumbh. And we were exactly where we were meant to be.

The next challenge—getting ourselves to the Mahakumbh.

Honestly, it was absurd. People were charging outrageous prices for just a few kilometers. And even if we hired a cab, car, or rickshaw, we'd still have to trudge a kilometer or more on foot. Considering my current state—a sleepy head, stomach cramps, and a migraine creeping in—that was an immediate no-go.

Then, like some divine intervention, two young guys appeared out of nowhere, following us. "We can drop you off at the doorstep. 500 per person."

I paused. "Excuse me, who even are you?"

Imaan stepped in, cool and composed, and grilled them on details. The boys explained: a two-wheeler, we go wherever we want.

Both **Imaan** and I locked eyes—and simultaneously blurted, "Bikes."

"Done," we said together, as if we were the rulers of this city and the universe had just handed us the keys.

Then came the next question: What about the luggage?

My suitcase wasn't huge, but it wasn't exactly feather-light either. They shrugged and said, "We'll manage." That was all the confidence we needed.

And just like that, we climbed onto the bikes, settled in like we owned them, and zipped through the chaos of Prayagraj, the night air whipping past, lights blurring, and the pulse of the city syncing with our own.

By the time we reached the ashram, I couldn't decide what I was more exhilarated about—the fact that we'd made it, or that I hadn't toppled off a speeding two-wheeler mid-Mahakumbh.

Either way, we had arrived.

"Food is ready. You both can freshen up; we'll heat it and serve. Kulhad chai (tea in an earthen cup) or haldi doodh (turmeric milk)—your choice," one of the ashram helpers called out.

We arrived around 3:45 a.m. The ashram was steeped in silence; everyone was fast asleep. Only the main hall had a soft, warm glow. There were around eighteen rooms—twelve with small washrooms, a main kitchen, a verandah, a dishwashing area, and a large living room where mattresses were neatly folded, alongside three or four khaats (woven cots) and a single regular bed without a mattress. Swami ji—the one I'd been coordinating with—was resting, ready to wake at 4:30 a.m. for the morning rituals.

No sooner had I tried to steady myself than my body staged a revolt—I threw up. My strength evaporated like mist in the early morning. Both **Imaan** and the helper were immediately by my side, looking like angels in a low-budget thriller. "Tonight, just rest. Holy dip can wait till tomorrow post-lunch—or even the day after," **Imaan** said, calm but unwavering.

There was no debate. She sized me up like a commander surveying a battlefield. "No point attempting the dip in zombie mode. Let's rest first; we'll decide later," she said.

We ate quietly—khichdi for me, simple but comforting—and were shown to the mattress-less bed in the living area. With a couple of bedsheets layered to make it slightly soft, I braced myself for the icebox of a floor, woolen socks doing their best against the cold. I wrapped my head in a warm shawl, and somehow, **Imaan** and I ended up sharing the bed. Exhausted, shivering, but quietly reassured by each other's presence, we drifted into a tentative sleep, the night outside whispering promises of the Mahakumbh that awaited.

By 8:30 a.m., we woke to a world already in overdrive, moving faster than our groggy brains could comprehend. **Imaan** and I stirred together, half-asleep, half-excited, and almost immediately, tea and coffee appeared as if conjured by magic. My stomach was still staging a protest, so I politely declined, earning a knowing smile from the helpers, who quickly substituted fresh fruits and juice—life nudges, subtle but effective.

Showers done, we geared up for Triveni Sangam. By 9:30 a.m., the biting early-morning cold had been replaced by a sun that felt like it was on a mission to test our resolve. My head throbbed, my body ached, yet my soul? My soul was electric. Every step felt like walking through centuries of devotion, faith, and whispered stories of millions who had come before.

Imaan asked what I planned to wear. I held up my simple white salwar kameez. She glanced at my other kurtis, and I offered, "Want to try one of mine?" A tiny smile curved her lips as she picked an indigo-blue floral print. Shades on, phones in hand, we decided to carry only one small sling bag, a water bottle, and some cash—ready, but minimal.

The streets leading to the Sangam were alive—a chaotic carnival of devotion. Beads, malas, Shivlings (Shiva symbols), flowers, garlands, incense, diyas, and devotional books jostled for attention alongside empty containers for Gangajal (holy water of the Ganga). Vendors called out, children darted past, and the aroma of marigolds mixed with smoke hung in the air. I had decided to carry two cans of Gangajal for my family and myself, and before I knew it, we were at the riverbank.

"You go first," **Imaan** said.

"Are you sure?" I asked, a twinge of nervousness sneaking in.

"Yes. I'll click your pics, take your videos—you lead. I'll follow," she said, steady and calm.

And then came the hilarious chaos. Dodging people, slipping on wet steps, almost dropping the water bottle more than once, laughing at our own clumsiness—it felt like the universe was testing us. But under the laughter, a quiet awe settled. The river gleamed, chants floated in the air, sunlight danced on the water, and the world shrank to just this moment, this shared adventure.

Before stepping in, we saw someone offering chandan (sandal paste) and kumkum tikka (red vermilion mark), along with the stamp for Shiva's imprint on the forehead. I draped my late grandmother's peach dupatta over my head, whispered Krishna, said "Shiv," placed my right hand on my head, and bowed. **Imaan** mirrored me, a silent echo of devotion.

I placed a small diya adorned with flowers on a pattal (leaf plate) and set it afloat on the water, a humble offering, a small gesture of devotion. Folding my hands, I whispered Om Namah Shivaya, letting the mantra guide me, anchoring me, reminding me why I was here.

I stepped into the river, and the cold struck me like a thousand tiny needles. My breath caught instantly, and for a moment, I questioned my own sanity. I have always feared water—never learned to swim—but this was not about skill or survival. It was about surrender.

The icy current brushed against my skin, jolting every nerve awake. And yet, beneath the shock, there was something strangely alive in it—an awakening, as if something deep within me had finally been stirred after a long silence.

The three sacred dips I took at the Mahakumbh Mela were not rituals. They were rebirths.

People speak of the Mahakumbh as a gathering of millions, a spectacle of faith, a river overflowing with devotion. But for me, it became something far more intimate and terrifyingly beautiful—it became the place where I finally met myself without noise, without masks, without escape.

The first dip shattered me.

The moment the holy water touched my skin, it felt as though years of exhaustion hidden inside my spirit rose violently to the surface. Every fear I had carefully buried, every silent guilt, every sleepless thought, every wound I kept decorating with fake strength—it all came rushing out of me at once. And for the first time in my life, I stopped resisting it.

As I stepped into the water, the only thing leaving my lips was: Om Namah Shivaya.

I did not pray for success.
I did not pray for love.
I did not even pray for happiness.

I prayed for release.

And somewhere beneath those sacred waters, I felt an emptiness so deep, so pure, that it frightened me before it healed me. Not the emptiness of loneliness—but the emptiness that comes after a storm destroys everything false inside you. The kind that leaves your soul standing naked before God.

The second dip felt like surrender.

Not defeat. Not weakness. Surrender.

The kind where you finally stop arguing with life. The kind where you loosen your grip on pain because carrying it has become heavier than letting it go. Standing there, surrounded by chants, prayers, and the echo of centuries of faith, I whispered once again:

Om Namah Shivaya.

I forgave people who had hurt me.
I forgave moments that broke me.
And for the first time, truly and completely—I forgave myself.

I forgave myself for being cruel to my own heart.
For expecting perfection while silently falling apart.
For carrying shame that did not belong to me.
For surviving things I never even spoke about aloud.

And then came the third dip.

The most powerful one of all.

By then, I was no longer entering the water as the same person. Something within me had already begun dissolving. Old habits, old fears, old versions of myself that had become prisons disguised as comfort—I let them go one by one.

As the water embraced me for the third time, my soul repeated only one thing:

Om Namah Shivaya. Om Namah Shivaya. Om Namah Shivaya.

I released the memories my mind kept clinging to like unfinished funerals.
I released the grief that had quietly settled into my identity.
I released every thought, every attachment, every invisible weight that was disturbing the harmony of my soul.

And when I rose from the water, I could not explain what happened in words that fully do it justice.

I did not feel "fixed."
I felt free.

Free from the exhausting need to hold everything together.
Free from the guilt of not being enough.
Free from the fear of becoming someone new.

It felt as though my soul had finally exhaled after years of suffocating in silence.

The Mahakumbh did not change my life in one dramatic second, the way films often show transformation. It changed me in a quieter, more permanent way. It emptied me of everything that was poisoning my spirit and made space for something softer, calmer, and infinitely more honest.

Those three sacred dips were not about washing away sins.
They were about burying the version of me that survived only through fear… and allowing a new self to rise through surrender.

And somewhere between the holy waters, the chaos of faith, and the silence inside my chest…
I understood something eternal:

Sometimes, before life can rebuild you, the soul must first agree to drown.

And maybe that is where this chapter truly ends—not at the riverbanks of the Mahakumbh, but in the quiet rebirth that followed after. Because the person who stepped out of those sacred waters was no longer carrying the same fears, the same guilt, or the same heaviness. I arrived there searching for peace, but I left with something far greater:

A soul finally willing to begin again.

And before I could even make my way back home, while the sacred echoes of Om Namah Shivaya still lingered within me, life revealed something I had been searching for without even realizing it—
One of the biggest purposes of my existence.

Even today, it feels unbelievable to me that I would one day stand at the sacred banks of the Mahakumbh Mela, taking holy dips beside a girl I had once met casually in a hostel room.

We were complete strangers when life introduced us. No history. No expectations. No grand beginning. And yet, somehow, we never truly felt like strangers. It was as if certain souls recognize each other long before words ever do.

Among millions of people gathered there, it still amazes me that destiny chose our paths to cross in that moment of faith, surrender, and transformation. Sometimes life builds its deepest connections in the most unexpected ways—not loudly, not dramatically, but quietly… like two souls simply arriving where they were meant to be.

CHAPTER 05

Harley & We

Thursday, 25th MAY, 2017 | Mumbai

BEEP!!

My phone lit up with a picture of a jet-black puppy with innocent eyes.

"Yeh kaun hai?" (Who is this?) I texted Goru Bhai immediately, like I had just discovered classified information.

"Kaisa laga? Isko final karun?" (How do you like it? Should I finalise this one?) he replied, with the seriousness of a man selecting wedding attire and not a dog.

"It's your birthday gift, you decide." I barely knew two or three dog breeds — for me, every dog was a cutie. I just loved them all. End of research.

"GSD," he replied proudly. German Shepherd Dog.

Another message followed instantly, just to ensure that I was properly impressed.

"Okay, whatever makes you happy," I said.

And that was my mistake.

Because within the next five minutes, he entered full emotional manipulation mode — puppy pictures, funny videos, dramatic reels, and silent propaganda.

I had planned something meaningful for his 17th birthday. Instead, I somehow became the unwilling CEO of his "please-let's-get-a-dog" campaign, fully aware my parents would say a strict NO, and I would eventually be the one getting audited.

Because in Indian households, when parents refuse something, the elder sibling is no longer a sibling.

They become the official soft target.

His birthday falls on 31st March, and for the last two months I had been procrastinating. But that excuse expired the day he casually landed up at the pet shop, ready to bring one home himself.

"Thank you, didi (elder sister), best birthday gift ever."

Gaurav has always been dangerously obsessed with dogs, cats, and honestly, any living creature with four legs and an attitude. He is the kind of person who spots an injured stray and suddenly behaves like a full-time veterinarian with zero qualifications.

Hungry dog? Fed.
Injured dog? Hospital run.
Lonely dog? Emotional support provided.

Of course, bringing one home was practically illegal in our house. Thank God. Otherwise, in a four-bedroom apartment, at least two rooms would already be occupied by animals.

The funniest part? The moment Gaurav steps onto a street, dogs just appear around him like he has some secret membership card to the canine universe.

And irony? He had already been bitten twice as a child — once at five and once at nine — but clearly those incidents failed to leave any emotional impact.

If anything, they probably strengthened the obsession.

When Harley finally came home, Mom was shocked… but happy.

Chai had absolutely no idea because we had successfully hidden him from her. Dad was away in the United States for three months, which honestly felt like divine timing.

So naturally, we decided to hide Harley until we physically could not anymore.

Imagine that — two siblings secretly hiding a living, breathing German Shepherd puppy inside the house like it was some classified operation.

Every tiny sound became suspicious. Every movement felt illegal.

Coincidentally, Harley himself stayed unusually quiet, as if he too understood the assignment and had willingly entered "silent survival mode."

The weekend arrived, and with it came our first vet visit.

Both Goru Bhai and I were ridiculously excited. We bought treats, toys, leashes, food bowls — everything.

We had even bought a basket for him, though Harley looked personally insulted every time we tried making him sit inside it.

The vet looked at him and smiled.

"Very handsome… just like Gaurav."

I burst out laughing.

"Same same but different."

Gaurav immediately gave me a look so sharp that my laughter converted itself into a professional poker face.

Then came the real battle.

"So, what name are you keeping?" the vet asked.

"Mars," I said confidently.

"Dexter," Gaurav replied at the exact same moment.

We looked at each other.

"It's my gift and he is mine," he argued.

"But I gifted him, so technically I get voting rights," I replied.

We barely fight in life. Most of the time, we function like twins accidentally born in different bodies. But clearly, destiny had reserved this disagreement for a dog-naming ceremony.

The vet laughed. "I already have two Dexters and one Mars… all German Shepherds. You guys might want to think of something else."

Silence.

Then I quietly said, "Harley."

Without blinking, Gaurav replied, "Harley it is."

No debate. No ego. No negotiation.

And somehow, the best part happened immediately after.

The moment I said "Harley," the tiny puppy started licking me as if he himself had approved the name.

Case closed. Name approved.

One fine day, my mother casually asked the trainer, "How big will he grow?" (Oh God!)

Both Goru Bhai and I slowly turned towards each other.

That was never a casual question in our house.

That was a pre-disaster announcement.

The trainer calmly showed her a picture of an adult German Shepherd.

Silence.

A long, emotional silence.

Then my mother whispered, "Hey Bhagwan (Oh God)… he's going to be the size of a small horse!"

She looked at both of us in betrayal.

"Why didn't you both tell me earlier?"

At that exact moment, we knew peace had officially left the household.

And honestly? She wasn't entirely wrong.

Harley was growing frighteningly fast.

One day he fit inside our arms like a soft cloud, and the next day he was sprinting through the house like a furry missile with absolutely no brakes.

GSD puppies are not normal dogs.

They are pure energy disguised as cuteness.

They don't walk — they patrol.
They don't run — they launch emotional attacks on furniture.

Harley's greatest obsession in life was the ball.

Nothing else mattered.

Sit? Only if the ball was visible.
Stay? Depends on emotional condition.
Come? Only if the ball was participating.

The moment a ball appeared, training officially ended.

Even the trainer once laughed and said, "He's not stubborn… he's just convinced he owns the house."

And slowly, we realised he actually did.

Days turned into weeks, and before we knew it, our entire routine revolved around Harley.

The house no longer felt like just a house. It had a heartbeat now.

If someone was upset, Harley would quietly sit beside them. If someone laughed, he would instantly join the celebration like he personally understood the joke.

Slowly, without realising it, he stopped being just a pet.

He became family.

And somehow, 31st March no longer belonged only to Gaurav.

It became Harley's day too.

Every year we celebrated their birthdays together — double cake, double excitement, double chaos. Harley would run around like he fully understood the concept of birthdays and believed the entire event was organised exclusively for him.

And honestly… maybe it was.

Once every two or three months, we would take Harley to the beach early in the morning. **Saloni** would often join us.

I have known **Saloni** for almost ten years. We met at a yoga studio near my place and somehow connected instantly.

She is calm in a way very few people are. Thick dark-brown hair falling till her waist, a soothing voice, sharp expressive eyes — the kind of person who notices everything without needing to say much.

The three of us would sit peacefully for exactly two minutes before Harley transformed into complete public entertainment.

The second he spotted someone playing with a ball, his soul would leave his body.

Children, strangers, random people peacefully minding their business — nobody was safe.

Harley would sprint across the beach, steal their ball with full confidence, and proudly return as if he had completed national duty.

And the funniest part? He genuinely believed every ball belonged to him emotionally.

Meanwhile, Gaurav would be running behind him apologising to strangers like a customer care executive handling complaints.

Around the same time, we also started taking him to pet-friendly cafés and restaurants.

Harley loved attention.

The moment someone called him "cute," his entire personality changed. Suddenly he would sit properly, tilt his head slightly, and behave like a very cultured gentleman who definitely did not destroy cushions at home.

But the funniest transformation happened around Chai.

Harley — the same creature who treated our house like a racing track — suddenly became unbelievably obedient around her.

No jumping. No madness. No zoomies.

He would quietly sit near her, lower himself respectfully, and behave like a disciplined student attending military school. She was the only person Harley genuinely respected.

The rest of us were simply staff members managing his lifestyle.

Around this time, I told **Saloni** everything.

She listened patiently and then simply said,

"Only you could turn life into a full-time situation like this."

And honestly, she wasn't wrong.

Then came Dad's call.

"I am back on the 20th November. Do you guys want anything from the States?"

Till then, we had somehow managed to hide Harley from him.

But suddenly, our temporary secret started feeling like a ticking time bomb. Dad is strict — not loud strict, silent strict. The kind where even a pause feels dangerous.

Then he casually asked Goru, "Do you have anything to say?"

"No."

"Anything you want to disclose or admit?"

Still no.

Exactly as planned.

Because I had already instructed him — we would reveal Harley together once Dad came home. Maybe seeing Harley in person would emotionally manipulate him better than explanations ever could.

But destiny had other plans.

Dad found out through the CCTV camera fixed near the corridor.

Yes.

A full HD exposure.

He saw me and Goru Bhai sneaking Harley out and bringing him back repeatedly like amateur criminals handling classified material.

Not through confession.

Not through honesty.

Through surveillance footage.

The moment Dad confronted us, Goru immediately said,

"It was didi (elder sister) who gifted him…"

Then began his legendary stammering performance — half explanations, half panic.

Before the situation could collapse further, Dad calmly interrupted.

"Since you both have got him, ensure you both take proper care of him. And take him to the vet regularly."

That was it.

No anger. No shouting. No lecture.

Just responsibility.

And suddenly, Harley was no longer a secret we were trying to hide.

He was family.

Then Dad asked the most important question of all.

"What is the correct spelling of his name?"

"H-A-R-L-E-Y," we replied together.

He nodded quietly.

Because Dad, being Dad, was already getting his name tag made. And somehow, in that small moment, everything changed. Harley was no longer just Gaurav's birthday gift. He had quietly become the heartbeat of our home.

Harley is genuinely such a good boy.

Chaotic? Absolutely.
Dramatic? Without question.
Slightly convinced the world revolves around him? One hundred percent.

But beneath all the madness was the purest heart.

The kind that quietly sits beside you when you are low, without ever being called. The kind that turns ordinary evenings into lifelong memories without even trying. The kind of love that asks for nothing except your presence, your time, and maybe your ball — if you are emotionally prepared to lose it forever.

Somewhere between the stolen slippers, beach zoomies, destroyed cushions, birthday celebrations, and endless chaos, Harley stopped being just a pet.

He became family.

He became home.

Note: This chapter will continue in the next book…

CHAPTER 06

Diljit Dosanjh – My Role Model

Some families pass down heirlooms.
Ours passed down weekend movie rituals.

It all began in our living room—where time slowed down, the aroma of home-cooked food filled the air, and the television became a doorway to Punjab. My siblings, my parents, and my late grandmother would gather like clockwork, ready for our weekly dose of Punjabi cinema. In a typical Punjabi household, this wasn't just entertainment—it was an event. A full-blown, no-tickets-required, laughter-guaranteed celebration.

We've watched everything—from the timeless charm of Mamla Garbar Hai featuring Gurdas Maan Ji to the unstoppable energy of Jatt & Juliet starring Diljit Dosanjh Ji. And somewhere between those films, between the laughter and the tears, between the "oye hoye!" moments and the emotional silences—I found a part of myself.

Now, let me be honest—no matter how many films I've watched, my heart always bows down to Punjab 1984. That film did far more than entertain me; it stayed with me long after the subtitles disappeared from the screen. The emotions lingered quietly in my mind, making it feel less like a movie and more like a deeply personal experience.

Before watching Punjab 1984, I admired Diljit Dosanjh for his music, charisma, and screen presence. But this film revealed a completely different side of him. He showed that he was not only a celebrated entertainer but also an actor capable of carrying deep emotion with remarkable honesty. Without dramatic dialogue or exaggerated expressions, he conveyed fear, helplessness, love, and confusion in a way that felt natural and real.

What impressed me most was the simplicity of his performance. He did not appear as a larger-than-life hero; he felt like someone from an ordinary Punjabi family. Through subtle expressions and quiet moments, he brought authenticity to the character, and somewhere during the film, admiration slowly turned into genuine respect. That was the moment I truly became his fan.

The film also reminded me that Punjabi identity is not defined only by celebration, music, and laughter, but also by resilience and endurance. Beneath the warmth and energy often associated with Punjab lies a history shaped by struggle, and Punjab 1984 portrayed that reality with sensitivity and dignity.

Equally unforgettable was the portrayal of the mother by Kirron Kher. Her performance carried the emotional soul of the story. She captured the quiet pain of a mother living between fear and hope with such restraint that even her silence felt heartbreaking.

Watching Punjab 1984 left me with both sadness and pride—sadness for the suffering reflected in the story, and pride in the strength that continues to define the Punjabi spirit. More importantly, the film changed the way I viewed Diljit Dosanjh. It made me admire him not just as a singer or star, but as an artist capable of leaving a lasting emotional impact through sincerity alone.

And that's where Diljit Dosanjh became more than just an actor to me—he became a role model in the truest sense.

To me, Diljit is not just a performer on screen. He feels like a presence, a reminder that success does not require abandoning where you come from. Instead, it can come from carrying your roots with pride, no matter how far life takes you. In a world that often chases trends and reinvention, he stands grounded in his identity—unapologetically Punjabi, effortlessly authentic.

What makes him stand out is his balance. One moment he makes you laugh with his natural charm, and the next, he leaves you thinking deeply with the sincerity he brings to his performances. There is no forced image, no attempt to fit into a mold—just a quiet confidence in being himself.

Watching him made me realize something simple but powerful: you don't have to become someone else to succeed. You only need to embrace who you are fully and express it without hesitation.

Being Punjabi, for me, has never been a subtle experience. It's loud, vibrant, full of life—and yes, a little dramatic. Okay… a lot dramatic 😄 Punjabi cinema captures that spirit perfectly. When I hear the language, it doesn't feel like dialogue—it feels like home. When I see the culture on screen, it doesn't feel like performance—it feels like memory.

From buttery paranthas that somehow look and taste real even through a screen, to phulkari dupattas that instantly remind me of family weddings, to accents that feel like they've walked straight out of my own living room—I connect with it all. Deeply. Instantly. Effortlessly.

And the Punjabi lehza… uff. I fall for it every single time. Maybe it's because it echoes so strongly in my own home, shaped by the most powerful presence of all—Meri Jhaai (my grandmother). The head of our family. The keeper of traditions. The kind of person who didn't just "teach" Punjabi culture; she embodied it so fully that we had no choice but to inherit it, proudly and permanently.

Looking back now, those movie nights were never just entertainment. They were quiet lessons wrapped in laughter—on identity, on pride, on staying rooted no matter how far life tries to pull you.

And somewhere in all of this, Diljit Dosanjh slips in like a reminder I didn't know I needed. Not preachy, not loud about it—but effortlessly consistent. He shows that you can walk into any world, any stage, any screen, and still carry your roots like they are your signature.

And if there's one thing Diljit unknowingly taught me, it's this:
Be so deeply rooted in who you are that the world has no option but to recognize you.

Because trends will come and go. Languages may fade. Cultures may blur.
But when you carry your roots in your heart—with pride, with passion, and maybe a little Punjabi tadka—you don't just exist in the world… you rise.

One of my absolute favorite looks of Diljit Dosanjh till date is his Met Gala appearance, where he wore a deeply rooted Punjabi-inspired traditional outfit. What made it unforgettable for me was not just the fashion, but the emotion behind it. It felt like he was not just attending an international event—he was representing Punjab on a global stage. That aura, that pride, that quiet confidence… it felt like history meeting identity. It was not just style—it was statement.

It truly felt like: "Main hoon Punjab" (I am Punjab).

And honestly, that energy is what defines him everywhere he goes.

Because when he shows up, it always feels like:
"Punjabi aa gaye oye!" (The Punjabis have arrived!)

But if I'm being completely honest, there's one small regret I carry.

I wish my parents had spoken to us more in Punjabi than Hindi while we were growing up.
Because while my grandmother—meri Jhaai—wrapped us in the warmth of Punjabi with every sentence she spoke, my parents had their own "special timing" with the language. Punjabi would come out fluently… but only during scoldings or punishments. The moment things got serious—boom—pure Punjabi mode activated! Otherwise, it was mostly Hindi running the show in our day-to-day lives.

And English? Oh, that's a recent guest appearance in our family—especially after my brother-in-law entered from Canada. Now suddenly we're all like, "Excuse me… what is happening here?" 😄

But jokes apart, language is not just about words—it's about identity. And somewhere between Hindi conversations and Punjabi scoldings, I learned to feel Punjabi more than I spoke it.

And maybe that's why I hold onto it so tightly today.

Coming Back to My Role Model

Okay, let's get real. What exactly is a role model? I'm not talking about the usual textbook answer—someone you look up to, or someone who inspires you with fancy quotes on Instagram. No. A role model, for me, is someone who hits you right in the soul, someone who makes you laugh, think, cry, and get up all at once.

Someone whose energy connects with yours so perfectly that it feels like… destiny.

For me, that person is none other than Diljit Dosanjh. And I say that with my full chest—no hesitation, no filter, only pride.

I don't usually fall for celebrities. I don't worship fame. I don't lose myself in fandom. But Diljit? That connection is different. It is not obsession—it is inspiration. It feels like a quiet force in my life, like someone reminding me, without even speaking directly to me, that I can rise above my own doubts.

He feels less like a celebrity and more like a Guru in disguise—someone who lifts your mood when you're sinking, who makes you laugh when you don't even feel like smiling, and somehow, without preaching, pushes you back toward your strongest self.

And then there's the magic of how he exists in this world.

Forget the songs. Forget the films. Forget the comic timing that lands effortlessly in the middle of chaos. Forget even the designer kurta pajamas that scream effortless charm. And yes—forget those unforgettable moments when he steps onto a stage wearing a chadara and a white pag (turban), carrying Punjab on his shoulders like it is not an outfit but a statement. In those moments, he doesn't perform culture—he becomes it. Quiet. Proud. Unshakable.

There is something almost spiritual in him. Not loud spirituality—no preaching, no noise. Just a simple truth he seems to live by: life is temporary, God is one, and we are all just playing our roles… so why not play them fully, wildly, honestly?

Now mix that philosophy with discipline, relentless hard work, raw talent, and a sense of humor that can break tension in a second—and you get a man who is impossible not to admire.

Not in a fan way.
In a pause-and-reflect-on-your-life way.

He makes you ask yourself uncomfortable questions like:
"Am I even trying hard enough?"
"Why am I complicating life so much?"
"Why don't I just… be real?"

And the twist is—he never forces it. He just exists like that.

His simplicity is loud without being loud. His confidence is calm but unshakable. His values feel inherited, not performed. And somewhere in that authenticity, you start seeing something strange… a reflection. Not of him—but of who you wish you were.

And then he switches gears—because of course he does.

One moment, he's making you laugh with effortless charm. Next moment, he's singing a line that somehow lands directly in your chest. Then he's acting in a scene that doesn't feel acted at all—it feels lived. And before you even realize it, you're emotionally invested in a man who doesn't even know you exist.

That's the problem with him.
He doesn't just entertain you. He occupies you.

I'll be honest—he played a huge role in me writing this book. His speeches, his concerts, his words like "Sapne vadde vekho" (dream big)—they didn't just inspire me, they shook me awake. They reminded me that life is vast, full of possibility, and waiting for you to step into it fully. And the most powerful part? He does all of this while staying grounded, humble, and completely real.

And that's why Diljit is not just my role model. He is a teacher, a motivator, a soul connector, and an unstoppable force of inspiration.

Watching him is like drinking chai on a rainy day in Punjab—it warms you, it wakes you up, and somehow, you feel like you can take on the whole world.

And I say that with immense pride.

Because Diljit doesn't just represent success—he represents roots. He represents the courage to stay original in a world that constantly asks you to fit in.

In a world full of filters, he showed me the power of being real. In a world chasing validation, he taught me the strength of self-belief.

And somewhere between his journey, his voice, and his unapologetic Punjabi spirit…

I didn't just find a role model—
I found a reflection of who I want to become.

Honestly, Diljit Dosanjh truly lives up to his name… Dil Jeet (winner of hearts) indeed. Every single time. Without fail. Again and again, he manages to conquer our hearts.

Apart from publishing this book and seeing it reach readers around the world—which is one of my biggest dreams—there is another dream tucked quietly in my heart. A slightly softer, slightly more personal, and absolutely non-negotiable one: having a cup of coffee with Diljit Ji.

Just one hour. No cameras. No crowd. No stage. Just a table, two cups of coffee, and a conversation about life, dreams, failures, music, and everything in between.

I feel like I would sit there pretending to be calm while internally my brain is buffering and my soul is probably doing backflips. The idea of actually looking at him while he speaks? Let's just say my composure would need serious emotional support.

And my friends? Oh, they know this dream very well. Every time his name comes up, they tease me, laugh a little, raise their eyebrows, and go, "Let's see." And I just smile. I don't argue. I don't over-explain. Because deep down, in a place I don't even question anymore, I carry a quiet certainty.

Before I leave this world, that coffee will happen at least once in this lifetime.

And maybe that is what makes it beautiful—not how close it looks, but how strongly it already lives in my heart. Because some dreams are not meant to be defended. They are just meant to be felt.

If life ever decides to be kind enough to make it happen—one hour, one coffee, one conversation—I know I won't have anything perfectly rehearsed to say. I will probably just sit there, quietly overwhelmed, thinking:

So this is what peace and panic feel like at the same time.

And that is where this chapter rests—not in certainty, but in belief. Because some dreams are not measured by how close they are, but by how deeply they shape you while you wait for them. Maybe that coffee will happen tomorrow, maybe years later, or maybe in a way I cannot even imagine yet. But I know this much: it is not just a wish anymore—it is a part of me. And sometimes, the most powerful endings are not when dreams are fulfilled, but when they become strong enough to quietly promise: I am still on my way.

CHAPTER 07

Meri Jhaai (My Grandmother)
Part I: Between Her Last Breath and Mine

"Hasti reh, khush reh. Dekh, kitni badhiya lagti hai tayyar hokar."
(Keep smiling, stay happy. Look how beautiful you look when you get dressed up.)

She used to say that to me every single time I got dressed up.

There was something about seeing me ready—bangles, kajal (kohl eyeliner), a little lipstick, and finally, the delicate sound of panjebain (anklets) around my ankles—that filled her with quiet joy.

Maybe it reminded her of something innocent, or maybe it was just her way of saying she was proud. She'd sit back, smile at me with those kind eyes, and I swear the world felt softer in that moment.

But she wasn't just my grandmother.

She was my everything.

We called her Chai. Or Jhaai (grandmother).

She was my anchor, my comfort, my home.

The safest place I've ever known.

People often talk about soulmates like they're always romantic—like they must be lovers.

But my soulmate was her.

And I'll say this with every breath I take, in this life or any that may come—

No one has ever, or will ever, love me the way she did.

She didn't just love the version of me that smiled brightly for the world. She loved the messy, unruly me. The moody, unpredictable me. The jhalli (crazy/silly), clumsy, and vulnerable me—the one tangled in restless thoughts and quiet storms of overthinking. She loved me when I was too much for others—and not enough for myself. She saw through me like light through glass. She understood the tremble behind my laughter and the silence between my words. She knew my fears, my quirks, my preferences, my moods—everything. She recognized my innocence and my fire. My ambition, my stubbornness. My defeats, my dreams.

She knew how easily I could hurt, how deeply I could care, how obedient I always was—soft-spoken, gentle, but sharp when wounded. She knew I couldn't harm an insect—and that I'd flip the house upside down if I ever saw a cockroach.

I'd jump onto the bed in sheer terror, crying and shrieking—while she sat nearby, laughing softly, trying to calm me down with her soothing presence.

She was my secret-keeper.

My better half.

The one who finished my sentences—and understood the ones I couldn't finish. The missing piece that made me whole. She could read my eyes like scripture—knew instantly when something was wrong or when my heart felt light.

She wasn't just a grandmother.

She was my breath.

My shadow.

My prayer.

My light.

Not God, not family, not friends, not lovers—no one has ever held the place in my heart that she did.

And the day I lost her in the physical world...

I didn't just lose her.

I lost a part of myself.

I've always written from emotion, never logic. My words usually spill out like a river—but today, my hands hesitate. Not because I don't know what to say—but because how do you even begin to describe someone who was your entire universe?

Where do I start?

Which memory do I pull from the thousands she left me with? How do I explain the kind of love I had for her—the kind that I would trade my life for, just to hold her hand once more?

To rest my head on her lap. To hear her say my name again—Sonia—like no one else ever will.

Today, as I write, my hands tremble.

My eyes blur.

My chest tightens.

Because she's not just a memory.

She still is.

She's in the scent of slow-cooked food on a winter morning.

In the tang of achaar (pickle) she kept in her favorite martabaan (ceramic pickle jar). In the folds of her warm shawl. In the way she said "Sonia"—a sound only she ever got just right. I never say "my late grandmother." Because for me, she never truly left. I don't need to close my eyes to find her. All I have to do is whisper, "Chai," And she's there—right beside me. Smiling, holding me. Grounding me. Loving me still. I don't know if I'll ever be able to love someone the way I loved her. What we had was something beyond words.

It was sacred.

Timeless.

Unshakable. Beyond the logic of this world.

Even now, I try to walk the path she showed me.

And yes—it's hard.

The right path usually is.

I got wounded. I often feel like a stranger in my own world. They call me old-fashioned. Some say I'm too rigid, too blunt, too brutally honest. Because this world wasn't crafted for hearts like mine—soft, unwavering, and fiercely genuine. It celebrates masks and manipulation. People who speak sweetly and sting silently. Those who calculate relationships with their heads, never their hearts.

But I don't want to fit in.

I want to live in a way that would make her proud.

Because one day, when it's my time to go...

I want to look into her eyes again and say—with a steady voice and a full, open heart:

"Chai, whatever you taught me—I tried to live by.

With sincerity in my soul.

With truth in my heart.

I couldn't be perfect.

But I was yours."

And if there's one thing I know with absolute certainty—

She will return to me—not in some faraway lifetime, but in this one.

She will find her way back into my life, and into my arms.

And when our souls meet again—in a glance, a touch, a silence only we understand—I will know.

Without question. Without doubt.

I will know it's her.

Because some bonds are written not in time, but in eternity.

Meri Chai (My Grandmother) — My Power, My Peace

She was strong—but not the kind of strength that needed to shout.

Her silence could still a room.

Her voice? Calm, yet commanding.

Her attitude? Fearless.

Even most men today don't carry the kind of presence she had without effort.

She lived by values no one could shake—not society, not convenience, not even time.

Rooted in righteousness, she walked a path paved with principle. If something wasn't right, it simply wasn't done. No bending. No pretending. No shortcuts.

She was an old soul with a forward mind—

Disciplined, sharp, and fiercely independent.

Hisab-kitab ki pakki (someone meticulous and disciplined with accounts and responsibilities).

She had her ways, her rules, her wisdom—carved in stone and wrapped in love. She didn't change them for comfort or to please others.

She lived with clarity.

And she loved unconditionally.

Whenever life knocked me down—when I felt lost, small, or broken—she'd sit beside me, composed and still, and say gently:

"Koi baat nahi, roti kyun hai? Rone se hum kamzor nahi hote, par phir bhi hamesha haste raho—kyunki hasne se aur himmat milti hai. Badi se badi mushkil bhi asaan hone lagti hai."
(It's alright, why are you crying? Crying does not make us weak, but still, always keep smiling—because smiling gives us more strength. Even the biggest difficulties begin to feel easier.)

Whenever people around me hurt me or misunderstood who I truly was, she had her own gentle way of guiding me through the storm.

She would say,

"Never explain yourself to someone who doesn't want to understand."

Then, with that unmistakable twinkle in her eye and a shrug full of quiet wisdom, she'd add,

"Behas-baazi mein kuch nahi rakha, Sonia."
(There is nothing worthwhile in pointless arguments, Sonia.)

But her favorite mantra, the one she lived by, was timeless:

"Ek chup, sau sukh."
(One moment of silence can bring a hundred comforts.)

Not a silence born of surrender, but one rooted in dignity and profound understanding.

And finally, her unwavering truth that stayed with me always:

"Sach sach hota hai. Chahe koi jitna bhi dhoka de, kitne jhooth bole—tu sach bolne se kabhi mat ghabrayiyo."
(Truth remains truth. No matter how much others deceive or lie—never be afraid to speak the truth.)

She found quiet joy in the simple act of watching me truly live—not just exist, but breathe life into every moment.

She adored seeing me dressed to the nines, laughing freely, savoring food with a fullness of heart, and sleeping peacefully, a calm serenity softening every line of my face.

Her happiness was interwoven with mine—like threads in the same fabric.

She didn't just wish for my success.

She wanted me to be happy. Fearless. Bold. Independent.

She encouraged both my sister and me to never stop dreaming—to chase ambitions and build a life that belonged solely to us.

She would often say with quiet conviction,

"Kabhi apne sapne, apni naukri, apni khwahishein mat chhodna.
Hum khushnaseeb hain ki jee rahe hain—toh puri tarah se jiyo.
Zindagi badi khoobsurat cheez hai. Usse sirf guzarna nahi, jeena seekho."

(Never give up your dreams, your career, or your desires.
We are fortunate to be alive—so live fully.
Life is a beautiful thing. Don't just pass through it, learn to truly live it.)

And then came the time when her body began to slow, but her soul remained fierce.

She had grown weak—bedridden now—but my resolve was strong.

I had decided, without hesitation, to leave my job.

I wanted to be with her every single minute. To soak in her wisdom, to learn from her presence, to just sit near her and be.

I remember telling her, "No job in this world can offer me what your companionship can. I'd rather be by your side."

She looked frail, but her gaze didn't waver.

And with the same strength she had always carried in her voice, she said:

"Naukri mat chhodiyo.
Chahe kuch bhi ho jaaye, kisi ke bharose kabhi mat rehiyo.

Apne pairon par hamesha khadi rehiyo—chahe duniya kuch bhi bole."

(Never leave your job.
No matter what happens, never become dependent on anyone.
Always stand on your own feet—no matter what the world says.)

That was her—soft at heart, iron-willed in spirit.

Even as her body failed her, she was still preparing me to stand on my own. To walk this world with strength, dignity, and grace.

We had our own little tradition, a quiet, beautiful ritual that belonged only to us.

Every milestone, every joy, every celebration—was incomplete until it was shared with her.

Report cards. The first mangoes of the season. A new outfit. A new car.

Even a freshly stitched kurti (traditional tunic) wasn't official until Chai had seen it.

I still remember that day—January 2012.

My final MBA exams loomed at the end of April, but before all that pressure could settle in, life had already whispered its promise to me.

My very first job offer had arrived through the college placement: EIH Limited.

I was the only student selected out of the 132 who sat for the interview.

And believe me, getting shortlisted—let alone selected—by EIH Limited wasn't easy. It was a long, demanding process, designed for those with endurance and quiet determination.

It began with several rounds of preliminary screening, followed by a high-pressure panel interview. Then came the General Manager's round—formal, precise, and deeply probing.

Just when I thought the toughest part was behind me, there was the Skype interview—the kind that makes your pulse quicken even before the screen lights up.

But even that wasn't the final step.

After all the approvals came through from every level, they administered a thorough psychometric test—evaluating not just your aptitude, but your instincts and resilience.

I had applied for this role back in October 2011. But because I'd already been shortlisted at Zee for a space-selling role, the college placement cell didn't allow me to sit for any more interviews.

Still, somewhere deep inside, I held on to the hope of making it to EIH Limited.

I couldn't explain it clearly then. Maybe it was the brand's legacy. Or maybe it was the way the process unfolded—deliberate, unhurried, almost as if they were testing not just your skills, but your patience and perseverance.

Unlike most companies, where decisions come within a month or two, EIH moved at its own pace—slow, thorough, and highly selective.

It took four long months.

And somehow, I made it.

The email blinked on my screen like a beacon of hope, and my heart felt like it might burst from the sheer joy coursing through me.

I ran to her, the laptop trembling in my hands, my eyes wide and shining—like a child discovering a whole new world for the very first time.

"Chai, dekho! Naukri lag gayi!"
(Chai, look! I got the job!)

She looked at the screen, her eyes welling up with a haunting mix of pride and prayer.

Then, as always, she placed her hand gently on the laptop—not to read, but to bless.

Her gaze locked onto the screen with unwavering focus, as if she were reading every letter with the solemnity and authority of a judge passing final verdict.

And then, in her calm, firm tone, she said:

"Paise chahe jitne marzi milen, tu sirf apne haq ke paise liyo.
Kisi se bura ni bolna. Na chugli karni. Na kabhi khud ko kam samajhiyo.
Apna kaam imaandari aur khushi se kariyo."

(No matter how much money you earn, only ever accept what is rightfully yours.
Never speak ill of anyone. Never gossip. And never think less of yourself.
Do your work with honesty and happiness.)

She pulled me close and chuckled softly:

"Aaj kal computer pe bhi naukri pakki ho jaati hai… hamare zamane mein toh milkar hoti thi."
(Nowadays, jobs get confirmed on computers too… in our time, it all happened in person.)

We both burst out laughing like children.

And then, true to tradition, she added with a sparkle in her eye,

"Goru se keh… pizza order kar dega… aur thodi mithai le aayega."
(Tell Goru… he'll order pizza… and bring some sweets too.)

That was her.

A perfect blend of old-world charm and new-world sparkle.

A woman who could bless your future and laugh about email job offers—all in the same breath.

She was always anchoring me. Always celebrating me. Always seeing me.

No matter the moment—whether she was offering life-altering wisdom or a gentle reminder—she would always end her words the same way:

"Hasti reh. Khush reh."
(Keep smiling. Stay happy.)

Those weren't just blessings.

They became the pillars I leaned on.

The words that built me from within.

Maybe that's why I am who I am today.

Maybe her love still surrounds me—like an invisible shawl wrapped around my shoulders on hard days.

It's true what they say:

"Strong women raise strong women."

And I know, deep in my bones, that I was blessed beyond measure—

To live 31 years under the roof and in the arms of a woman like her.

She lives in every inch of me.

In the cadence of my voice.

In the steadiness of my walk.

In the way I fall—and in the way I always rise.

And on days when life feels loud, overwhelming, or just a little too cruel—

I don't need to close my eyes to remember her.

I simply whisper,

"Chai…"

And there she is.

Still.

Beside me.

Always.

Friday, 8th FEBRUARY, 2019

(The fate I could not change)

7:30 p.m. Mumbai

I had just wrapped up my lobby PR at the Trident, Nariman Point—a customary task where I met VIP guests, gathered their feedback, and explored future prospects. Usually, this stretched until 8 p.m., but tonight, I finished right on time at 7:30.

We had a farewell planned for one of our team members, so I hurried to get ready and leave for BSE, Colaba. A few of us were leisurely goofing around, clicking pictures. I was draped in a vibrant parrot-green saree and heading off to change.

By 8:30 p.m., we left. The traffic was relentless, causing us to run late. My phone died due to low battery—a rare, almost unheard-of situation for me. I handed over the car to the valet and stepped into the pub.

Everyone was gathered; I ordered myself a Coke, planning to leave by 11, mindful of work the next day.

Then Goru Bhai's frantic calls began—incessantly pinging my phone. This was unusual. He never called my friends or my colleagues; it was always just me.

"Your brother is calling—it's urgent! Why is your phone off?" my Director of Sales approached me, concern etched on his face.

I grabbed my phone from the charger, thinking it might be something trivial—a question about when I'd get home, or maybe he needed the car or something.

Rupali, one of my closest friends, handed me her phone.

On the other end, I heard Goru's voice, heavy and trembling:

"Didi, sab kuch chhodo, jaldi ghar ke liye niklo!"
(Didi, leave everything and come home quickly!)

It wasn't a prank. The gravity in his voice was unmistakable.

"Are you okay? What happened?" I urged.

"Didi, drive carefully," he said, his voice cracking like it was being held together by sheer will.

My heart skipped. Something was off.

"Just tell me! What happened?" I yelled, panic lacing every word.

I started blurting out questions without stopping to breathe—"Are you okay? Is Harley alright? Did Mummy say something? Did you have a fight with anyone?"

Silence. Just his breath. Heavy. Uneven.

And then, the question I dreaded the most slipped from my lips:

"Is Chai okay?"

He paused.

Then said, almost in a daze,

"Didi… woh Chai na… neend se uth nahi rahi."
(Didi… Chai… she isn't waking up from her sleep.)

I froze.

My heart started pounding so loudly I could barely hear my own voice.

"Arey! Aise kaise? Tu jagaa na… unko utha, kuch bhi karke! Paas mein baith… haath pakad... kuch bol!"
(What do you mean? Wake her up… do something! Sit beside her… hold her hand… say something!)

His breath hitched.

And then, his voice broke completely.

Silence followed—thick, deafening, final.

That was it.

My stomach dropped. My hands went cold.

"Kya hua Chai ko?"
(What happened to Chai?)

I asked again, desperate, begging for him to lie to me.

But he started crying.

And I knew.

My voice cracked open—

"Is she still breathing?"

"I don't know," he choked out. "Please… just come home safe."

I froze.

Rupali looked at me, concerned.
"Is everything okay?"

I couldn't see or hear anything clearly except my little brother's shaky voice and my grandmother's presence echoing in my mind.

I whispered to myself,
"No, no, no! This can't be how she leaves me! Nooooo!"

Word had spread—she was gone.

It felt like the ground shifted beneath me.

Goru had broken the news, but his voice was trembling, unclear—maybe on purpose, maybe because he didn't want to say it out loud.

He urged me not to travel home alone, but his words barely registered.

I ran further ahead.

Heart pounding. Breath short. Somewhere between disbelief and dread.

As I reached the exit, a colleague caught me. I don't even remember who—just warm hands on my arms trying to steady me.

And then, I collapsed.

Right there—knees to the floor, grief ripping through me like glass. The weight of the news crashing down louder than any scream.

Someone offered me water. I splashed it on my face over and over, as if I could wash away what I had just heard—as if the cold shock would wake me from a dream.

I kept telling myself, maybe it's a mistake. Maybe her breathing is just shallow. Maybe they got it wrong. Maybe... she's still alive.

But deep down, I knew.

And then another wave of panic hit—I had to call Daddy. He was in the States.

How do you tell your father—his mother, his backbone, his everything—is gone?

How do you break someone else's world when yours has just fallen apart?

I called him.

Busy.

I dialed my mother.

Unreachable.

I tried Goru again—no answer.

I left a message for Dad:

"We need to speak… Chai isn't well. Please call ASAP, Daddy!"

After that, everything blurred.

I don't know who helped me into the car, where my own car was parked, or how I left.

For nearly ten minutes, I was in a trance.

Slowly, as if surfacing from underwater, I became aware that I was seated in the back of a cab.

The world outside blurred past in streaks of light and motion, but inside, time had stilled.

Rupali sat beside me, gently holding my hand, coaxing me to sip some water, while Pooja sat in the front, guiding the driver and whispering instructions with quiet urgency.

I reached for my phone with trembling hands and dialed **Amruta**—my best friend for over 28 years.

A sister in spirit.

She was supposed to visit my home that day to invite our family to her wedding, scheduled for February 14, 2019, in Nagpur.

The plan was to hand over the wedding card to Chai personally—

that card, now, would never meet her hands.

My voice was already cracking under the weight of what I feared.

My throat tightened as the phone rang—once, twice—and then she answered.

But she said nothing.

"Will I get to see her? Is Chai… is she still alive? Am I too late?"

There was silence.

A pause too long, too heavy.

Amruta didn't answer immediately—I could feel her holding her breath, trying not to break.

But something in me shifted.

My voice, suddenly steadier, sharper, pushed through the silence.

"Tell me. Now. Please… tell me the truth."

Her voice cracked.

"She's gone," she whispered. "The doctor declared it about 30 minutes ago."

A silence fell between us—quiet, final, unforgiving.

I took a deep breath.

Somewhere inside, a wall went up.

Grief was pushed aside—not forgotten, but folded away.

I steadied myself and spoke softly, but with authority, like a different version of myself had stepped forward.

"**Amruta**, you know, right? You cannot stay there. Your wedding is next week. Please go home, take a bath, and don't let this break you. Not now."

Even in the middle of heartbreak, I found myself protecting her.

Perhaps that's what Chai would have done—and so I did it too.

There was no time to weep.

No room for collapse.

Daddy was still in the States, more than 24 hours away.

Until he arrived, I had to step into the role Chai had quietly been grooming me for all along.

I had to be the man of the house.

Take charge. Manage everything. Hold my younger brother together. Be my mother's strength.

My phone buzzed again.

It was Kake, my sister, calling from Canada.

Her voice tumbled out, panicked and breathless, grief bursting through every word.

"Didi, are you okay? Is it true? Are you home? Can I see you on video? How did it happen? What's happening now? Please tell me... please..."

Her questions came like waves, crashing faster than I could answer.

I closed my eyes for a moment and said the only thing I could manage.

"Yes… she's gone."

And then silence.

"I'm booking a flight," she said. "I'm coming!"

I hesitated.

She had undergone nasal surgery just the night before.

Her body was healing, but her heart had just broken—how could I stop her?

Still, I tried.

"Kake…" I said softly, "let us think this through. Should you really travel like this? Alone? Especially now, just hours after surgery?"

There was a pause.

"I know," she whispered, ending in tears, "but this is the last time I'll get to see her. I want to touch her, seek her blessings one last time. I want to be with you all, Didi."

I swallowed hard.

My voice stayed calm, even though my soul was torn apart.

"I know. And if I could, I'd put you on the next flight myself. But think, Kake, now is not the time to be impulsive. Would she want you to risk your health? You know her. She would want you to be wise, not emotional. To be present, yes—but to be safe. I'll show you everything—every ritual, every prayer—on video. I promise you won't miss a thing. Let's do what's right and what's required, not out of haste."

She didn't argue.

But I knew her silence was soaked in helplessness.

And then I turned into someone else—or maybe into the very version of me that Chai had been preparing all along.

Without shedding a single tear, I began calling our relatives.

One by one.

Voice steady.

Tone respectful.

Words mechanical.

I was doing what needed to be done.

I wasn't grieving.

I was functioning—hollow, yes, but present.

My friends in the cab didn't speak.

They just watched quietly, sensing that something inside me had gone still.

Then came Daddy's call.

I braced myself.

His voice, when it came through the line, felt like it had aged decades in mere hours—weathered, fragile, carrying the weight of something too vast to name.

"How are you, Nona?" he asked gently. "Don't worry about anything. I'm making all the arrangements. I'll be with you all soon."

He was trying to stay strong, holding himself upright on words alone.

But I could tell—he was skirting around the mention of Chai, as if saying her name aloud would shatter him completely.

"I'm here, Daddy," I said softly. "On my way home."

"I've just been coordinating everything... booking flights," he explained, the weariness in his voice unmistakable. "That's why I hadn't called earlier."

I closed my eyes and exhaled.

"This will be the hardest journey of your life, Daddy. But don't worry—I've got everything covered until you arrive. Goru is with us. Mummy is safe. Just get here."

There was a long, aching silence.

The kind that stretches across oceans and grief.

Then, barely a whisper:

"I love you, Nona."

Tears welled up before I could stop them.

"I love you too, Daddy," I said, my voice trembling. "Come safely."

I don't remember who paid the cab fare, or where I'd left my car, or even when my phone was last charged.

Everything was a blur, fragments slipping through the cracks of my mind.

But as I stepped out of the vehicle, I remember two things with piercing clarity—the hollow, burning ache in my chest... and Pooja and Rupali's hands gently holding mine.

"I'm okay," I said quietly, my voice steady though everything inside me was unraveling.

I didn't want to be held—not because I didn't need comfort, but because I didn't know how to receive it just then.

I was barely holding myself together, and if anyone embraced me, I feared I might fall apart completely.

But I couldn't find the words to say that.

So I just stood there, letting the silence do what words couldn't.

As I walked toward the building, I saw Goru Bhai coming down the steps to meet me.

In that moment, he wasn't just my younger brother.

He was my elder—steady, red-eyed, but standing tall, holding himself together for my sake.

He walked straight up to me and gripped my shoulders, firm and grounding.

"Didi," he said quietly, "don't cry. Not even a little. Daddy will be here tomorrow night. Until then, you and Mummy—you're both my responsibility."

Something clenched inside me.

But not a single tear escaped.

I simply nodded, letting his strength wrap around my breaking heart.

"Let's get everything ready before Daddy comes," I whispered. "Let's make sure she gets the farewell she deserves."

We embraced—no drama, no weeping.

Just strength. Quiet, solid strength.

I stepped into the house.

I was still in my red top and denim, unchanged from work—untouched by the storm that had swept through our world.

The moment I entered, my eyes searched for her.

And there she was.

Lying on a thin mattress on the floor, wrapped in her soft pink nighty, she looked almost ethereal—peaceful in a way that made the ache in my chest even sharper.

Her face held a strange kind of glow, not of this world—as if some quiet light had taken residence beneath her skin.

Beside her, an agarbatti (incense stick) burned slowly, its gentle smoke curling upward like a prayer.

The scent—earthy, sacred, heartbreakingly familiar—filled the room.

A small aate ka diya (a traditional lamp made from wheat dough) flickered steadily at her side.

I moved closer, wordless.

My instinct was to sit beside her, just like I always had.

"Goru," I said softly, "can I get some Gangajal (holy Ganges water)?"

Before I could even finish, he was there, placing it gently in my hand.

"Didi," he said, "I've already given her a little. But please… you do it too."

Around us, neighbors stood quietly.

Some wept.

Others whispered prayers.

The room was heavy—not just with grief, but with love unspoken, memories pressing in from all sides.

I looked up and spoke, clear and calm.

"Please don't cry. Let's not send her off with tears."

Then I leaned in, kissed her forehead, and gently placed my hand over it—as if I could will life back into her, as if the warmth of my palm might stir something in her spirit, just one last time.

I kissed her lips once… twice… and then a third time—each kiss trembling, reverent, aching.

As if my soul was trying to meet hers mid-journey.

As if, in that fragile silence between us, love might still be louder than death.

"Dekho, Chai," I whispered, "main ab bhi nahi ro rahi."
(See, Chai, I'm still not crying.)

Later, I changed into a plain white salwar kameez (traditional tunic and trousers with a scarf).

In the other room, Mummy sat trembling, her tears falling silently, endlessly.

She urged Goru and me to let it out—

"Ro lo thoda, beta… don't hold it in…"
(Cry a little, child… don't hold it in…)

But I had turned to stone.

No tears.

No trembling hands.

No fear.

Just stillness.

She had passed everything to me—strength, dignity, silence, and love.

And now, it was my turn to carry it forward.

Goru Bhai and I sat down to discuss the practicalities—how to take her to the hospital and keep her safe for the next 24 hours while arranging for her Antim Sanskar (last rites/funeral rituals).

We called Daddy.

Despite the unbearable weight on his shoulders, he managed to organize everything—the hospital, the ambulance, the formalities.

He was due to board his flight within two hours, and yet, with a calm resolve that stunned and humbled me, he handled it all.

I sat quietly by her side, fingers gently tracing the soft silver strands of her hair, when suddenly, there was—

a scream.

Raw. Guttural.

It tore through the stillness like lightning slashing open a quiet, dark sky.

Moments later came the crash.

Glass shattering. Steel clanging. Something heavy collapsing to the floor—the sound of a heart breaking, made physical.

Grief had entered the kitchen like a storm.

Loud. Uncontrollable. Wild with disbelief.

It didn't speak in words—it screamed, it broke, it shattered.

But I stayed beside her.

Still. Silent. Unmoving.

It was Goru Bhai.

Her laadla (beloved one/darling).

Her eklauta pota (only grandson).

The one she had named at birth, with joy and ceremony.

Their bond was different—sacred in its own way.

A bond of affection woven with laughter and endless indulgence.

And while I had always been her "number one," her "favorite grandchild," it was Goru Bhai who held that special corner of her heart—one no one else could touch.

I didn't move.

I had known this moment would come.

I know my brother—every crack and corner of his heart.

And since I couldn't cry, couldn't scream, I knew he would do it for both of us.

People began to gather around me, whispering with concern.

"Sonia, thoda ro lo... please cry a little."
(Sonia, cry a little…)

They reached for me, tried to hold me, console me.

But I pulled away.

"Let me be," I said quietly. "I don't feel like crying. So why should I?"

Instead, I asked someone to bring me a cup of tea from their home.

The gas hadn't been lit since the news—a tradition observed during mourning—and we wouldn't be allowed to cook for several days.

I knew I wouldn't sleep.

Neither would my brother.

And I wouldn't be able to leave her side, not even for a moment, not until Daddy arrived.

The neighbors understood.

They had known me since childhood—since 1995—and they knew the depth of my love for her.

They didn't question my silence, only worried about the weight I carried within it.

Eventually, Goru Bhai emerged from the kitchen, his voice hoarse but steady.

"Didi," he said, "let's take her to the hospital now so that she is safe."

It was 1:00 a.m.

I nodded.

The ambulance was on its way.

He would follow on his scooter.

I would go with her.

Mummy would stay back, surrounded by friends and neighbors who refused to leave her side.

All of this was decided by Goru Bhai, and I simply supported him.

A close friend accompanied me, along with a neighbor.

We reached the hospital in silence.

And as the minutes passed, I began to notice the shift.

People stopped calling her Maaji/Maata ji (mother/respected elder mother).

They began referring to her as "the body."

I looked at Goru Bhai, and in that instant, we shared a silent cry—a quiet, wordless understanding of loss that needed no expression.

How strange it is, I thought—how swiftly a beloved person becomes "a body."

How names dissolve into cold, clinical labels.

How, in the moment of greatest sorrow, only the family truly bears the depth of the ache.

We have all lost someone dear.

We've all stood in that unbearable silence where the world seems to move on without pause.

Yet how mechanical people become—like cogs in a well-oiled machine, executing their duties with practiced detachment.

No one gives the family time.

Not even an hour.

The instant death is declared, the person you love becomes an object.

A thing.

A task.

A body.

Yes, life moves forward.

Yes, reality must be accepted.

Yes, grief eventually folds itself into memory.

But in that first hour, in that fragile, sacred space between breath and burial—does the family not deserve a moment of grace?

A sliver of time to still call them by name?

To whisper Maa ji, Chai, Dadi, Maata ji (mother, grandmother, respected elder mother)—whatever they were to us, rather than what they've become?

Is it so difficult to offer that final dignity?

To allow the soul to depart with the same gentleness it offered in life?

In that moment, I made myself a quiet promise:

I would never call a loved one "a body."

I would pass this belief down in my family, like a ritual, like a prayer—this insistence on reverence, even in parting.

Maybe I can't change the world.

But if I can uphold dignity within my home—if that brings solace to the grieving and honors those we've lost—then perhaps that's enough.

We were led to a cold, dim room—the mortuary.

The air was heavy, laced with a scent I couldn't quite name.

The walls were lined with stainless steel drawers, each one holding someone's ending, someone's story paused in stillness.

It was my first time seeing such a place.

And in that moment, my nineteen-year-old brother became a man.

Without hesitation, he took charge—speaking to officials, signing documents, making arrangements.

All while holding me steady with a glance, a gesture, a quiet courage that spoke louder than words.

I don't know how he kept his tears at bay.

Perhaps the same way I did—not by strength, but by becoming numb.

By surviving the moment rather than feeling it.

We had no parents physically beside us, and yet we managed somehow.

When life thrusts something this heavy into your hands, you don't always know what you're doing.

You just do it.

You either fly or fight.

Maybe we were doing both.

At our core, we were just trying to honor her—with dignity, with love, with the softness she had shown us every day of her life.

She was the Mukhia (head/matriarch) of our home—the matriarch, the anchor, the soul.

And we were not just mourning her.

We were protecting her.

Even in death, we were fiercely possessive of her—as if to say: she was ours. Ours alone.

Her slightest call would send us scrambling to her side—eager, unquestioning, like loyal subjects answering their queen.

She never demanded this of us.

But the love she gave, the values she instilled, the unwavering faith she lived by, the quiet life lessons woven into everyday moments—they shaped us.

Our obedience wasn't fear or duty.

It was love returned.

A reflection of the boundless affection she had poured into us, day after day, year after year.

We were asked to choose a drawer—a compartment in the cold storage.

Goru Bhai and I exchanged a glance, a silent understanding passing between us.

Without a word, we both reached for the middle drawer—not too high, not too low.

It felt instinctive, as if we both knew this was where she would find peace, where she would have wanted to rest.

Some might wonder: she's gone—what comfort can there be?

We do not presume to know how others grieve, nor the rituals they follow.

But for us, she remained the same—breathing or not, present or gone—alive forever in our hearts and souls.

I held a peach shawl I had brought back from a trip to the north—a small gift meant to wrap her in warmth.

Once she was placed inside the drawer, I told Goru Bhai I wanted to cover her with it—to protect her from the cold that seeped into that room.

The same cold she never allowed when alive, never letting the fan blow too strongly in her room.

Goru Bhai, with surprising maturity, spoke to the hospital staff.

"Meri Didi yeh shawl Dadi ji pe daalna chahti hai, aap madad karoge daalne mein?"
(My sister wants to place this shawl over Grandmother. Will you help us cover her with it?)

The men immediately replied,

"Didi ji, aaiye, aise odh dijiye."
(Sister, please come and drape it like this.)

In a quiet voice, I asked,

"Thand toh nahi lagegi na?"
(She won't feel cold, right?)

And then my brother broke.

Tears streamed down his face as he grabbed my hand, whispering,

"Aapne shawl de di, ab thand nahi lagegi."
(You've given her the shawl now, she won't feel cold anymore.)

We all understood what had just transpired—a simple act layered with so much love and finality—yet no one spoke of it.

They took me out of the room while Goru Bhai stayed behind to handle the formalities.

"Didi, aap theek ho? Ro lo, mujhe hug kar ke," he urged.
(Didi, are you okay? Cry if you need to—hug me.)

The same brother who always ran from hugs.

I shook my head.

"Rona kyun hai? She was eighty-eight. She was happy. She lived her life with us, and she left happily. Why should I cry and

disturb her peace?"
(Why should I cry?)

I honestly don't know why I couldn't cry.

Perhaps I was still in shock, or maybe I had already accepted what was happening.

Or maybe I was trying to be strong for everyone else.

Everyone around me—my father, sister, brother, mother—worried because they knew I was the one most affected by her passing.

Yet they were shocked to see I had shed no tears.

When we finally reached home, the tea was ready.

I drank it quietly with everyone gathered there.

Our helpers—who had cared for her tirelessly over the last six months—stayed with us through the night.

One from the morning shift, the other from the night.

They kept urging my mother,

"Please make her cry. It's not a good sign to hold it all in."

I finished my tea and quietly slipped into Chai's room.

I sat down on the mattress where she had taken her last breath.

Suddenly, I remembered the baby-pink nighty she had worn—the one I had bought her three or four months ago.

A pang of guilt hit me like a storm.

Why had I bought this?

If only I had known I was buying clothes for her final moments...

Just days before, she had asked me to show her some sarees she wanted me to start wearing at work.

She'd been talking about organizing her wardrobe—something I had promised to do that very weekend.

I had planned to take her out for a drive, a promise I had made upfront.

And now, I was filled with regret, feeling like I had failed as a granddaughter.

I should have done it all sooner.

My brother entered quietly.

"Didi, thoda rest kar lo. Tomorrow is going to be full of arrangements, and it's already 4 a.m."
(Didi, get some rest for a while.)

I nodded and said,

"Bas thodi der aur…"
(Just a little while longer…)

I sat at the side of the bed where we would usually sit together, laughing and joking.

I held her pillow close and hugged it tightly.

The scent of her lingered faintly—a fragile ghost of presence.

I found two white strands of her hair on the pillow.

I didn't know what to do with them.

Her dentures lay soaking in water nearby—she had the habit of soaking them every night and cleaning them in the morning before wearing them.

Her stick—the sotti (walking stick/cane)—was propped in the corner.

She rarely used it except to turn the fan on or off, to scare Harley so he would stop jumping on her, or sometimes to playfully gesture at my brother and me when we fought.

She never actually hit us, but the stick was enough to make us stop.

My grandmother hated dependence on anyone.

She would rise at 5:30 every morning, pace around the house, check on me, and wake me gently.

Every day, as she brushed her teeth, I'd hug her and whisper,

"Good morning, Chai."

Even now, I kept this ritual alive—a simple tradition she'd brought home from London in 1991.

Our routine was quiet but sacred:

first, a warm hug, then a soft "Ram Ram" (a traditional Hindu greeting invoking Lord Ram).

It was an unspoken rule we all followed.

My father and Goru Bhai performed the pairi pauna (touching the feet of elders as a mark of respect and blessing).

But I preferred greeting her with a hug and a kiss on the cheek before the prayers began.

Her hugs were magic—the kind that carried a silent message:

I love you, and you are my favorite person in the world.

Eventually, my mind shut down completely.

Pooja and Rupali gently coaxed me to lie down with them.

I rolled out a mattress on the floor.

Goru Bhai said he'd take it, while I could rest on the bed with Rupali and Pooja.

Chai's room was left untouched—a quiet shrine.

The helpers chose to rest in the living area.

My mother and a neighbor retired to her bedroom.

Even Harley was unsettled, making strange noises and refusing to eat.

Mummy tried feeding him, but he barely touched his food.

None of us had the strength to comfort him properly, so she took him to her room and put him to sleep.

My body felt numb.

My hands and feet were icy cold, though the AC was off.

Suddenly, I murmured,

"Goru, Chai ko thand lag rahi hai."
(Goru, Chai must be feeling cold.)

This time, my brother lost his composure.

"Didi, so jao, woh theek hai!" he said firmly.
(Didi, go to sleep, she's okay!)

Then softer,

"Close your eyes. Recite the Gayatri Mantra. Try to rest for a few hours."

I don't know how Goru Bhai managed to stay so composed.

By now, Pooja and Rupali were asleep, and even I could hear Goru softly snoring—a gentle rhythm in the quiet room.

But I was wide awake—trapped in a storm raging fiercely inside my chest.

Every breath was shallow and uneven, as if the air itself were slipping through my fingers.

Suddenly, I realized—

I was having a panic attack.

I rose slowly, legs trembling beneath me, and walked toward the kitchen.

My hands shook as I poured cold water into a steel glass.

My heart pounded unbearably heavily—as if it might burst.

Each breath was short, like gasping underwater.

Instinctively, my right hand pressed gently against my chest, trying in vain to soothe the chaos swirling inside me.

I stumbled to the washroom, splashing icy water on my face, lifting my hands over my head—desperate for relief.

But nothing calmed the turmoil.

I loosened the knot of my salwar (traditional trousers) to give my lungs space.

I removed my dupatta (scarf/stole) and kept it aside—but the suffocating tightness lingered.

It felt like drowning—sinking deeper into an invisible ocean with no lifeline in sight.

My breaths came in quick, shallow gasps.

My mouth barely opened.

For a terrifying moment, I thought I'd lost my voice altogether.

Then suddenly, an overwhelming urge to run outside overcame me—to escape this suffocating space and find open air where I could finally breathe.

I tried praying—quietly, desperately.

It didn't help.

I began reciting the Gayatri Mantra, but by the third repetition, the tightness in my chest worsened, and my words became trembling whispers.

I grabbed my phone and played the Hanuman Chalisa (a Hindu devotional hymn dedicated to Lord Hanuman), hoping the sacred verses would calm my racing mind.

But no comfort came.

Wrapping my dupatta around myself again, I grabbed the Activa and house keys, determined to run away—to find fresh air, to breathe.

But the helpers woke.

One of them caught my arm firmly; the other rushed to call Goru Bhai and Mummy.

I struggled fiercely, desperate to be free.

But she held me tight, enveloping me in a fierce, tender embrace.

She clasped my hand—

and in that single touch, everything inside me shattered.

I broke.

I cried like a newborn—a raw, aching sound torn from somewhere deep beneath my ribs.

A wail so primal, it didn't just echo in the room—

it split through it,

like something sacred had been ripped from the world.

My back hit the wall as my knees gave way, and I slid down slowly, folding into myself—like paper surrendering to fire.

I sat crumpled on the floor, palms pressed tightly to my face, as if I could somehow contain the grief, as if holding it in would stop it from swallowing me whole.

The sobs came in waves—violent, uncontrollable.

My face flushed red, hot from the pressure of crying.

My eyes swelled, lashes sticking together, tears pouring without pause.

My voice had gone hoarse from screaming into the silence.

My hair unraveled from its bun, falling wildly around my face.

My dupatta (scarf/stole) slipped off my shoulders, pooling beside me like I'd melted out of myself.

My hands were freezing.

My feet were numb.

My body was there, but I wasn't.

I couldn't hold back the tears.

I couldn't catch my breath.

I couldn't sit still.

I couldn't lie down.

And in that moment—that hollow, unending moment—

I truly didn't know how to live in a world she was no longer part of.

It felt impossible.

Unbearable.

Unthinkable.

Not like this.

Not without her.

I was desperate for my father to be there.

For his voice, his hands, his grounding presence—the one person who could make even the worst things feel manageable.

But he was still thousands of miles away.

And I was here, unraveling.

Goru Bhai came out first, his footsteps soft but urgent.

Then Mummy followed, her eyes wide with worry, her face pale in the dim light.

They knelt beside me—no questions, no panic—just steady arms wrapping around my trembling shoulders, just warm palms resting gently on my back.

Their voices were soft, soothing, like a lullaby meant for grief.

Goru reached for my hand and asked quietly,

"Do you need anything? Can I help?"

His voice cracked on the last word.

And for the first time that night, I let myself lean into them.

Into the family.

Into the safety of being held.

Through the choking tears lodged in my throat, I whispered,

"Mujhe meri Chai wapis laa de, Goru...
Tu mera sabse accha bhai hai...
Tu meri har baat manta hai...
Bas ek baar, sirf ek baar Chai ko wapis le aa..."
(Bring my Chai back to me, Goru... You are the best brother in the world... You always fulfill my every wish... Just once, only once, bring Chai back to me...)

He pulled me close, wrapping his arms around me, and held me like he never had before.

Tears streamed down his cheeks as he cried with me.

That moment shattered us—all of us.

The walls we'd carefully built around our grief came crashing down.

We held each other tightly, trembling—raw, fragile, broken.

I buried my face into Goru Bhai's chest, sobbing,

"Don't let go of me… please don't let go…"

Somehow, through that storm of sorrow, he and Mummy held me steady—like anchors in a sea that threatened to swallow me whole.

One of the helpers gently touched my shoulder and said softly,

"Agar aap itna toot jaayengi, toh Chai ko aur zyada dukh hoga…"
(If you break down this much, Chai will feel even more pain.)

But the tears kept coming—harder, faster.

"I wasn't a good granddaughter," I wept. "I wasn't there enough. She died because I went to work. Because I didn't come home on time. She died because of that nighty I bought her… it wasn't a nighty—it was her kafan (burial shroud)."

Mummy and Goru Bhai looked on helplessly—terrified to see me unravel so completely.

Goru reached for a glass of water and gently brought it to my lips.

I sipped mechanically, still shaking.

Then, in a quiet voice that somehow pierced through all the noise in my head, he said,

"Didi, agar aap Chai se pyaar karte ho, toh meri ek baat dhyaan se suno."
(Didi, if you truly love Chai, then listen carefully to what I'm about to say.)

At first, I could barely hear him.

But something in his tone—calm, unwavering—reached me.

He said,

"Chai jahan bhi hain, theek hain… aur khush hain. Agar aap itne pareshan hoge, toh sabse zyada dard unhe hoga. Hum sab dukhi hain, par abhi ke liye, unhe haste-haste jaane dena zaruri hai. Agar aap roogi, pareshan hogi, toh unka raasta swarg tak mushkil ho jaayega."
(Wherever Chai is, she is okay… and she is happy. If you stay this distressed, she will feel the most pain. We are all heartbroken, but for now, it is important to let her go with smiles. If you keep crying and suffering, her path to heaven will become difficult.)

I looked up at him, my voice small and trembling, like a child's:

"Toh agar main rona-dhona band kar dungi toh woh swarg mein chali jaayengi?"
(So if I stop crying, then she will reach heaven peacefully?)

He could barely smile, but he did—eyes glistening, warmth breaking through the grief.

"Haan!!!… Let Daddy come first. Tab tak hum milke sab taiyyari karte hain."
(Yes… Until Daddy comes, let's prepare everything together.)

Everyone in the family knew—Chai had entrusted me with her locker keys.

Not because I was the eldest.

Not because I was the most capable.

But because, somehow, she had seen something in me—a quiet attentiveness, a promise I never even knew I had made.

I was the keeper of her last wishes.

The only one who knew the full picture—not written down, not formally handed over, just softly spoken between shared meals and quiet afternoons.

She had told me which suit piece she wanted to be offered at her funeral—the one that came from her brother's side many years ago, who was no more—a pista-green suit piece with delicate threadwork, folded carefully in her Godrej almari (wardrobe/cupboard) behind the old shawls.

She had told me who should receive what:

a pair of bangles each for me and my sister,

her favorite sari for Mummy,

things for Goru's future wife whenever he married,

her woolen wrap for the helper who stayed with her through winter nights,

and gifts for Sangeeta Didi, our house help who had been with us for over twenty-eight years.

It was all in my memory.

Every detail.

Every instruction.

Every soft goodbye hidden within her words while she was still alive.

Goru Bhai sat next to me, his voice low, but carrying the weight of an elder brother, a son, and a boy who had just lost the woman who had named him.

"Didi," he said gently, "you're the custodian of her wishes. She trusted you with her heart. You're the only one who knows what she truly wanted."

I looked at him, eyes swollen, heart pounding.

I didn't feel capable of anything.

I felt like a child.

A broken, trembling child who had just watched the sky collapse.

But he kept going, his words like a hand reaching through the fog of my sorrow.

"Abhi bas thoda rest karo. Kal subah hum sab milke taiyyari karenge."
(For now, just get some rest. Tomorrow morning, we'll prepare everything together.)

His voice cracked slightly as he added,

"All I've been doing is thinking of her. The way she held my face when I came home late. Of how she never called me by name, 'Goru,' only by love—I want to honor all of that. And I need you with me to do it."

Tears slid silently down my cheeks.

This wasn't just a goodbye.

It was a sacred duty.

A final act of love we were planning.

Chai and I were inseparable.

Back in 1996, when I was just eight, she suffered a cardiac arrest and was rushed to the hospital, where she remained in the ICU for almost a week.

That was the first time I tasted fear—the kind that sits on your chest and doesn't move.

I prayed with a desperation no one else could see, with a fire only a child's love can kindle.

When she recovered, I made an unspoken vow:

I would never take time with her for granted.

I would bring light and laughter to her days, always.

From that promise, a ritual was born—sacred and secret.

I had heard somewhere that ghee (clarified butter) from a jyot (sacred flame/lamp) held healing power.

And so, each morning, after lighting the diya (oil lamp) at our home altar, I would dip my little finger into the warm ghee and gently touch it to her forehead and neck.

It was my way of blessing her.

Of protecting her.

At first, I thought I was discreet.

She let me believe it for a while.

But soon enough, she caught on.

And when the rest of the family noticed, they would smile, teasing,

"Sonia is protecting her Chai and will never let her go."

Sonia—the name she gave me.

My favorite name in the world.

When she said it, it wasn't just a nickname—

it was a lullaby,

a love letter,

a home.

We shared a bond filled with whimsy and wonder.

I still can't bring myself to say "late grandmother," because in my heart, she never truly left.

She exists in the folds of my memories, in the language of my habits, in the corners of every room where her presence once lingered.

As a child, I would often tell her,

"Chai, you and I will go to God's house together."

And she'd laugh in that way only she could.

"Theek hai, Puttu."
(Alright, Puttu.)

Puttu—that tender, affectionate word, short for puttar (child/ beloved child), that elders in Punjabi homes use for their little ones.

I would watch her sleep, vigilant, holding my breath until I saw her chest rise.

If it didn't move right away, I'd inch closer to hear the soft hum of her snoring.

Sometimes she'd wake up with a start and whisper,

"Jundi aan hale, dardi kyon hain?"
(Sonia, I'm still alive. Why are you so afraid?)

We'd laugh.

I'd wrap my arms around her and kiss her cheeks.

And I'd whisper into her ear,

"Don't you dare think of leaving me alone. You're not allowed to go without me."

But life doesn't make deals with devotion.

It teaches us through loss.

Even on February 8, when I found her lying still on the mattress—silent, breathless, her warmth already fading—I reached for the diya (oil lamp).

My hands were trembling.

I dipped my finger into the ghee (clarified butter) and touched it gently to her forehead.

Maybe it meant nothing.

Maybe it was too late.

But the child inside me... she wasn't ready to give up.

She still believed that love—if strong enough, if pure enough—could wake the dead.

But this time...

she didn't move.

Not even a flicker.

And that silence—her silence—was the loudest thing I've ever heard.

I had other ways, too, of checking on her well-being during my childhood.

If she was unusually quiet while watching her daily soaps—Uttaran, Kyunki Saas Bhi Kabhi Bahu Thi—I'd softly whisper,

"Chai, haso…"
(Chai, smile/laugh…)

And if she smiled back, I knew all was well.

I couldn't bear the thought of her holding even a sliver of sorrow.

Our evenings were sacred—no gossip, no drama.

Chai detested gossip.

Instead, we shared conversations that spanned everything:

Partition, undivided India, my father's childhood, how Goru Bhai was always causing mischief, the mangoes she secretly saved just for me, my dislike of certain habits in people, and how my mother's affection sometimes felt uneven among my siblings and me.

We spoke of cooking sabzi (vegetable curry) on a low flame to deepen its flavor, and of how she carefully selected her sarees.

We were each other's closest companions—sitting for hours, exchanging stories and sentiments.

Though she has departed from this world, she remains alive within me—

in my heart,

in my memories,

and someday, I believe, in my dreams.

Chai was the very first person to gently prepare me for the quiet changes that come with growing up.

I remember one peaceful night when I was eleven years old, just before we drifted off to sleep, when she spoke softly about a time in a girl's life when her body begins a new rhythm—a cycle that marks the beginning of womanhood.

She explained that I might one day notice a small stain on my innerwear, or feel cramps in my lower belly, and that these were signs of my first period.

She said it gently, without fear or shame, as if she were passing down a secret that all women share.

"It's something natural," she told me, "and something to be proud of. If you ever feel unsure or have questions, you can always come to your mother or me."

Such conversations are often avoided in many families, wrapped in silence or embarrassment.

But my grandmother was different—wise, grounded, and unafraid to speak with honesty and kindness.

Her openness gave me comfort.

Her calm gave me the confidence to meet the changes ahead with understanding rather than fear.

Her hands taught me how to fold dough, how to light a diya (oil lamp), how to calm a racing heart.

Her love taught me how to stay strong—

even in silence,

even through grief.

And even now, though her bed is empty and her voice no longer fills the room, Chai remains with me—

in every diya I light,

in every saree I wear,

in the yearly ritual of making achaar (pickle),

in the slow-cooked sarson ka saag (mustard greens curry) that I make every winter.

One of my fondest pastimes with Chai was sitting together to watch Pakistani dramas.

We were completely drawn in by the depth of emotion, the beautiful storytelling, and the richness of language.

Those moments would often drift into long, heartfelt conversations—about food, family, culture, and everything in between.

Later, I came to understand why we enjoyed them so deeply.

The language—so familiar, a blend of Punjabi, Sanskrit, Persian, and Urdu—mirrored Chai's own speech: her pauses, her accent, her careful choice of words.

Even the sets—the kind of suits worn, the architecture of the homes—reflected the world she had grown up in.

Despite differences in caste, community, or upbringing, there was a striking resemblance to the stories she used to tell me about her childhood.

Watching those dramas allowed me to glimpse her past.

Through them, I could live a version of her youth.

And maybe that's why both Chai and I were so drawn to those shows—

they weren't just entertainment.

They were a bridge between lifetimes.

We would laugh over the old bade-ponche wali salwars (wide-flared traditional salwars)—those graceful, flowing garments now more fashionably referred to as farshi salwars.

She'd tell me how elegant they looked, and how she and her cousins would wear them to weddings and festivals, twirling and laughing in the courtyards of her childhood.

And then, sometimes without warning, the conversation would shift to something heavier.

She spoke of Partition—those painful, irreversible years of loss.

With sadness in her eyes, she'd refer to it simply as,

"Jab raule pade the."
(When terrible unrest and suffering happened.)

She told me how her family had to leave behind their grand home, their land, and their legacy.

Chai came from a wealthy and well-respected family.

They had cows and buffaloes in their own courtyard, and a three-story dry-fruit shop when she was just six or seven years old.

Her father and brothers bathed in milk, curd, and ghee—a life of luxury by every standard.

Among four brothers, she was the beloved little sister, the heart of the home.

She'd light up as she recalled playing kikli (a traditional Punjabi folk dance/game where two girls spin while holding hands), hide-and-seek, and even... cricket with her siblings and neighbors. Her stories brought the old Punjab to life for me—vivid, colorful, and heartbreakingly distant.

She made the most delicious pickles—tangy, spicy, and full of love. But she always kept them hidden, even from me. Whenever I asked, she'd chuckle and say, "I'll give it to you myself—gille hath na paayi achaar vich!" (Don't put wet hands in the pickle jar and spoil it!)

That little act of mischief between us became its own language of love. Each time, she'd tuck the martabaan (pickle jar) away in a corner, hoping I wouldn't find it—worried I'd overeat and fall sick. And every single time, I'd eventually track it down. With the stealth of a thief and the glee of a child, I'd lift the lid just enough to take one tiny piece, thinking I'd gotten away with it.

But she always knew.

She'd catch on from the slightest shift in its position, or how loosely the lid was placed back. And with that familiar mix of mock scolding and laughter, she'd say, "Sonia... tu pher labh lita? Dhakkan te kass ke band karna si, Puttu!" (Sonia… you found it again? You should've closed the lid tightly, dear!)

Another thing was that Chai stitched all my salwar kameez with her own hands. She had an instinct for fabric—soft cottons, vibrant silks, delicately embroidered chiffons. Her cupboard was always stocked with unstitched suit pieces and bolts of thaan (fabric), folded meticulously and saved for special occasions, family functions, or simply because she couldn't resist a beautiful print. There was something ceremonial in the way she handled fabric—as though she wasn't just sewing clothes, but preparing a gift of love.

In 1997, one quiet afternoon while walking back from the market, Chai paused mid-step. A little girl in our colony was wearing a Patta Pavada (traditional South Indian silk skirt and blouse set), bright as marigolds and glinting in the sun. Her eyes lingered on the outfit with that familiar look I had come to recognize—the kind that always preceded a burst of inspiration.

That evening, she went to the girl's mother, gently inquiring about the fabric and design. And without saying much else, she retreated into her sewing room, where two precious pieces of fabric—saved for years—were quietly unrolled. In just a couple of days, she had stitched matching Patta Pavadas for me and my sister: a deep orange one for me, and a soft pastel green for her.

We wore them proudly on Ganesh Chaturthi. Our skirts fanned out with every step, the silk rustling softly as we moved through the house like little queens. Chai had thought of everything—jasmine gajras (flower garlands) for our braids, shiny plastic bangles that caught the light, and little bindis she helped us press gently onto our foreheads. I still remember the weight of those new clothes, the cool touch of fresh silk on my skin, and the warmth of her hands as she dressed us. We didn't just feel beautiful—we felt cherished, seen, loved.

Chai's sense of style was always ahead of its time. The salwar suits she stitched for us followed the latest cuts; her cardigans and sweaters—hand-knit or crocheted—were so intricate they could've come straight from a designer catalog. Every winter, as the temperature dipped, she'd open her big tin of wool and begin working on a new set for each of us. Stripes, florals, sometimes pastel, and sometimes bold—each one reflected her artistry.

My favorite was the magenta one. A solid, regal color with heart-shaped buttons that sparkled like little diamonds. It had a round neck and full sleeves—tight at the wrists, slightly loose at the elbows—giving the look of royalty. But more than the look, it was the warmth of her love, woven into every thread, that made it unforgettable. She used to call it rani pink koti (queen pink sweater), and when I wore it, I didn't just feel warm—I felt wrapped in her.

We still have all her handwoven sweaters. They now belong to my sister, who has a little daughter, Maya, in Canada, barely five years old. And we've made our own quiet promises: when I have a daughter someday, I'll dress her in them too. And then we'll pass them on to Goru Bhai's kids.

It's strange, the kind of commitments we siblings make: "You take it for now, I'll use it later," or "Let her wear it this winter, I'll keep it safe after that." Touch wood (a phrase used to ward off bad luck), in our family, we've only ever fought to let the other person have more. Not once—not once—have we shown greed or claimed a bigger share. That's just how we were raised.

Our father had firm rules. If you threw a tantrum, you wouldn't get the toy, the dress, or the picnic. But if you behaved—if you were kind, patient, and understanding—you'd get stars and diamonds from the sky. We were taught to accept a "no" with grace. If any elder refused something, that was the end of the discussion. No arguments. No negotiating.

The only person who could ever melt that "no" into a "yes" was our grandmother, Chai. And even she did it only when she believed it was right. She lived by the old saying: "Bin maange mile moti, maange mile na bheekh." (Pearls come unasked for; what is asked for may not even bring charity.) And believe me, we lived that. We were granted more than we ever dared to ask for—just not always in the ways we expected.

Chai's taste was impeccable—subtle, refined, distinct. She noticed the extraordinary in the ordinary—not out of extravagance, but because everything she did was rooted in love and meaning. Her choices were thoughtful, deliberate—anchored in both elegance and emotion.

Even now, when I run my fingers over her old shawl or wrap a leftover strand of yarn around my wrist, I feel her presence. She didn't just leave behind belongings—she left behind values, memories, a way of living that was rich, generous, and full of grace.

When we lived in Delhi until 1993, our home was filled with quiet rituals—the kind that stitched together days, seasons, and years. During the hot summer months, we would gather on the terrace to roll papads (sun-dried lentil wafers) and slice potatoes into thin chips, laying them out to dry under the burning sun. Our fingers would tingle with salt and spice, and Chai would hum old Punjabi songs as she worked, her voice soft and steady, as if it carried memories from another time.

"Suhe Ve Cheere Waliye Main Kehni Aa" (O red-clad beloved, I am calling out to you) and "Sui Ve Sui" (traditional Punjabi folk songs) were the songs most sung in our culture.

In winter, the kitchen would fill with the smell of roasted wheat flour and warm ghee—clear signs that pinni season had begun. As soon as the first tray cooled, she would call me over with a quiet smile and break off a small piece from the edge. I was always the first to taste it. It wasn't something we talked about—it was just understood. A small, special privilege I held close to my heart.

Looking back, I see now that it was never just about food, clothes, or chores. It was about the way she cared—the way she gently folded us into her world through her cooking, her stitching, and her presence. Everything she made carried her love. It was never loud or dramatic. It was quiet, steady, and full of grace. She gave so much of herself in small, everyday moments—and that's what made it unforgettable.

Chai also had her own way of speaking—a mix of languages and made-up words that became part of our family's story. The bathroom was always the gusalkhaana (bathroom; literally "washing room," from Urdu). A knife was a karad or sometimes just a churi (knife). She switched between Punjabi, Hindi, Urdu, and even Persian without thinking. It wasn't just language—it was music; it was comfort.

No matter how often we corrected her, she always called the microwave the microne. Safety pins were baksua (safety pin)—a word she used so often and so confidently that we never questioned it. Even burgers weren't safe—she called them burgal (burger), said in such a sweet, proud tone that Goru Bhai and I would burst into laughter. And instead of being embarrassed, she'd repeat it even louder just to make us laugh harder.

These words became our inside jokes—our little treasures. Even today, I still say baksua sometimes without thinking. And when I do, I smile. Because in that small, silly word, she's still here—tucked inside my voice, living quietly in the corners of my speech, reminding me that love has many languages. And hers is still speaking.

Sonia & Ruchi | Nona & Kake

In our family, there were quiet allegiances—unspoken loyalties, invisible threads.

My sister, two years younger than me, was officially named Ruchi. But when she arrived in our lives in early 1990's, my parents introduced her to me with a single, fateful sentence:

"Dekh, Sonia—yeh kaka hai."
("Look, Sonia—this is the baby boy/girl.")

And just like that, she became Kake—the little one.

Chai, our grandmother, had her own term of endearment: Gudiya (doll).

As for me, I was Sonia. Of course I was. You could throw a stone into any Punjabi household from Ludhiana to London and hit a Sonia, a Kake, a Gudiya—maybe a Sweety, Bittu, Sonu, Nimmo, Baby, Golu, or Pinky thrown in for good measure. We weren't just a family—we were a Punjabi greatest hits album.

Still, those names—as common as they were—meant something. They were given without ceremony but full of affection. The way Punjabi families do everything: loudly, generously, with zero volume control, and always with food involved.

Now, while Ruchi (Kake, Gudiya, etc.) was unmistakably Mom's favorite, I was Chai's. That bond didn't need explanation—it just was. Quiet, steady, grounding. Like an underground spring that kept everything alive from below.

Like most younger siblings, Kake grew up watching me—innocently copying everything: my clothes, my expressions, even the way I walked. At first, I thought it was sweet, like she was trying to learn from me, not compete.

Because really, that's how it goes in most families: the younger ones follow the older ones. It's natural, harmless, and often full of quiet admiration.

But Chai—wise as ever—made sure we didn't get lost in each other's shadows. She wanted us to grow into ourselves, not into each other.

Whenever she caught Kake mid-mimicry, she'd raise an eyebrow and say, with a glint in her eye:

"Rees paresi, dubb maresi."
("If you imitate others blindly, you'll sink yourself.")

It wasn't scolding—it was her gentle, cheeky way of reminding us: admire each other, yes—but never forget who you are.

And in simpler words that still echo in my mind:

"If you blindly copy others, you'll only drown yourself," she'd laugh, as my sister pouted and I smirked. But her teasing was always wrapped in affection—never sharp, only soft. It was her way of drawing us closer, of turning rivalry into gentle laughter.

I had my nicknames too—even my nickname had a nickname. Whenever my dad wanted to melt me, he'd call me Nona. A name so soft it wrapped around me like a hug. In Punjabi, nona can mean well-behaved, sweet, or beautiful—though I personally leaned more toward the first interpretation.

We were so deeply loved, so thoroughly spoiled, we had pet names for our pet names.

I've lived with very few regrets, mostly because I never waited for the perfect moment. Jo hai, abhi hai. Kal ka kya pata? ("What is now is enough. Who knows about tomorrow?") That belief shaped every hour I spent with her. I never let a day pass without making space for her, whether in celebration or in the quiet comfort of everyday life.

I'd take her on drives, always opening the car door with a mock bow and calling it her throne. We shopped for fruits, vegetables, suits, dupattas, and anything else that caught our fancy. We watched films together—often with her asking me to explain the story three times—and wandered through parks where she'd pause to admire bougainvillea as if it bloomed only for her.

Sometimes, late at night, I'd quietly tiptoe into her room, the floor cold beneath my feet, the silence wrapped around the house like a blanket. I wouldn't say a word—just slip under the blanket beside her. She wouldn't ask why. She never did.

She'd simply shift ever so slightly, barely opening her eyes, and murmur, "Tu aa gayi?"
("You've come?")

That was all. No questions. No conditions. Just presence.

And then, like muscle memory, her hand would find my back and begin to gently pat it—slow, steady, reassuring—like she was lulling the world's noise out of me.

Within minutes, I'd drift off—safe, small, and entirely held in her arms.

I'd massage her tired feet with warm oil, gently braid her grey hair while we watched Balika Vadhu, or invent the most ridiculous hairstyles just to hear her laugh. And her laughter—loud, uninhibited, full of joy—was the sweetest music in the world to me.

Whenever Goru Bhai scolded, "Chai ko tang mat karo!"
("Don't trouble Chai!"), she'd smile protectively and reply, "Yeh tang nahi kar rahi, meri seva kar rahi hai."
("She is not troubling me; she is taking care of me.")

And I'd smile proudly at him, triumphant as ever.

We took countless photos—selfies, videos, blurry moments between giggles and hushed conversations. I'd proudly show her sarees I bought, sometimes pretending they were cheaper than they were. And Goru Bhai, of course, would spoil the act with the truth. But she'd just smile knowingly and say, "So what? She earns her own money. Shouldn't she wear what she loves?"

Nothing in the world—not time, not distance, not even death—could ever turn her against me. Our bond was sacred. Rare. Pure, deep, and utterly timeless. Even now, when I try to put it into words, they fall short. Because how do you describe something that felt like home, like shelter, like your very beginning?

And the most magical part? She's still here.

The moment I think of her, I feel her presence—gentle and steady. I feel her in the breeze when I walk alone, in the warmth of tea shared in silence, in the quiet blessings that follow me everywhere I go. She protects, she guides, she watches over.

Some relationships don't end.
They simply change form. Ours is one of them.

The moment I placed my phone back on the charger, it began to tremble with life—blinking, buzzing, lighting up with missed calls and unread messages, as if the world had sensed the rupture before I had found the strength to acknowledge it aloud. Voices I hadn't yet heard, fingers reaching through glass, names I didn't want to see.

I knew what I was expected to do: reply, inform, explain. But my hands wouldn't move, and my voice had gone still inside me.

The night before, I had managed only a short message to my extended family. A few plain words: She's gone. That was all I could bear to write. I said nothing about the hour, the breathless stillness of the moment, or the quiet unraveling of something eternal. Not because I wanted to hide it, but because remembering it felt unbearable. Naming it made it too real.

It was around 6:30 a.m. The world beyond our walls was already beginning its day. Milkmen rattled down the lane, birds filled the air with their busy calls, and the sky was shifting from gray to gold.

But inside our home, time had stopped.

Pooja and Rupali were still asleep. I hadn't seen Goru Bhai. I assumed he was downstairs with Harley for a walk or still in the bathroom. I didn't ask. I didn't stir. I didn't want to acknowledge anything outside the four walls of my silence.

Grief had arrived not as an outburst or collapse, but as something heavier—denser. It wasn't loud. It was suffocating. It hung in the air like smoke, like fog, like the remnants of a fire that no longer needed to burn to destroy.

I couldn't sit. I couldn't cry. I couldn't even think in full sentences. My body felt alien, uncooperative. The world around me dulled and blurred. Every surface felt unfamiliar.

For a moment—a single flicker—I felt the gentlest whisper of peace: At least she's no longer in pain. At least she's free.

But it passed quickly, like a breeze that leaves no trace.

What remained was weight. A heavy, relentless ache lodged somewhere between my ribs and my throat. A migraine was building behind my eyes—sharp and pulsing—from too many tears held back and a night without rest, only silence.

I wasn't hungry. I wasn't thirsty. I didn't want sympathy, comfort, or even kindness. I wanted stillness. I wanted time to freeze long enough for me to understand how the world could still spin when she no longer walked in it.

No one tells you how strange grief really is. People talk about sadness, about loss—but not about how it feels to become unrecognizable to yourself. It doesn't strike like a thunderclap. It seeps in slowly. Quietly. It lingers. It rearranges you. It makes you forget how to be whole.

And I knew—even in those first hours—that I wouldn't come back from this entirely. Some piece of me had gone with her, buried in her silence. I didn't know who I was anymore. Only that I would never again be who I was before.

I felt like a silhouette of myself—faded, frayed at the edges. A girl shaped by grief.

Then I heard the flush. A door creaked open.

Goru Bhai stepped out of the bathroom. His eyes were swollen, bloodshot from tears neither of us had witnessed. His voice, when it came, was raw and threadbare.

"What do we do for breakfast?" he asked gently, not looking at me.

"There are people at home; we need to arrange breakfast at least. I'll go out, get some tea, something light. Then we'll shower and leave," he said.

It wasn't just what he said—it was how he said it. Measured, almost rehearsed. Like someone walking across thin ice, afraid that if he stopped speaking, he would fall through.

I didn't answer. I only nodded.

He was trying. And maybe that was all either of us could do now—try.

The day had begun. But for me, those few quiet minutes of stillness before the world fully woke were where the real grief lived. In the breathless silence between knowing and accepting.

And even as the day moved forward, I remained suspended there—with her—in the space between presence and absence.

There was so much to do. Too much. The kind of tasks that feel impossibly heavy when your heart is already splintered, when your body moves but your spirit lags far behind—stuck somewhere between memory and disbelief.

We had to get her photograph framed for the rituals. It sounds simple, almost routine, but choosing that picture—just one image to represent a whole life—was its own heartbreak. We finally settled on one where she was smiling softly, her eyes lit with that quiet knowing she always carried. But even then, it felt impossibly small. How could a single frame contain the vastness of who she was to us? Her voice, her warmth, her presence that filled every room—none of it could live behind glass.

Then came the calls. We had to reach out to the pandit ji (Hindu priest), speak through the lump in our throats, and ask about rituals, timings, and customs we were suddenly expected to understand. We had to coordinate the cremation, make arrangements that felt clinical and hollow in the face of such raw grief. Everything was urgent. Everything had to be done correctly. The list of ceremonial items felt endless—each one precise, each one steeped in meaning: sandalwood, tulsi leaves, specific grains, clarified butter, white cloth… each whispering centuries of belief, carrying weight far heavier than its name.

And all the while, all I wanted was to stop. To sit in silence. To cry without being needed. To freeze time just long enough before the world forced us to let go.

I had to find that pista green suit piece—the one Papa ji (her brother) had gifted her just a few years ago. She had treasured it like something sacred, folding it with quiet care and intention. It lay deep inside her almari (wardrobe), the fabric still crisp at the edges, as if untouched by time. That was the outfit she had chosen for her final journey—a soft, graceful farewell wrapped in the color of new leaves and old memories.

In our culture, the final garment—a suit piece or saree—must come from the paikke (maternal home). It is a tradition rooted not only in ritual, but in belonging. It is the brother's final gesture of love and honor—a last offering from the home where her story began. For her, that pista green suit was not just beautiful—it was symbolic.

Now, it was my responsibility to take it to the tailor for kacchi silai (half-stitching performed before cremation). But finding someone willing to do that work wasn't easy. Not every tailor agrees to stitch clothes meant for death. Some politely refuse; others decline outright, afraid of the energy it carries. I didn't blame them. This wasn't just cloth. It was ritual. It was belief. It was a thread connecting the living and the dead—a farewell stitched in silence.

There was more. We had to consult Daddy to confirm the tervi (ritual performed on the 13th day after death) dates, call relatives, and draft the message that would carry the news. Just a few lines to announce something that had torn through our world. Simple words. Flat. Powerless.

Each task felt like a betrayal of the stillness I craved. Each call, each decision, each list item felt like movement when all I wanted was to freeze—to curl up inside the ache and remain there. But grief doesn't wait. It arrives with demands—urgent, relentless. It forces your hands to move even when your soul is still anchored in mourning.

In the middle of that blur, a message from Daddy lit up my phone. I hadn't even realized he was halfway through his journey.

"I've reached London. You guys must be resting. Just a few more hours, and we'll be together."

I remember sitting there, completely still—paralyzed not by shock, but by the sheer weight of absence. It didn't scream. It didn't break. It simply sat on my chest—heavy, unmoving—making it hard to breathe, hard to think, hard to exist.

How cruel it is, I thought, that grief comes hand in hand with logistics—with paperwork, rituals, and lists of things to do. When all you want is stillness, the world demands motion. It demands decisions. You're asked to function, to coordinate, to respond, when every cell in your body is screaming to pause.

No one prepares you for this part.

Not age, not experience, not strength or spiritual insight. Loss doesn't care how wise you are or how many goodbyes you've already survived. This kind of grief isn't something you reason with—it bypasses understanding and undoes you from within. In those first few days, even the act of staying alive can feel like betrayal, like you're defying their memory simply by continuing to exist.

This is where acceptance truly begins—not as a moment of clarity, but as collapse. Not as grace, but as a quiet, hollow nod to a reality you never asked for.

Ting-tong.

The doorbell rang. I didn't move.

A neighbor stepped in, holding a steel tray with warm tea and a simple breakfast. She had brought an entire jar of tea with it—as if she knew, intuitively, that we'd need more than we thought. She didn't say much. Just placed it gently on the counter, gave me a look that said I know, and left.

That kind of silence holds more compassion than a thousand well-meaning condolences. It doesn't ask questions. It doesn't offer platitudes. It just is—present, patient, and deeply human.

Slowly, the house began to stir.

The helpers woke. Pooja and Rupali stepped out of the bedroom, faces still soft with sleep and disbelief. Mummy was already in motion—quiet, composed, slipping into the rhythm of responsibility, her grief folded beneath layers of ritual and necessity.

But the loudest grief that morning didn't come from any of us.

It came from Harley.

He wandered the house, restless and confused, as if trying to piece together a version of the world that made sense again. In and out of Chai's room he went, again and again—nose lowered, tail still, steps hesitant. He sniffed her bed, circled it once, twice. Then he lay down by her walking stick—the one she always kept beside her, leaned gently against the wall like a loyal companion.

He waited.

Still. Patient. Hopeful.

As though, at any moment, she would walk in and softly call his name.

As though this was just another morning, and not the first of a forever without her.

And somehow, that broke me more than anything else.

Because grief doesn't always arrive in sobs or keening wails.

Sometimes, it's quiet.

It's a dog sitting by a door that will never open again.

It's a teacup left untouched on a tray.

It's the faint scent of her warmth in the folds of a shawl.

It's the eerie stillness of a room that used to breathe with presence.

That morning, I learned that loss echoes loudest in the smallest things.

And yet, even in that ache, life moves forward—awkwardly, gently, and sometimes against your will.

Not because you're ready.

But because time, unlike us, doesn't wait to be whole again.

No one had the heart to even entertain the thought of breakfast, let alone eat. Yet, amid her own silent sorrow, my mother quietly assumed command. There was a weary resolve in her movements, a fragile strength that wrapped around us like a protective embrace. She gently ensured each of us took at least a few bites. I managed a cup of tea and some hesitant spoonfuls of poha. With every swallow, my stomach rebelled; my head felt heavy, clouded by a dense fog of grief. The very idea of food—or conversation—was unbearable.

I couldn't trust my voice. Not because I lacked words, but because I feared anything I uttered would come out raw, jagged, and undeserved. I had already warned everyone, "Please don't speak to me or ask me anything unless it's urgent. I just... can't. Let's wait until I'm a little steadier."

After breakfast, my friends departed quietly—gracious and gentle, their presence a tender offering of love and empathy. Goru Bhai calmly instructed the household staff to return home, rest, and come back the following day for the funeral.

We washed up, changed, and sat down to confront the day's grim necessities. Each task felt monumental. First: choosing her photograph for the frame. There was no hesitation—no debate. Goru Bhai and I instinctively settled on the same image, as if she had placed it before us herself, guiding us even now. As though her presence still orchestrated every detail with quiet grace.

The duties were divided. I went to the tailor to arrange her suit's kacchi silai (half-stitching required for the funeral ritual), while Goru Bhai went to meet Pandit ji to finalize the cremation arrangements. Most tailors refused to take on a half-stitched suit on such short notice, especially for a funeral. Drawing a deep breath, I found a local tailor who had known her. Saddened by her passing, he accepted the task as a gesture of respect and asked me to collect the suit in a few hours.

My sister, Kake, called several times that day, her voice a fragile thread of concern and longing. I missed her calls at first, then tried to return them, hoping she might be asleep, at peace. But she was awake—restless and waiting, craving some sign from us. When we finally spoke, her voice cracked with a raw vulnerability I hadn't expected. "Didi… can I still plan to come? Maybe at least by the time of asthi visarjan (immersion of ashes) or chautha (ritual on the fourth day)?"

I froze, caught between wanting to say yes and the crushing weight of helplessness pressing down on me. Did I need her here? Without a doubt. She and I had woven our childhoods tightly around Chai—sleeping beside her, listening to her stories, inseparable like two halves of the same soul. People used to say we were twins. I knew my sister was drowning in her own sorrow, just as I was, but I was too depleted to hold her pain as well.

So I passed the decision to her, telling her to speak with Mummy. She agreed quietly, but I already knew what Mummy would say—her voice gentle but firm, urging Kake to stay, especially after her recent surgery. And Kake, ever obedient and loving, would listen to Mummy above all else.

In that moment, I realized grief doesn't just fracture a heart—it spreads its cracks wide, touching everyone connected, each one struggling in silence, each one waiting for a way to heal.

By 3 p.m., all the tasks were checked off—on paper, at least. But nothing about the day felt done. As I stepped through the front door, the air inside the house clung to me like grief made physical. In the far corner, Harley lay curled up—motionless, silent, refusing food, company, or comfort.

My mother looked utterly drained—the kind of exhaustion that doesn't just sit in the body, but seeps into the bones. She had spent the entire day on her feet—managing Harley, receiving visitors, attending relentless phone calls, and offering the kind of quiet hospitality expected of her.

Unlike me, she didn't have the luxury of retreating into silence.

I bent down to fill Harley's bowl with his usual food. He didn't even lift his head. I tried offering vanilla ice cream—his favorite indulgence, normally enough to earn a tail wag—but he turned his face away. I sat beside him, waiting. What could I say to him? He had lost her, too. Maybe in his own way, he understood more than we did. I stroked his head gently, whispering nothing in particular—just a sound to remind him he wasn't alone.

Eventually, I slipped out and picked up two new balls, hoping a familiar game might shake him out of his stillness. It worked, if only slightly. We played fetch, half-heartedly at first, until he finally accepted a few reluctant licks of the ice cream. I don't know how I managed to mask my own breaking heart—to play, to coax, to soothe. But I did. For him. Because Harley had no words, no rituals, no closure—only an empty room, a missing voice, and a scent fading from the bedsheets.

He barely ate. But I let it be—not because I didn't care, but because I knew he needed time. And because I knew he was feeding off Goru Bhai's energy, mirroring the quiet despair of the one he obeyed most. Until Goru Bhai found his footing again, Harley wouldn't either.

Later, I spoke with his trainer, Aishwariya, the one who had helped raise him when he was just a four-month-old pup. She lived in Chembur, and we agreed to give him one more day. If nothing changed, he would go to her for a week. She would care for him, love him, give him the kind of comfort only familiarity could offer.

Now, when I look back, I wonder how we managed to keep everything afloat—her final rites, the endless to-dos, the fragile emotional terrain of the household—without letting anything slip. Sometimes I believe it wasn't us at all. It was her. Chai. Still here, still guiding, still stitching every broken thread into place from somewhere just beyond the veil.

But as the sun dipped below the skyline, the ache returned—low and relentless. That's the thing about grief: it gives you false reprieve. A few hours of numbness, a moment of distraction, and then—without warning—it strikes again, reminding you that you're not done hurting.

By evening, I was spiraling back into that trance-like state I had lived in the night before. Only this time, there was one difference: a faint light at the edge of the dark. Daddy was going to be home soon. In a few hours, I would no longer have to be the strong one. I would no longer have to pretend I could carry all this alone.

I grabbed the car keys and stepped out—not for fresh air, not for peace, but to run. I couldn't bear the house anymore. I couldn't bring myself to face her empty bed, or the quiet corner of the living room where she used to sit—peeling peas into a steel bowl, humming old songs that felt like lullabies to the house. The dining table stood like a ghost, mocking me with its stillness. Her seat—the spot where she would sip her evening tea, slowly and thoughtfully. A mustard-stained napkin still folded exactly as she had left it—tucked under a plate, untouched by time.

Even the small basin near the living area—where I would hug her each morning and whisper, "Good morning, Chai"—now felt like a cruel reminder. A ritual abruptly halted. A rhythm stolen mid-beat.

The house hadn't just lost her presence. It had lost its pulse.

Everything around me screamed of her presence. And that was the hardest part. She was everywhere, and yet, she wasn't anywhere.

"Sonia beta, dhyan se drive karna… aur zyada door mat jaana."

My mother's voice followed me to the door. She didn't try to stop me—she knew better by now. When I needed air, when I needed distance, no one could reason with me. Not even her. Still, she called out those familiar words, a soft echo of concern trailing behind me.

I walked toward the car park with my head lowered, eyes locked on the concrete, dodging every glance, every footstep, every shadow that moved too close. I couldn't bear the sympathy—not the quiet nods, not the softened stares, not the unbearable kindness in someone's eyes. I wasn't ready to smile politely. I wasn't ready to hear the hollow comfort of "She's in a better place."

What place could be better than right here beside me?

I didn't want anyone to see me—not like this. Not cracked open and stripped bare. I didn't want anyone to notice how my world had caved in on itself. How the girl who once filled every room with her laughter now walked like a ghost in her own skin.

I couldn't bear the thought of someone looking at me and seeing my grief—seeing how utterly broken I was.

Because buried beneath the devastation was something even heavier.

Shame.

Yes, shame.

And even now, I still can't explain it—not fully.

It was this unbearable weight pressing down on my chest, whispering in the darkest corners of my mind that maybe… maybe I hadn't loved her enough.

Because if I had, wouldn't I have known? Wouldn't I have seen it coming? Wouldn't I have done something—wouldn't I have saved her?

How fragile, how foolish, how small my love must have been—if it couldn't even protect her.

And suddenly, the whole world felt like a cruel stage.

As if every eye was watching me—not in pity, but in quiet judgment. Mocking the way I'd lost the one person I couldn't imagine living without—and done nothing to stop it.

I slid into the driver's seat, shut the door harder than necessary, and cranked the music up—full blast. Volume 30. Maybe more. The car pulsed with the beat of Michael Jackson's "Black or White." Why that song? I don't know. Maybe because it had once made me feel invincible. Maybe because I just needed noise—anything to drown out the silence she left behind.

I drove hard. From Sanpada to Moraj, then on to Palm Beach Road. The speedometer climbed: 80… 100… 120. The world outside blurred. Traffic lights flickered like ghosts, and at one point I ran a red signal—something I never do. That jolted me just enough to snap out of the free fall.

I exhaled, hands still trembling on the steering wheel, and slowed down. My heart was racing, thudding against my ribs like a desperate knock on a locked door.

At the next signal, I finally stopped. The red light blinked like a warning I couldn't ignore. Just then, an old woman appeared at my window. She was dressed in a pista green saree—the same soft, calming shade Chai had chosen for her final journey. For a moment, my breath caught. She looked so much like her. Not exactly, but enough to stir something deep and primal.

She tapped gently on the window, and I rolled it down.

"Beti, kuch khane ko hai?" she asked softly.

I instinctively reached for my wallet—but of course, I had left it behind.

All I had was a packet of chips lying on the passenger seat.

I picked it up and handed it to her, a little embarrassed.

"I'm sorry… bas yahi hai," I whispered.

Then, with tears gathering in my eyes and my voice trembling under the weight of grief, I asked,

"Aapka naam kya hai?"

I didn't even know why I asked—maybe I was grasping at straws, hoping to hear something familiar… something that sounded like Chai.

She took the packet with a smile that was strangely kind, almost knowing—a quiet grace in her eyes.

And before I could say anything else, she said gently,

"Naam mein kuch nahi rakha hai, jaan kar karogi kya? Ro mat… jo beet gaya, use jaane do."

There is nothing in the name, child. And what will you do with my name? Don't cry… let what's gone be gone.

And just like that, she turned and walked away—leaving me holding my breath and my broken heart in the stillness she left behind.

My body went completely still, and my throat tightened with a pain I couldn't shake.

Those words—they weren't just comforting; they were her words. Different phrasing, but the same soul in them. The same soft lift, the same tender rhythm that had always wrapped around me like a warm embrace.

I blinked hard, half afraid it was just a cruel trick of my mind, a fragile whisper in the storm of my grief.

But when I looked again, the old woman was gone.

Was I losing my mind? Had the weight of sorrow finally cracked something deep inside me? Or… could it really have been her? Not in flesh and bone, but in some other, quieter way—a gentle light, a whisper of love sent from beyond.

I stayed frozen in my car at the signal long after it turned green, letting the moment flood over me. Whether it was real or a mirage didn't matter anymore. I needed to believe it was her.

Because sometimes, when the world feels unbearably empty, the ones we've lost find a way back to us—in the kindness of strangers, in fleeting signs, in the exact words we didn't even know we desperately needed to hear. And in that fragile, aching moment, love feels alive again.

My phone started ringing again—first Goru Bhai, then Mummy. One after the other. Frantic, persistent.

They were worried. Rightfully so.

I knew I couldn't disappear on them, no matter how much I wanted to vanish into the stillness of the lake that lay just beyond the road.

So, with a heavy heart, I turned the car around. As the early evening shadows stretched across the city and the cool breeze brushed against the closed window, something inside me finally broke.

Michael Jackson's "They Don't Care About Us" started playing—loud, furious, unapologetic. I turned the volume up even more, almost in defiance of the silence that had wrapped itself around me these past two days. It wasn't just about the song. It was about drowning out the noise inside.

I needed something louder than my grief.

I pulled the car over to the side of Palm Beach Road and broke.

I screamed—until my throat burned raw. I slammed my hand against the steering wheel, my body trembling with the force of everything I'd been holding in. It wasn't poetic. It wasn't graceful. It was grief in its rawest, most desperate form: ugly, human, unstoppable.

And then my phone buzzed.

A notification blinked on the screen.

"Sonia beta, himmat nahi harni. Shanti se kaam lena. Woh hamesha tere saath hain."
("Don't lose courage, child. Be calm. She's always with you.")

It was from Chai's sister-in-law.

And in that moment, it didn't feel like a coincidence. It felt like Chai was there—in the passenger seat beside me—whispering those words through someone else's fingers. The timing. The phrasing. The calm. It was all too precise. Too her.

I froze.

A strange warmth settled over me, even as tears kept falling. Maybe it was a sign. Or maybe just a fragment of comfort I chose to believe in. But it didn't matter. In that instant, I believed it. I needed to.

She hadn't left me entirely. She was still here—around me, inside me, finding ways to reach me when I was unraveling.

Maybe that's what grief is.

Not the end of connection, but the reshaping of it.
Not silence, but learning how to listen differently.

I reached home without a word. I didn't look at anyone, didn't pause to answer questions or explain. I walked straight to the bathroom like a ghost returning to a place that once felt safe.

Still clothed in my white salwar kameez, my sky-blue dupatta drenched and heavy with tears, hair twisted loosely into a tangled bun, I stepped into the cold shower without hesitation. I didn't have the energy to undress. I didn't want to. This wasn't about cleansing. It was an act of surrender. A quiet unraveling.

The first icy rush slammed into my shoulders—sharp and cruel—sending a shudder down my spine. I gasped but stayed rooted, letting the cold slice through every layer of soaked fabric, as if the water could flood the hollow places inside me where grief had burrowed deep and poisoned everything.

Slowly, I collapsed to the slippery floor, knees drawn tight against my chest, forehead pressed hard into the curve of my legs. My arms curled protectively around myself—tiny, defenseless—trying to disappear, to vanish. The cold tiles pressed into my skin, water pooling and swirling around me, a relentless storm I no longer fought.

Hands trembling and numb, I reached for my phone and pressed play. The Hanuman Chalisa began—steady and sacred—followed by Jagjit Singh's "Hey Ram." His voice, raw and soaked with devotion and sorrow, filled the bathroom, weaving into the roar of the water and the heavy silence lodged deep in my chest.

I sat there motionless, the minutes blurring together—twenty, maybe twenty-five—time lost beneath the cascade. My eyes fixed on the drain, watching it swallow the endless torrent—water, sorrow, silence—as if it might carry away the unbearable weight crushing me.

But the cold didn't wash away the ache. It only deepened it, hollowed it out, made the dark inside me grow darker still.

I didn't cry. Not there. Not then.
I didn't scream either.

I just sat—somewhere suspended between numbness and the distant noise of the world beyond the bathroom walls. Outside, I had to hold everything together—be strong, composed, present.

But in that small, locked space, under the cold weight of water and the steady rhythm of familiar verses, I was allowed to unravel.

I wasn't trying to feel better.
I wasn't even trying to feel anything at all.

The water soaked through me, chilling every part of my skin, but the ache beneath that cold was heavier than any temperature. Slowly, I peeled myself from the damp floor and slipped into Dad's oversized T-shirt—soft, worn, comforting in its familiarity—and a loose pair of pajamas that hung on me like a cocoon.

Mummy came in quietly, her voice gentle and tentative.

"Sonia beta, chai le le… aur thoda aaram kar le."
("Sonia, dear, have some tea… and rest a little.")

I didn't answer. I just sat down on the living room floor and took the cup from her outstretched hands. The warmth of the chai was a faint contrast to the cold that still lived in my bones. I sipped slowly, deliberately—each swallow feeling like a small, exhausting task.

Later, I made my way to the bedroom, my footsteps heavy and slow. I lay down on the bed, letting the world fall away bit by bit—the noise, the weight, the expectations.

Finally, I surrendered—to the silence that pressed against me, to the stillness that stretched like a vast ocean beneath my skin, to the exhaustion that had been quietly waiting, ready to pull me under the moment I stopped fighting.

My eyelids felt impossibly heavy. I didn't have the strength to keep them open, nor did I want to.

What felt like peace was only the thin veil of fatigue pulling me under—soft, dark, and complete.

Somewhere in that space between heaviness and release, I drifted off.

Into sleep.

"Didi, jaldi utho… Daddy aa gaye hain."

Goru Bhai's voice broke through the heaviness of my sleep—soft yet urgent, soaked in the weight of everything this day had been. It was around 11 p.m., and I jolted upright, my heart suddenly racing. Without a word, I rushed to the living room, then instinctively turned into the kitchen. My hands moved mechanically as I put water on the stove for Daddy's black tea—something small, something familiar, something to anchor us in the chaos.

I stood quietly in a corner of the living area, my back pressed against the wall for support. Mummy sat motionless on the sofa, her face a portrait of stoic exhaustion. Her silence screamed. In the other room, Harley slept restlessly, his unease a quiet echo of our shared sorrow. Goru Bhai had gone downstairs to receive Daddy and bring up his suitcase.

And then the door opened. Daddy stepped in.

He looked at me—and in that one glance, something in both of us gave way. The grief that had been brimming beneath the surface came rushing out. I ran into his arms, and we clung to each other as though the world might collapse if we let go. I sobbed like a child—loud, broken, guilt-ridden.

"I'm sorry, Daddy… I couldn't save her," I whispered through tears. "I wasn't even home. I was out… I wasn't with her."

He held me tighter, crying with me. And in that moment, I wasn't the strong one anymore. I was just his daughter, broken in his arms.

Goru Bhai came back in quietly, placing glasses of water before us—the only thing any of us could offer one another that night.

We gathered in the living room, emotionally wrecked, our voices low as we went over the details for the funeral the next morning. Every word felt heavier than the last.

A video call came from Kake. Her face was streaked with tears, her voice barely holding itself together. She wanted to come home—she begged to.

Mummy and Daddy spoke to her gently, their own voices heavy with sorrow, as they tried to explain why it wasn't possible right now. They turned down her request with love, not refusal.

But we didn't want her to sit alone in that silence, wrapped in grief with no one by her side. We urged her to call one of her friends and stay with her. Thankfully, her roommate was there with her.

None of us had the appetite, but we forced ourselves to eat a few bites—just enough to get through. And then we sat together, the four of us, for what felt like a suspended eternity.

We talked about Chai. Just her. Nothing else. No logistics. No obligations. Only stories, memories—the way she laughed, the way she scolded us, the scent of her clothes, the softness of her touch. Her presence filled the room, as though she was seated among us one last time.

Around 2 a.m., Daddy looked at all of us and said gently but firmly, "We need to rest. Tomorrow will be a long and tiring day. Let us all get some rest."

And he was right. The darkest night was only a prelude to the morning that would follow.

CHAPTER 07

Meri Jhaai
Part II: A Soul Waiting to Be Set Free

2018-2019

She needed someone with her around the A-clock—not just for company, but because her age and health demanded it.
And I wanted to be that person.

Because I knew.
Somewhere inside me, I already knew.

That our time together was slipping, grain by grain, through my desperate fingers.

I didn't want a career. I didn't care for recognition, for ambition, for applause. I would have given up everything—every title, every promotion, every plan—if it meant I could sit beside her, just watch her exist. I wanted to spend every waking second by her side.

I wanted to learn how she crocheted—with a rhythm that only her fingers knew, with patterns that made no sense to anyone but still came out perfect every time. I wanted to learn how she stitched suits, her needle always finding its way with quiet precision. I wanted to learn every recipe—every pinch of salt, every simmered moment—because her food didn't just feed us, it healed us.

Not just watching her—but learning her. Absorbing her. Memorizing her.

I wanted to carry her forward in me.

Because the child inside me, foolish and pure, believed that if I learned enough—if I became her student in life—I could keep her alive long after she was gone.

That somehow, she'd never really leave me.

But a part of me also knew the day was coming. And I knew I wouldn't survive it.

I used to cry into my pillow at night, silently begging God to take me too whenever He decided to call her. Because what was I without her? What was the point of my breath if it no longer mingled with hers?

She wanted me to live. To grow. To chase dreams. Even knowing that my biggest, brightest dream was her. Just her. I would've brought the stars down for her and laid them at her feet if I could. She knew that.

And she knew losing her would shatter me.

That's why she began preparing me in her own quiet, deliberate way—not through lectures, but through gentle, fragmented moments. Conversations threaded with subtle guidance—about the roles I would one day inhabit: as a daughter, a sister, a granddaughter. Eventually, a wife, a mother, a daughter-in-law. Each time she spoke of it, I resisted, not yet ready to hear it. But beneath every word, every pause, her deepest wish was unwavering—that I grow into a kind, grounded, and compassionate human being.

I'd snap, "You're not going anywhere."
I'd cry.
I'd throw little tantrums.
I'd deflect with humor.

I wasn't ready to hear it. I don't think I ever would be.

I'd get up and walk away, and she would slowly follow behind.

She'd say gently, "Udaas na ho, hale te main jundi aa. Chal, puttar, main nai boldi marne da bas."
(Don't be sad, I'm still here for now. Come on, my child, I'm not talking about dying, that's all.)

I'd look at her stubbornly and mutter, "Main aapse katti hoon. Baat mat karo mujhse."
(I'm not talking to you. Don't speak to me.)

And she'd just laugh and say, "Accha, accha, nai marungi bas. Khush? Tere saath hi hoon."
(Alright, alright, I won't die, okay? Happy now? I'm right here with you.)

And I couldn't help but smile—and laugh—right back at her.

No matter how stubbornly I resisted, her words still found their way in.

What she said slipped quietly into my bloodstream.

Every little instruction, every story, every example she shared—they tucked themselves into the folds of my mind and wrapped gently around my heart.

She wasn't just speaking.

She was imprinting.

She was laying out a quiet map.

Preparing me to live without her—even as she remained fully present in the time we still had.

She knew the storm was coming.

And like only the purest kind of love can, it begins to prepare without ever saying so directly.

she began building me a shelter—quietly, gently, one word at a time.
Preparing me in ways I couldn't yet understand.
Preparing me for a day I refused to believe would ever come.

From 2018 onwards, I began begging her.
"Let me stay. Let me care for you. Choose me, Chai. Let me be the one who walks with you till the end."

But she'd always refuse—softly, lovingly, yet unshakably firm.
"Nahi, Puttu, tujhe apni duniya banani hai, office jaana hai, apne pairon par khade rehna hai."

As if chasing dreams could ever mean more to me than sitting beside her feet and wrapping her in a shawl of love.

Eventually, we arranged for two attendants—one for the day, one for the night. It broke me. Because while someone else watched over her body, I knew I was still tied to her soul. And she was to mine.

I was still the child who whispered, "Good morning, Chai," before doing anything else each day.

Even when she was too weak to rise, she remained the first person I'd wish every single morning.

"Good morning, Chai," I'd whisper at her bedside. She'd try to sit up, her arms twitching with the instinct to hold me like she always did, but her body betrayed her.
"Utho mat… aaram karo. Main bas office jaakar jaldi se aati hoon. Phir hum saath mein khaana khayenge."
(Don't get up… just rest. I'll be back soon. Then we'll eat together.)

I used to say it with a smile, but inside, I was bargaining with time.

Promising myself moments I wasn't sure I'd still have.

Telling her we still had dinners to share. Telling her I'd return.

As if I could stop the clock.

As if I could trick fate with love.

Each morning, just before leaving for work, I'd step into her room.

I'd lean in, kiss her cheeks, whisper a silent prayer—asking God to take care of her—and light a small diya in the temple beside her bed. I'd play the Gayatri Mantra softly, its sacred rhythm weaving peace into the room's stillness.

Then, as I turned to leave, I'd call out, "Bye, Chaiiii…"

And almost every time, her voice—faint but laced with warmth—would follow:
"Arey, jaati jaati, paani toh pilati jaa…" (At least offer me water before you leave.)

This used to be her tone; I can still hear her saying this.

It didn't matter that I'd already slipped into my sandals, my office bag slung over one shoulder, house keys lost somewhere in the chaos. It didn't matter that the carpool was waiting somewhere I had to meet. The moment I heard those words, I'd drop everything—right there in the hallway—and run back into her room.

"Main aa gayi… yeh lo, paani piyo," I'd say, holding the glass to her lips, my eyes drinking her in. ("I'm here… here, drink some water.")

I'd watch her sip slowly, her hands delicate, her eyes meeting mine with quiet affection.

And in those moments, time stilled. Nothing else mattered.

That little exchange, that tiny ritual—it became the heart of our mornings.

A sacred rhythm. A shared breath.

Even now, just the memory of it makes my heart ache and flutter at once.

It is, without doubt, the fondest thread I hold from her final year.

The one that still lives in me like muscle memory, like prayer.

I would rush home straight from the office—without even changing out of my work clothes—just to make sure I made it in time to have dinner with her. That one meal meant everything. Sitting beside her, sharing bites, watching her eat—it was more than routine; it was sacred.

Every single day, I'd call home at least two or three times.

"Mummy, how's she doing?"

I'd ask one of the helpers, too, needing constant updates, needing to feel involved even when I couldn't be there physically.

Sometimes, I couldn't resist and would say, "Put the phone near her ear."

And then I'd whisper, softly but urgently,

"Chai… I love you, okay? Accha, bye… khana acche se kha lo." (" Granny I love you…Ok! Okay bye, please eat well ")

I never wanted her to forget—not even for a second—how deeply she was loved.

Those calls weren't just check-ins.

They were lifelines. For her, and for me.
She had made her decision—quietly, firmly.
She would never let me quit my job.

And so, she did what only someone with a mother's soul—or a grandmother's love—could do.
She acted like she was getting better.
She feigned strength, smiled through pain, forced herself to look "okay," just so I wouldn't bring up the one thing I kept pleading for—to leave everything behind and sit beside her, day and night.

But the truth was clearer than ever:
She wasn't saving herself.
She was saving me.

Because she knew that if I allowed myself to stay, if I gave in and spent every second wrapped around her shadow, I'd never recover from losing her.
She knew I would fall to pieces.
And she knew I wouldn't know how to gather myself again.

So she pushed me gently toward my dreams, even when I begged to stay.
She hid her pain behind a brave face—because what she feared more than her own death… was mine.

She was preparing me to survive a world without her in it, even if it broke her heart to do so.

She was simply selfless—and so was I.

We both carried within us an unwavering desire to place the other before ourselves. Not out of duty, but out of love—the kind of love that isn't loud or boastful, but quiet, constant, and all-encompassing. All we ever wanted was for the other to be happy. That was our joy. That was enough.

Looking back, I know how rare that kind of bond truly is. I was fortunate. Because in many families, that selflessness is not always present. Too often, love is replaced by fear—and fear, when left unchecked, turns into control.

Many elders, often unknowingly, act from a place of deep insecurity. In their need to feel relevant and central in their children's lives, they begin to hold on too tightly. Not out of malice, but out of fear. In doing so, they sometimes confuse authority with love and end up limiting the very growth they once nurtured.

They forget that while they may still influence today through tradition, guilt, or emotional dependence, tomorrow they will no longer be here. But their children will remain—left behind in the aftermath, carrying hearts shaped by control rather than quiet confidence and freedom.

Even when they grow up and build lives, something within them often remains restrained—unable to fully trust their voice, choices, or worth, because they were never truly allowed to.

And how will such children raise their own children?
How will they teach freedom if they were never given it?
How will they understand unconditional love if they have to earn it?

Unhealed pain does not end with one generation—it becomes legacy. What is not transformed is inevitably transmitted.

This cycle often becomes most visible in defining life moments like marriage or choosing a life partner. Instead of support, there is resistance. Instead of trust, control. Children do not leave because they do not love their parents—they drift away when love begins to feel like confinement.

What is needed is not control, but trust. Trust in the values once given. Trust in the foundation built. Trust that children carry invisible threads of connection, even when they walk their own path. New relationships should be welcomed, not resisted—because they expand love, they do not replace it.

True love does not grip out of fear or ego. It does not suffocate. It gives space. It listens. It allows growth.

And something remarkable happens when love learns to let go—it does not lose people. It brings them back.
Not out of obligation, but out of choice. Not out of fear, but out of love.
Because love that releases with grace is the love that is always returned to.

Jhaai was among those rare souls who allowed her children and loved ones to grow freely. She never held anyone close out of insecurity or selfish need. There was no possessiveness in her love, no fear of being left behind. She simply gave space—quietly, naturally, without conditions.

She was never insecure in her affection. Her love did not demand, it did not control, it did not confine. It trusted.

And what we gave her back, in return, was only love—pure, effortless, and unmeasured.

She used to wear her soft, faded nighty—the kind with tiny flowers printed across it, its fabric loose and familiar, almost like a second skin. Her hair was always tied into a tight, slightly thinning bun. No dupatta. No fuss. Just her.

Her large, round glasses rested heavily on her face; she used to call them "ainak," often slipping down her nose as she moved—slow, careful—through the kitchen. Age had made her cautious. She was slightly plump, slower on her feet, always alert to the floor beneath her.

"Bas, Puttu, pair phisal na jaawaan," (Just hope I don't slip, my child) she'd murmur, steadying herself by gripping the edge of the fridge or leaning gently against the counter.

But even then, she refused to let go of her role in the kitchen. That space was hers. Her temple. And she cooked not just to feed, but to love.

She would ask me to sit by the dining table, just within her sight.

"Tu baith ja, beta, main sab kuch kar laan gi."
(You sit down, my child, I'll handle everything.)

Her hands moved with age, yes—but also with grace. Those thin gold bangles on each wrist jingled softly with every stir of the spoon, every lifted lid. A single band adorned her right-hand ring finger—always there, always shining. And in her ears, thick, round baaliyan swayed with her movements. Her piercings had widened over the years, so she couldn't wear studs—only those classic loops she'd had forever.

As she stirred the daal slowly, she spoke—her voice light, matter-of-fact.

"Kam theek chal reha? Koi pareshani toh nahi?"
(Is work going okay? No one troubling you?)

And then, almost without transition, a life lesson would slip in between the turmeric and the tadka.

"Vekkhin, Sonia… asli khana hamesha dheemi aanch te banda ya. Slow gas te. Jiven pyaar—ghut ghut ke pakda."
(Real food is always made on a low flame, child. Slow gas. Just like love—it simmers slowly, gently.)

She would add:

"Namak ghatt paayi da, baad ch hor pa sakte ne."
(Add less salt. We can always add more later.)

The first bite of every meal was always for Goru Bhai and me—whichever one of us happened to be near her at the time.

It didn't matter what she was eating—her love always made sure we were fed first.

And you didn't get to argue.

You couldn't say you were full, or that you didn't like something, or that you'd eat later.

She'd just smile and tease, "Maa ne sikhaya, Dadi ke haath ka khana nahi khana?" ("Did you mother teach you not to eat food cooked by Grandma?")

Then she'd laugh, and somehow, we'd all end up laughing too—eating straight from her hands, like always.

Whenever we told her, "This is amazing—what did you put in it?"

her answer never changed:

"Kuch bhi nahi—nimak (salt), mirach (pepper), haldi (turmeric), jara jaya jeera (and just a pinch of cumin)."

And then she'd say, every single time:

"It's not about how many ingredients you use. What matters is the energy you cook with—your love, your intention. And always, always on a slow flame, with patience."

Her big glasses would fog up with steam as she leaned over the pot.
The gold bangles shimmered under the kitchen light.
Her baaliyan would softly clink against her cheeks whenever she tilted her head.

All these little things—so ordinary back then—feel sacred now.

She never rushed.
Not with food. Not with love.

She taught me that care takes time.
That patience is an ingredient, too.

And as I sat watching her cook—her hands aged but sure, her voice weaving between stories and spices—
I began to understand: this wasn't just routine.

It was an inheritance.

Not just recipes or instructions.
But a way to love.

Slow.
Sacred.
Eternal.

Slowly, around 2018, the roles began to shift.

What once was me at the dining table, watching her cook, became her sitting—then lying down—while I stood at the stove instead.

At first, she was still in the kitchen doorway, giving tips, guiding me with her eyes and her voice.

And then, eventually, she was listening from her bed—her body too tired, too fragile to move.

But even as her limbs began to fail, her will never did.

We kept a small bell by her bedside, which Daddy had got from Ikea, so she could ring it whenever she needed something. And each time it chimed, Goru Bhai would leap from the living room, halfway through watching TV, and rush to her.

"Kya hua, Chai?" he'd ask, slightly out of breath, concern etched across his face.

She'd smile faintly and say, "Sonia nu bula jara…"
(Call Sonia for me, just for a moment.)

And I would come running into her room, wiping my hands on the end of my kurta, hair pulled back, a spoon still in hand.

She'd look at me with that same sparkle in her eyes—the one that never left—and say gently,

"Koi jaldi nahi hai. Aaram naal banai… man laga ke banai. Aur phone te na lag jaayi, kadchi hilaati rahiyo."
(There's no rush. Cook slowly, with love. And don't get distracted by your phone… keep stirring the ladle.)

She would effortlessly weave Punjabi, Hindi, and Persian—a beautiful, seamless blend of languages, often without even realizing it. Yet both Goru Bhai and I understood every syllable, every nuance. And we would always respond to her in Hindi.

And then, laughter would fill the room.

Her words, her delivery—always laced with that perfect mix of tenderness and mischief—never failed to bring us joy.

She might have stopped standing by the stove, but she was still in every meal I made—in the salt I measured carefully, in the flame I kept low, in the taste I paused to check twice.

Even when she could no longer lift a kadchi, she was still holding everything—our family, our rhythm, and me—together.

From those evenings spent watching Pakistani dramas side by side, it slowly became just me, alone on the sofa, staring at the screen while her room remained quiet. She began spending more time sleeping, her body giving in even as her spirit clung on.

Each time I sat there, I told myself—just a week more, just a little rest, and she'd be back beside me. We'd laugh again at those overdramatic dialogues, argue over the storyline, and she'd lovingly tell me, "Bas ab band kar de, kitna TV dekhegi?"

But the truth lingered quietly in the corners of the house—I just wasn't ready to accept it.

Once old age pins you to a bed, it rarely lets go. And yet, even at 88, her presence filled the home like sunlight through a sheer curtain—soft, fading, but still undeniably there.

Her eyes still held command. One glance from her, and Goru Bhai and I would straighten up like scolded children.

She still insisted her clothes be hand-washed—"Machine da kapda nai paune." (I won't wear machine-washed clothes.)

She'd wake up with the doorbell's chime, her senses sharper than ours.

She still managed to control Harley with just her sotti, tapping it on the floor like a gentle warning.

She didn't miss a single video call with Kake—her Gudiya. Or with Daddy.

Even lying in bed, she would correct Mummy on how to cook special food for Goru Bhai and me.

And yet… behind all that, time was slipping.

Quietly. Steadily.

Like sand slipping through cupped hands, no matter how tightly we tried to hold on—she was fading.

Her body had begun to slow. But more than that, her spirit seemed to gently loosen its grip on life. She was no longer interested in food, in conversation, in the small joys that once kept her tethered to the world. Gradually, quietly, she was detaching herself from the pleasures of the living—like a bird preparing for its final flight.

Both Goru Bhai and I would try, in our own ways, to pull her back—sometimes with her favorite dish, sometimes with old songs, sometimes just with silly stories. But we had started sensing it. Her silence wasn't just tiredness. Her stillness wasn't just weakness. It was a surrender.

It felt like she had already made peace with the idea that her time had come. She didn't fight it. She was preparing herself, and—without saying it—preparing us too.

Old age doesn't just weigh heavily on the one enduring it—it quietly lays its burden on the hearts of the family too. I don't mean the duties or the routines. I mean the slow, aching awareness that someone you love deeply is slipping away. That every shared meal, every touch, every word… might be the last.

It is a kind of slow grief—a death that begins before the final breath.

And in that space, what's needed from us isn't just care. It's patience. Deep, deep patience. Acceptance. Perseverance. Kindness. But above all, consideration. A willingness to hold space for them, even when it breaks something inside us.

It's not easy. It drains you—mentally, emotionally, spiritually, physically.

But when it's someone you love with all your heart, you find a way. Somehow, you always find a way.

All of us began making small, quiet adjustments—reshaping our lives in subtle ways just to spend more time with her. Duties were shared, rotated, and passed between us with care. And somehow, each of us wanted to do more than we were capable of, as if love alone could keep her from slipping further away.

Her needs had started to change. She needed her hearing aid now, almost constantly. Her glasses had to be replaced—the numbers higher, her gaze softer. The list of vitamins grew, and prescriptions changed. The doctor, once an occasional visitor, now came home every month. He'd check her gently, say a few kind words, and for a few days after, she'd perk up—as if his presence brought her a sense of hope.

But it never lasted. Within a week, she'd fall quiet again, drifting into a silence that felt heavier than before. There were days when she seemed to lose the will to even be.

Her food changed too. Gone were the rich curries and warm rotis. Her meals were now soft and simple—khichdi, boiled vegetables, light soups. Nourishing, yes, but without the flavor she once delighted in. The plate looked full, yet her appetite faded.

And still, we kept adjusting—not just the meals or the medicines, but our hearts. Stretching them in ways we never had before. Because loving her now meant learning to let go of the version of her we once knew… and embracing this quieter, more fragile one, who still carried the same soul, just wrapped in slower steps and softer silences.

We started arranging the doctor's visits every two weeks, hoping that the regularity would help her—if not physically, then at least psychologically. We thought that if she felt cared for, supported, and seen, it might lift her spirit.

Goru Bhai and I sat down and decided to book a full round of physiotherapy—sixteen sessions in total. She had just started becoming bedridden, and we knew that movement, even a little, could make a difference. But she refused to take it.

So we brought physiotherapy home—forcefully, through emotional persuasion, whatever it took. We just wanted to get it done, to be able to sigh in relief: Thank God, at least this problem is taken care of.

She agreed, reluctantly. She completed barely two sessions. By the third, she began to complain—about the therapist, about the pain, about everything. She insisted it wasn't working.

We knew the truth.

This wasn't really about the therapist. It was her way of gently pushing us away—of asking us, without saying it outright, to stop trying. To let her be. To stop hoping she might get better, because somewhere deep down… she no longer wanted to.

Still, we changed the physiotherapist—just to make her feel heard. Even when we knew it wasn't about them.

It was her quiet surrender.

And our quiet resistance.

Because even as she pulled away from life, we weren't ready to let her go.

Somehow, she sat through one more physiotherapy session. But that was the last. After that, it was as if something within her snapped—or maybe settled. She turned the house upside down in her quiet, firm way, making it clear that she was done with all of it. No more therapists. No more coaxing. No more trying. And once she made up her mind, there was no space for discussion. No room for negotiation. Her decisions, once made, stood like stone.

Questioning her was out of the question.

So Goru Bhai and I shifted our focus to what we could still do. We set a schedule between ourselves—deciding who would be there and when, who would take the lead on her care that day. Giving her medicines became a shared ritual. Sometimes it was as easy as placing them in her hand and watching her quietly take them. But most days, it was a dance—a mix of gentle pleading, playful banter, and stubborn insistence.

We'd joke with her, tease her as we used to when we were kids, just to make her smile before slipping the medicines into her palm. On harder days, we'd sit beside her, hold her hand tightly—

not forcefully, but with the kind of firmness that said: We're not giving up on you. Not yet.

There was love in every capsule we handed her. In every glass of water held to her lips. In every sigh, every smile, every rolled eye. This was how we fought for her now—not with doctors or therapies, but with laughter, with presence, and with relentless, ordinary devotion.

Because sometimes, love looks like showing up. Over and over again. Even when you know you're slowly being asked to let go.

Each day added another layer of difficult decisions for all of us. Every single day, we found ourselves struggling with one challenge or another. Our sole purpose was clear—to give her the utmost comfort and to hold onto hope that she might come back to us. But her purpose was quietly different. She had made a silent choice deep within her heart: that her time was drawing near, and when it came, she would finally reunite with Dada ji and her brother.

For a whole year, our lives folded quietly into the space around her. Every outing was canceled, every plan quietly set aside. I stopped stepping out after work, spending every weekend at home, simply close to her. Goru Bhai gave up cricket on weekends—his bat resting untouched, his laughter quieter. Mummy postponed her trips to Delhi, choosing to stay near, even though her heart longed to see her own brother. My father's calls grew more frequent, his voice a steady thread of care and worry. Each morning and evening, he would check the CCTV feed from her room—her silent guardian—streaming live to all our phones, binding us to her even when we were apart.

And whenever one of us noticed the faintest stillness, a quiet pause in her breathing or movement, it was like a ripple through our hearts. The moment the alarm went off, we would immediately reach out to each other, and someone would drop everything to rush to her side.

Our days became a gentle, relentless rhythm of watching and waiting—held together by love, hope, and the fragile desire to keep her safe as long as we could.

She began to say things that pierced straight through the core of our hearts—soft, fragile words from a soul growing weary. "Why are you all still taking care of me?" she whispered one day, her voice fragile, as if carrying the weight of a thousand silent nights. "My body is old… so tired. Just give me an injection—end this pain."

There were moments when she spoke of seeing Dada ji—not as a dream, but as a presence close enough to reach. "I see your Dada ji," she'd say, her eyes distant yet filled with a strange calm. "He's calling me. But you—your love is holding me back. You won't let my soul go."

And then, with a faint, almost sorrowful smile, she would murmur, "Koi baat nahi… mera jis din waqt aayega, tum mein se koi rok nahi paayega." ("Don't worry… when my time comes, none of you will be able to stop me")

Those words shattered me. I would sit there, trembling, tears flooding my eyes, feeling an ache so deep it left me breathless. And alongside that pain, a fierce anger would rise—the kind that comes from watching someone slip away while they tell you to let them go.

She would often speak in quiet, resigned murmurs: "Woh dekh, sab line se mujhe bula rahe hain… ab bas karo, mujhe baksh do, jaane do mujhe." ("Look, they're all calling me one by one… now stop it, please spare me, let me go.")

It was as if she were begging us silently, pleading to be freed from the weight of life itself. Her surrender was a raw wound laid bare between us—love and grief tangled so tightly that every word felt like a dagger, every silence a cry.

And in those moments, all I could do was hold her hand, swallow my own tears, and pray for the strength to keep loving her through the breaking.

Our hearts shattered a little more with every passing moment. We watched her bravely, wearing masks of strength in front of her, but when night fell and we were alone with our thoughts, the walls closed in. In those silent hours, tears would fall freely—tears born from a struggle to accept a reality that felt unbearable.

I was losing myself in the weight of it all. Sleep became a stranger; peaceful rest was something I could no longer claim. I would wake in the middle of the night, heart pounding, drawn instinctively to check on her. For an entire year, true sleep eluded me, as if my subconscious mind refused to let me rest—haunted relentlessly by the thought of her leaving, the thought of a tomorrow without her. I must have died a thousand deaths in those dark moments, each one heavier than the last.

Our festivals, once lively and full of laughter, shrank into quiet, intimate affairs. We celebrated only to catch a glimpse of joy in her eyes, only to coax a fragile smile from her lips.

But she saw through it all. She knew, in her heart, that each of us was wearing a mask—pretending to be brave when none of us truly were.

I found myself taking leaves from work more often than I wanted—sometimes just a few hours, other times a whole day—because the weight inside me was crushing. It wasn't just exhaustion; it was the heaviness of a heart that ached to simply be near her. All I longed for was to sit quietly by her side, to watch her breathe, to hold her hand and care for her in the small, silent moments that felt so precious.

But peace was a stranger. My mind was a storm of fear and anxiety, living constantly with the unbearable thought of losing her. Every time my phone rang—whether it was from home or Goru Bhai—I froze. My breath would catch, my heart would race, and a cold, sharp dread would claw its way through me, whispering mercilessly: What if this is the call that changes everything?

That fear lived with me like a shadow—relentless and raw—stealing sleep and hope alike.

In January 2019, I had to travel to The Oberoi, New Delhi. I had no choice. I had just closed a major piece of business—it was one of the most important delegations I had ever handled, and as their relationship manager, I had to be there. But nothing about those four days felt right.

The entire trip, especially the flights to and from Delhi, felt like a war inside me. My body was moving, smiling, performing the role I was expected to play—but my mind and heart were somewhere else, completely disconnected. I couldn't stop the thoughts—What if she leaves while I'm not there? What if this is the moment she chooses to go? I had no trust in fate anymore. No trust even in time. I used to say it half-jokingly, half with dread—She will go when none of us are around. She'll leave quietly. Alone. And I was terrified that I wouldn't be there to hold her hand when she did.

Before I left, Goru Bhai and I had already spoken—long, painful conversations where we tried to prepare ourselves for the unpreparable. We had made a pact, without saying too much. If one of us wasn't there when the time came, the other would step in—calm, mature, and focused. The first thing to do: call the doctor immediately, ask him to check her breathing. And until the doctor said the words we were most afraid to hear, we would not stop trying.

We had even kept Gangajal ready—in the temple drawer next to her bed. We had rehearsed this in our minds like a ritual: this would be the first thing we'd reach for, if it ever came to that. Then we'd call each other, and Daddy—without hesitation, without waiting even a second. No matter how much it broke us inside, we had promised to act without emotion, almost mechanically. We had agreed: we would not share the news with anyone else first, not until we had done what needed to be done.

We had also arranged for an ambulance—already connected to the nearest hospital and saved on speed dial. I still don't know how we created that checklist as siblings. It wasn't something we read or were told. It just… became instinct. It was love acting in survival mode.

One of us was always there. She was never left alone. Goru Bhai was still in college then, so he could be around more during the day, which allowed me to stay in the office when absolutely needed. But even then, my heart was never at peace. I constantly wanted to take leave and be with her.

But she wouldn't let me quit. Chai had taken that promise from me. "Don't quit out of helplessness," she would say. "You quit a job when you choose to—for your children, for motherhood, if your husband stands by you, appreciates you, and supports you. You quit when you want to. But never because you feel trapped."

Even in those final months, she was preparing me. Gifting me wisdom I didn't even know I'd need. Readying me for storms I hadn't yet seen. Lessons I carry with me even now—some I might share in later books. Some I may never have the courage to write down at all.

There was one incident that still haunts me—one of those moments you wish you could go back and undo, not because you didn't care, but because you cared too much and just didn't know what to do.

The doctor had come for a routine check-up, and the moment he looked at her reports, his expression changed. He was upset—genuinely disappointed. He asked us how long it had been since she'd taken her medicines regularly, and we hesitated… because we knew. We had let a few days slip by.

Not out of negligence. Never that.

But because Chai had started resisting so fiercely—every time we brought the medicine near her lips, she would turn her face away like a child. Some days, she would clutch her throat and pretend she couldn't breathe. Other days, she would cry or beg us to stop.

The first time it happened, Goru Bhai and I froze. It shook us to the core. Watching her struggle like that—our strong, stubborn Chai reduced to this fragile state where even medicine felt like a punishment—we didn't have the heart.

So we gave in. Just for a day.

And then another.

Telling ourselves maybe her body needed a break. Maybe her soul needed some peace.

But the truth is—we got scared. We were too scared to fight her resistance. Too scared to push when we could feel her slipping away.

When we confessed this to the doctor, he looked at us, paused, and then said something that cut deep—but stayed with me. "They do this sometimes," he said gently. "Not because they're being difficult, but because they've already started giving up on life. They've made peace with the idea of leaving. But you haven't. And so you have to act—not as children who love their grandmother, but as caregivers who cannot give up. You have to outsmart their resistance. You have to find ways. By hook or by crook, you give the medicine. You feed them. Even if it feels like force. Even if it breaks your heart. Just like you would with a newborn who refuses to eat. You don't stop trying. You just love them harder."

That moment changed something in me. It made me realize that caring for someone at the end of their life is not about grand gestures—it's about fighting silent battles every day, about holding the line even when they beg you to let go.

Old age—real old age—can look so much like childhood, but with a sadness that never quite leaves the room. She wasn't just refusing medicine. She was gently trying to leave… and we were doing everything we could to hold her back, even if it meant making mistakes along the way.

We didn't always get it right.
But every choice came from love. A desperate, aching kind of love.

The next week was harder than anything we had ever faced. Goru Bhai and I tried everything—we used humor, patience, gentle coaxing, even tears. We poured every drop of love we had into those moments, hoping she'd open her mouth, hoping she'd let us help her. But she wouldn't. She just wouldn't. Her lips stayed sealed, her eyes distant, as if she had already chosen to let go, and we were the ones still holding on.

Eventually, with tears welling in my eyes and a deep, painful heaviness in Goru's voice, we came to the hardest conclusion: we had to stop thinking like grandchildren and start thinking like caregivers. We had to treat her like a child—not because she wasn't strong, but because she had become so fragile, so unwilling to live, that we had no other way.

So, with broken hearts, we turned it into a task. A heartbreaking ritual. One of us would gently hold her hands—hands that had once fed us, held us, protected us—and the other would carefully bring the medicine to her lips. Sometimes we'd act like we were going to hold her nose shut, just to make her open her mouth. And the moment she did, we'd slip the medicine in and follow it with a sip of water.

It destroyed us. Every time.

It felt like betrayal. Like we were forcing her to stay when her soul had already begun asking for release. But what else could we do? Stand by and watch her give up? That wasn't love—not the kind we had grown up learning from her.

This quiet ritual—one of us holding her down, the other fighting back tears while pressing medicine to her lips—wasn't caregiving. It was heartbreak in slow motion. But we did it because we couldn't not do it. We did it because love, sometimes, means pushing past the guilt and the pain to do what must be done. Even if it leaves you bleeding inside.

And each time we walked out of her room, we didn't say much. We didn't need to. We just sat in silence, broken in our own corners, trying to hold ourselves together—because we had to be strong again tomorrow.

Feeding her had become another uphill battle—one layered with both emotion and exhaustion. She refused to eat anything we cooked at home. Her appetite had become so selective that she would only ask for restaurant food. And not just ask—she would insist, using her age like a weapon of charm and rebellion.

With a mischievous glint in her tired eyes, she'd say, "Mujhe swaad nahi aa raha, tum sahi tareeke se sabzi nahi bana rahe." ("I'm not enjoying the taste; you're not cooking the vegetables properly.")

And when we protested, she would threaten, half-seriously: "Watchman ko bulao... main usse keh dungi woh le aayega!" ("Call the watchman… I'll tell him, and he will bring it.")

But humne bhi kacchi goliyan nahi kheli thi. ("We weren't born yesterday either.")

We knew her ways—and we had our own.

So we took the watchman into confidence, made him a silent soldier in our little conspiracy of love. I began cooking food at home—but with a twist each day. I changed the presentation, the seasoning, and made it look and smell different. Then we'd pack it carefully in restaurant-style containers and hand it over to the watchman. He would dutifully ring the bell, walk in with the box, and announce, "Hotel se aaya hai." ("Its come from the restaurant")

She would light up like a child. A small smile would cross her lips, and she'd eat—sometimes slowly, sometimes reluctantly, but at least she would eat.

It became our daily play, performed without fail. But what looked like a harmless trick on the outside required so much patience—so much thought, care, and love. Every dish was not just food—it was a strategy. Every moment was a balance of emotion and exhaustion, of humor and heartbreak.

But we did it—because when someone you love stops choosing life, you start finding new ways to bring life to them. Even if it means pretending the food came from a restaurant just to see one little smile and a few more bites.

Goru Bhai and I were two very different people—cut from the same cloth, but stitched in opposite patterns.
He was quiet strength—the kind of person who didn't need many words to make his presence felt. He observed more than he spoke, thought before reacting, and always knew how to balance a storm with silence. There was wisdom in his calm.

And then there was me—loud in love, fierce in loyalty. I wore my emotions on my sleeve. I was upfront, stubborn to a fault, and unapologetically real. I didn't believe in stepping back—I charged forward, even when it hurt. Especially when it hurt.

He would bring his patience; I would bring my fire.
He'd know when to hold back; I'd know when to push.
Together, we found ways to make things work—even when nothing made sense.

We didn't need long talks to understand each other. A glance across the room, a half-finished sentence, or even just silence—we knew what the other was feeling. We knew when to step in for one another without asking.

There were days when I would lose patience, when the emotional exhaustion would drown me—and he would quietly take over, saying nothing, just letting me breathe. And there were nights when I saw him breaking quietly, staring at the floor too long, his voice softer than usual—and I would push myself to hold it all together, just so he didn't have to.

But even the strongest soldiers need rest.

So, some nights, we'd escape.
No big plans—just small rituals: drives under the dim city lights, windows down, music low, ice cream in hand. Those drives were our therapy. Our way of remembering that we were still young. Still siblings. Still human.

Sometimes we'd laugh about the absurdity of it all. Sometimes we'd sit in silence.
Other times, we'd park the car somewhere quiet, lean our heads back, and just say, "Yeh sab kab khatam hoga, Chai phir se kab

theek ho jaayengi?" ("When will all this end? When will things be okay again?")

We weren't trying to run away. We just needed to pause—to catch our breath before walking back into the storm.

In those moments, I saw my brother not just as a pillar of strength—but as a boy who loved quietly, hurt deeply, and carried more than he ever showed. And I think he saw in me the same girl he grew up protecting—still loud, still emotional, but now fighting her own battles with a kind of quiet courage.

But no matter how hard we tried, life always found a new way to test us. Just when we thought we'd figured something out, something would change—a new challenge, a new heartbreak, a new layer of helplessness.

Still, we came back every time. Stronger in silence, softer in love. Because this wasn't a responsibility—it was devotion. This wasn't just survival—it was our shared promise to her.

There is no pain deeper, no sight more gut-wrenching, than watching those who once carried the world on their shoulders slowly become fragile, broken shadows of themselves. Seeing your parents or grandparents—people who raised you, protected you, loved you unconditionally—fight a battle they never wanted, trapped in bodies that no longer obey, is a heartbreak that shatters every part of your soul.

We can survive losing a job, endure the collapse of a business, patch up broken relationships, even rebuild our lives from rock bottom. But this? This helplessness? Standing powerless while the people who once were your anchors fade away, watching them suffer pain you cannot ease—it rips you apart from the inside out.

It's the slow death of hope. The quiet surrender of someone you love. And with every weakening breath, you lose a piece of yourself too, swallowed by a grief so raw and relentless that it feels like drowning without ever hitting the bottom.

Sunday, February 10, 2019 - The Funeral Day

That day did not end like other days.
It ended like something sacred returning home.

We performed every ritual with trembling hands and heavy hearts—the bath, the Tulsi mala, the chandan tilak placed gently on her forehead. She was dressed in the semi-stitched green suit she had once spoken about, carefully kept aside by her, as though she somehow already knew it would one day become part of her final journey. It was brought from her maternal home, folded with love, now unfolding into farewell.

Her hands… her feet… still soft. Still warm in memory. So still that for a moment, it felt like she might simply open her eyes and smile at us, as she always did.

But she did not.

And yet, she was everywhere.
In every silence.
In every breath we struggled to take.
In every tear we refused to stop.

I remember placing the chandan on her, my fingers shaking, as if even touch had begun to understand the weight of goodbye.

And in that unbearable stillness, something ancient rose within me—the words of the Shrimad Bhagavad Gita:

"The soul is neither born nor does it ever die."

"Na jayate mriyate va kadachin…"
It is eternal, untouched by fire, water, wind, or time.
"Weapons cannot cut it, fire cannot burn it, water cannot wet it, wind cannot dry it."

In that moment, these were not verses anymore. They were the only thread holding me together.

Because if the soul cannot be destroyed… then she was not gone.
She had only changed form.

The body had returned to the earth. But something of her—something far beyond flesh—still lingered in the air, in the rituals, in us.

And yet, even knowing this truth, grief does not become smaller. It only becomes more sacred.

We were not just performing a farewell.
We were witnessing a transition the eyes cannot fully comprehend.

That day, I understood what Krishna meant when He said:
"Just as a person sheds worn-out clothes and wears new ones, the soul discards the body and enters a new one."

Nothing truly ends.
It only transforms.

And perhaps that is why, even in the deepest sorrow, there is a strange kind of stillness—as if the universe itself is reminding us… she has not vanished, only moved beyond what we can see.

But for those left behind, the silence is still loud.
And love… still remains unfinished in the language of this world.

And so this chapter does not end with closure.
It ends with a presence that refuses to fade.

Because some people do not leave life—they expand beyond it.

She was not just a memory we lost. She became the silence we now listen to more closely, the softness we try to carry forward, the love that no longer asks for form to exist.

And maybe that is the final truth she left us with—without words, without effort:
Nothing pure is ever lost. It only returns to where it always belonged.

A few days later, we carried her ashes to Haridwar for the asthi visarjan.

That journey felt unreal.

The same hands that once held us, fed us, and protected us… had now become ashes resting silently within an urn. And yet, even then, it did not feel like we were carrying an ending. It felt like we were accompanying her soul toward freedom.

As we stood before the holy Ganga, the air felt unbearably heavy and sacred at the same time. The sound of temple bells echoed in the distance, priests chanted mantras softly, and the river flowed with a calmness almost impossible to explain—as though she had witnessed millions of goodbyes before ours.

When the ashes touched the water, something inside me broke in a way words will never fully capture.

Because this was the final.
Not the hospital.
Not the funeral.
Not the rituals at home.
This.

Watching the Ganga carry away the last physical part of her that still remained with us.

And yet, somewhere between the flowing water and the tears I could no longer stop, the Gita echoed within me once again:

"For the soul, there is neither birth nor death. It is eternal, everlasting, and ancient."

In that moment, I realized something profound:

We were not releasing her.
We were returning her.

Returning her to the universe.
To the Divine.
To the infinite from where every soul arrives and where every soul eventually goes back.

As the ashes disappeared into the sacred waters of Haridwar, I folded my hands one last time and whispered quietly:

"Jhaai… thank you for loving us the way only you could."

And the Ganga kept flowing—
as if carrying both her soul and our grief gently toward God.

Monday, 25th February, 2019

I returned to work burdened by a heart weighed down with unbearable sorrow, though I had no choice but to push forward. I hadn't stepped into the office for nearly two and a half weeks, and truthfully, every ounce of my energy, passion, and motivation had withered away. Life felt hollow and devoid of meaning. Yet, for her—only for her—I summoned the strength to endure.

I couldn't even muster the will to apply lipstick or dress with care. How could I? My heart lay shattered, scattered in fragments too painful to gather. There was no appetite, no purpose, no solace—not even the refuge of sleep. When your world is broken, how does one find the resolve to care about appearances?

Every simple choice became an insurmountable ordeal: deciding whether to take an auto, navigating the train from Sanpada to CST, even packing my own lunch—each felt like a monumental challenge.

I refused to reveal my wounds to the world. I had no desire to engage with anyone. Yet my job demanded the opposite—my polished appearance, my social grace, my cheerful, positive demeanor. So I donned the mask. Because no matter how profound the pain, life's relentless march leaves no room for pause.

I confided in my manager that I felt like quitting. I told them I didn't know how long it would take to heal, or if I could even do justice to the work entrusted to me. They listened with such warmth and understanding, offering me the kindness I didn't know I needed. They told me to take more time—to breathe, to recover—and to return only when I felt ready.

I agreed, grateful for their compassion. But the very next day, I found myself back at my desk. Staying home was no comfort; it felt like slowly drowning in silence. Work, though exhausting, was at least a distraction from the pain that threatened to consume me.

We had two flats on the same floor, each with two bedrooms. One was where Chai lived, and I stayed there with her. Right next door, separated by just a single wall, was the flat where Goru Bhai, Mummy, and Harley lived. Honestly, it never really felt like two separate homes—it was more like one large house divided by a thin partition.

Daddy had been in Texas, USA, for nearly three years, returning to us only every three to six months.

Kake was in Canada, residing in a shared apartment. She had left in 2012 to pursue further studies, and now, with her permanent residency secured, she worked as a visual merchandiser.

But that day—returning home with the house keys in my hand for the very first time—was the most agonizing moment of all. Until 2018, she would sit in the living room, the door left wide open, waiting for me to walk through it. From 2018 to 2019, there was always a helper or caretaker to welcome me inside.

The next morning, I decided to go to work and try to divert my attention. It felt like a better idea than lying on the bed, watching the ceiling, and waiting for night to come. And when night came, I would only lie there waiting for the day to return. I knew I was slipping into depression, and I knew the only person who could pull me out was me.

So I decided to show up at work. The next day brought some distraction. And when the mind is busy, you automatically think less, or at least think differently.

Work, even in fragments, gave me something to hold on to.

But focusing was almost impossible at first. My mind would drift constantly—back to her, back to the house, back to the silence. There were moments when I would sit at my desk feeling completely hollow, and moments when I would feel everything at once, overwhelmed by the thought that maybe she was finally at peace, somewhere beyond this suffering.

Grief is strange. You don't even know what stage you are in. You only know that you are hurting, that you are lost, that life has lost its meaning. Everything becomes mechanical. You begin ticking off tasks like a machine, without heart or soul, without presence—just existing through the day.

And slowly, you stop recognizing yourself.

What makes it harder is that grief is invisible. People cannot see it, and often, they don't understand it. You want to scream your pain into the world, to show how deeply you are breaking inside, but you hold it back because it feels too personal, too sacred, too fragile to explain.

And even when you try, the answers are always the same.

"Time will heal."

"She is in a better place."

I know these are truths. I know people mean well. But when your heart is shattered, logic does not soothe it. The mind may accept reality, but the heart refuses to listen. It only wants to feel, to remember, to relive everything—even the pain.

That is what grief does. It keeps you bonded to what you lost, even when you are trying to move forward.

Daddy had to head back to the USA by the end of March. I had no heart to let him go. It suddenly hurt in a different way—watching our world shrink again. First it was my sister. Then Daddy expanding his life and work abroad. And now, after Chai, it felt like our family had been reduced to fragments of what it once was.

From six, we had become three.

And grief has a strange way of magnifying everything. Even the smallest inconvenience feels unbearable. Even a normal day feels like a battle. It waits for you to be slightly weak, slightly off balance—and then it pulls you right back into the depths.

For me, the real acceptance took nearly six months.

Six months of grieving.

And it wasn't linear. Some days felt like progress. Others felt like falling all over again.

It started with giving away her belongings. That was the first breaking point. Her wheelchair. Her walking stick. Her sewing machine—so old, so familiar, so full of her presence. Each item felt like a piece of her life being taken away again.

We gave them away to people who needed them, and in doing so, something inside me shifted slowly. Painfully. It wasn't about letting go of objects—it was about learning that love doesn't live in possession. It lives in impact.

If something she owned could bring dignity or support to someone else, maybe that too was a way of honoring her.

Still, it hurt. Everything hurt.

Her saris, her belongings, her room—we kept what we couldn't let go of. Some things were distributed, some preserved like fragments of memory we were not ready to release. Her room and her washroom remained untouched, exactly as she had left them. We never renovated them.

Even today, her space remains as it was.

And somewhere along the way, I began to understand two sentences I once could not accept:

Time heals everything.

She is in a better place.

Not instantly. Not easily. Not without breaking apart first.

But slowly, through sleepless nights, through crying spells, through loneliness, through therapy, through anger, through guilt, through everything I became and everything I lost in myself—I began to understand.

Grief changes you before it heals you.

And I had changed completely.

started going to the office. It became impossible to focus initially; my mind would simply drift to her. Sometimes I would feel hollow, and sometimes strangely full, convincing myself she must be in a better place.

Grief is strange; you don't even know what stage you are in. You just know that you are sulking, you are unhappy, you have lost your sense of purpose, and life feels almost impossible to live. You become so mechanical that you stop putting your heart or soul into anything you do. You begin ticking tasks off like a machine, working on things that no longer carry meaning.

A lot of times, we don't even realize that we are silently suffering or silently living in grief. We don't know it. We are clueless, directionless, lifeless.

We want to scream and shout, to tell the world our pain and suffering, to show how brutally we are breaking inside. But we hold ourselves back, thinking this pain is too personal. People might not understand it, might mock it, or might simply say, "It's okay, time will heal."

And believe me, the most common things I heard during that time were exactly this: "Time will heal" and "She is in a better place."

I know, I know—these are truths. I know people mean well. But how does one actually live through a pain like this just by hearing those words? The brain accepts reality, but the heart refuses to listen. It is shattered beyond logic. It only wants to feel, to relive, to stay in that pain—again and again.

With grief, even the smallest problem feels amplified. It waits for your weakest moment. And when you have even a slightly bad day, you fall back into that spiral—blaming life, asking why you, why this, why that, questioning how cruel everything feels.

It took me six months to accept that she was no more, or at least that she was in a better place. But those six months were a complete roller coaster.

6 Months of Grieving:

It was a hell of an experience. Every month felt worse at the beginning, but slowly, in its own strange way, it began to heal me too.

It started with giving away her belongings.

That broke me. I believe it broke all of us. It was painful, but it had to be done. In March–April, we began giving away her things to those in need, so that in some way, she would continue to be remembered.

Her brand-new wheelchair was the first item donated to an old-age home. Then her walking stick. Then her sewing machine—this one hurt deeply. It was nearly 70 years old. Daddy convinced me to give it to one of the helpers who had taken care of her. She knew how to stitch, and it could help her earn something for herself.

I refused at first. I couldn't let it go. But eventually, I agreed, thinking it might bring a small smile in someone else's life.

And slowly, that thought started changing something inside me.

If the person I loved the most was no longer here in physical form, what was the point of holding on to things for the sake of possession? If those things could bring even a small positive change in someone else's life, wouldn't that, in some way, make her happy too?

There were many saris. I kept a few that were close to her heart and distributed the rest to helpers and those in need. I kept four sets of suits, and the rest we gave away. Those four were kept as a form of her blessings—one sent to Kake, one taken by Daddy to the States, one kept in Mummy's almirah, and one I kept with myself.

Her almirah and her bed remained untouched. We never even broke the wall between the two flats. We kept everything exactly as she had left it. She wouldn't even allow us to renovate her washroom or room and would say, "When I die, you can do whatever you want, but not while I am alive."

The entire house was renovated, except her washroom and the tiles in her room. Even now, it remains untouched. It has become my sacred space.

It's been six years, and we have still not made any structural changes to her room or washroom.

Whether we agreed with it or not, whether we accepted it or not, those two sentences that once felt like knives in my heart slowly became my reality—and eventually, my healing:

1. Time heals everything.
2. She is in a better place.

And I say this honestly—it did not come easily.

It took sleepless nights, sudden crying spells, lonely coffee dates, long drives, poor eating habits, emotional extremes, therapy, anxiety, depression, continuous screen time, and complete disconnection from myself.

From being a people person, I became a shadow. From being courageous, I became fearful. I attracted people whose energy did not align with mine, and slowly realized they were toxic. I was at my lowest, and every day I saw myself slipping further away from who I used to be.

I had no love, no compassion—not even for myself.

I was becoming bitter. I was becoming rebellious. I was becoming someone I did not recognize.

I had forgotten how to live. I had forgotten how to smile.

At my lowest, I even reached out—to God, to astrologers, to therapists—hoping someone could help me connect with her, even once.

I know it sounds irrational, even maddening. But that was my reality. That was my rock bottom.

Thankfully, I was not into substance abuse, or I would have lost even more of myself.

I had no idea how to emerge from that depression.
It was my best friend **Amruta's** wedding on February 14 in Nagpur. I didn't attend. There was a reception in Mumbai in March 2019, which became the first outing I forced myself to attend—but I felt entirely hollow within.

Almost a month after her passing, I wore lipstick and something beautiful for the first time. And I felt an overwhelming sense of guilt, as though I had betrayed her, dishonoured the depth of love I held for her.

Gradually, I began dressing normally again for work. People started noticing subtle shifts. I began smiling occasionally. I resumed attending meetings, slowly returning to the cadence of life as it once was.

There were days I would go to the washroom and cry my heart out, wipe my tears, fix my makeup, look into the mirror, and

whisper:
"Sonia, you got this."

I started going for walks and jogs at Marine Drive after work, immersing myself in loud music, desperately attempting to forget her. But the more I tried to erase her memory, the more anger accumulated within me. I found myself blaming her—blaming her for loving me so deeply that losing her became unbearable. Somewhere along the way, I decided I would never love again. I would become emotionally detached. I would function like a machine, remain disciplined with my workouts, and never allow another human being to come close enough to wound me again.

There were days when I would beg God to quietly end my suffering and take me away, because I could not bring myself to end my own life. That was a boundary I refused to cross. Not out of fear, but because even in my deepest depression, I held onto certain non-negotiable principles: no substance abuse, and no transgression of that ultimate threshold of self-destruction. These two rules I clung to, though I cannot explain how.

One day in April, I decided to get a tattoo of her signature. On April 13, 2019, I scheduled my appointment at Aliens Tattoo in Nariman Point. I told no one. I took her signature from her Aadhaar card and had it inked onto my right wrist, directly over the nerve. I chose my right hand because I believe it is connected to karma—karmic energy. I wanted her blessings with me, and I felt this was the most sacred placement, as I intended to use my hands only to give—through charity, assistance, and support—and allow her essence to guide everything I offered to the world. I would strive relentlessly to act with righteousness, ethics, and moral clarity, so that if life ever placed me in moral ambiguity, her name alone would restrain me from wrongdoing.

I know it may sound irrational, but I cherished the idea, and her name, "Sumitradevi," remains the most beautiful name I have ever known.

There were days when I didn't want to meet anyone—not even those I once considered my closest companions. Some days, I couldn't even bring myself to sit with Mummy or Goru Bhai. I would simply wait to return home after work, collapse onto my bed, and silently hope I would not wake up carrying the same unbearable weight. I would wait for weekends and spend nearly twelve hours in front of screens, binge-watching just to escape reality.

There were days when I refused to step beyond my confined space—my bedroom, my iPad, and nothing else. I have always believed that electronic devices do not belong in the bedroom. It should be a sanctified space for rest, restoration, and renewal—not entertainment or distraction. Yet during those days, I would bring in my iPad, order pizza and Coke, and remain shut away for hours.

I would consume everything dark on certain days—Black Mirror, Saw, all installments of American Psycho, Peaky Blinders, horror films, anything that existed in the spectrum of darkness. And on other days, I would shift entirely to films like P.S. I Love You, and then restart F.R.I.E.N.D.S from the beginning again. That became my refuge. Not answering calls, avoiding conversations, and fabricating excuses to family and friends became routine. I had also withdrawn from Harley and Goru Bhai for a period. I do not know what was happening within me.

And then one day, **Amruta** called and asked to meet. I refused, but she persisted until I relented. I told her to come home so we could spend the night—I would cook for her. Even then, my love language remained cooking and feeding, though even that passion had begun to erode. Still, occasionally, I would force myself to cook.

She agreed, but later said, "Get ready, I am taking you out." Her intention was to pull me out of my grief; mine was to draw her into it. I have known her for more than 28 years, and she has witnessed facets of me no one else ever has. I have loved her and her family as my own. In every sense, she is an extension of my being. We are polar opposites, yet we fit. The love we share is once-in-a-lifetime. I am blessed to have her in my life. She is my school friend—we were in the same class, sat on the same bench, and later attended the same college.

But when one is consumed by pain, there arises a desire for others to feel that same anguish. So I pulled her into my world. She, however, had different intentions—to pull me out of it, take me on a date, and reignite my will to live. I was not ready, and I resented the idea. I said words I should never have said, telling her she could never comprehend my pain because I had lost my entire world, while she spoke of outings and joy. I did not stop there. I questioned her friendship and her understanding, and told her never to call herself my best friend again.

I became dramatic, without even realising it.

All I truly wanted was for her to step into my shattered world—to see me, hold me, and if not cry with me, at least wipe my tears or simply feel my pain. And all she wanted was to lift me out of it, make me feel alive again, help me rediscover the light I had long forgotten, remind me of who I was, and reintroduce love into my life.

We had a devastating fight the following week. Neither did she come home, nor did I meet her for dinner. For three long years, we neither spoke nor saw each other. She moved to Canada in June 2019 without seeing me. I clung to my ego, which is entirely uncharacteristic of me, and never reached out. We both blocked each other, vowed never to speak again, and as a consequence, our families also ceased communication. Grief has the power to dismantle far more than one can ever anticipate or comprehend.

I had lost my best friend.

I missed her. I cried for her. I prayed for her well-being. I even felt a sting of jealousy seeing her build a new life in Canada through social media updates via Goru Bhai. Her husband attempted to reach out a few times, and I later learned he would occasionally encourage her to speak to me. But we remained immovable.

Yet I know, without doubt, that we loved each other more than anyone else in this world.

I had given up on her too. I felt betrayed, shattered, isolated, and helpless. I began to believe that this version of Sonia was my reality, though it was not—it was only my grief speaking through me.

I went cold. I became mechanical. I felt numb. I slowly became fearless, and nothing seemed to touch me anymore.

It took me four months to return to my room again. I still remember one day, after returning from work, I decided to confront my fears and my sorrow. When no one was home, I entered Chai's room after four months. I broke down completely. I sat on her bed, and it felt horrifying and alien, as though I had stepped into a frozen realm that no longer belonged to her—or to me. I couldn't bear to look at it, and it shattered me further.

I sat there and cried. When my tears finally exhausted me, I looked at her photograph and said, "You wanted to see this version of me? Are you satisfied now, leaving me alone on this earth? Are you content seeing me helpless and broken at my lowest?"

I was simply unburdening everything within me. I do not even remember how I left that room.

I took a cold shower, made myself tea, returned to her room, and sat there in silence with that cup of tea.

After a few days of being back in that house, I slowly began to feel a fragile sense of acceptance. I do not know how my mind gradually surrendered to reality, and with acceptance came healing.

The more I accepted the truth, the more I healed.

I still miss her. I still cry at times, but it is different now. I have accepted it—gracefully.

Acceptance

Acceptance is not a quiet surrender or a shallow nod. It is a fierce, deliberate choice—a conscious opening of the heart to the full spectrum of life's truth, even when it burns. For me, acceptance was forged in the crucible of hitting rock bottom—not once, but three or four times. Each time I fell, the ground beneath me seemed to vanish, yet I rose each time, stronger and more unbreakable—like a phoenix blazing from ashes, reborn through fire and pain.

The death of my grandmother was one of those unbearable cracks in my world—a silence so heavy it felt as if the very air had been stolen from my lungs. You might ask, What makes death tragic? But tragedy is not simply the event itself; it is the meaning we give to suffering. It is the shattering of illusions, the breaking of what we once believed would never break. Tragedy is the cruel force that strips away our certainty and forces us to face the fragile, unpredictable nature of existence.

Yet, within the heart of acceptance, tragedy shifts. It becomes a sacred teacher—a portal to deeper wisdom and boundless compassion. It reveals that life's fragility is not weakness, but the fertile soil in which resilience, love, and grace take root and grow.

I have hit rock bottom four times in my life, counting 2022–2023, the peak of my rock bottom. 2019 was just a trailer. 2022 was the hardest and darkest year of my life. We will get to that a little later in life, when the time is right.

Acceptance comes with a lot of courage, with a lot of poor experiences, with a lot of maturity, with a lot of grief, with a lot of pain, with a lot of loneliness, and with a lot of failures and heartbreaks.

It doesn't mean you are helpless. It doesn't mean you simply accept, since you can't do anything about it. It purely means accepting with your heart, mind, body, and soul. It means you have come to terms with yourself, or a person, or a situation. It means you accept it gracefully and honor whatever life has to offer you or has offered without changing anything. It means believing in the universe that whatever has happened is for your best interest, and whatever will happen will be for your best interest. It means having unwavering faith in the universe and happily surrendering.

For example, if we like someone and we wish them to be a part of our life, we no longer beg the universe or God to send them into our lives. Instead, we pray that whatever is best for your soul and whatever is suitable for your peace, send that person. It's simply accepting and believing that you will be provided with the best. And if something isn't working your way even after a million attempts, don't worry. Either the situation will change, and you will get the results at the right time, or it's not meant for you, and something bigger and better is on your way. And you accept the failures gracefully and still work.

Accepting the self: this is also a form of self-love, fully accepting oneself, accepting the flaws and the positives of oneself, accepting yourself as a whole, accepting the scars, and also accepting the best version of yourself, accepting your mistakes, and also accepting your goodness.

No human on this planet will get to this stage in life until they have been through the darkest or the most horrifying things in life. Yes, the magnitude of your lows and rock bottom, or the number of times, may differ from each other, but to reach this stage of acceptance will cost you everything, and finally, acceptance will come. Mind you, there still will be days when, even after reaching this point of acceptance, you might go back to the old you for a brief moment, but with the experience and maturity in your hand, you will never fall in life ever again. And even if you do, you won't get damaged as you once did. You will protect yourself with every cell in your body to go back to the lowest in life.

Acceptance of self, then comes acceptance of others, and finally acceptance of life. Once you reach acceptance of life, no one on this planet can shake you or make you weak.

And even after reaching acceptance, I have stopped believing that life becomes easy or light. It doesn't. It simply becomes understandable.

The pain does not disappear. It settles. It becomes quieter, less violent, more familiar. Some days it still returns without warning, but it no longer destroys me the way it once did.

What has changed is not what I went through—but how I now stand beside it.

I no longer need life to make sense in order to keep going. I no longer need answers for everything I survived. I have learned to live with what remains unanswered, unhealed, and unfinished.

And maybe that is what acceptance truly is.

Not the end of grief.
Not the end of love.
But the beginning of living with both—without letting either take me down again.

I carry this feeling in every cell of my body—an unshakable knowing that she will return to me in this lifetime, no matter how or when, because some bonds are not bound by time, only by destiny.

CHAPTER 08

Kan Kan Mein Shri Krishn

How many encounters with Shri Krishna should I even begin with?

It's a strange question because, for me, He has never felt like a distant figure from stories or temples. He has felt... present. In timing, in silence, in chaos, in moments that made no logical sense, yet somehow felt perfectly placed.

Now the real question is—where do I even start?

Because choosing the "first" encounter almost feels impossible.

And I know what you're thinking. No, I haven't met Shri Krishna in a literal, ordinary sense—no dramatic introduction, no announced arrival. But there are moments in life so precise, so strangely guided, that even your doubt pauses for a second and listens.

You may not believe me when I say this.

But I have met Shri Krishna.

Not once.

Not in one form.

And certainly not in ways this world would call normal.

So let me take you through a few of those moments.

And I'll warn you now—this is not just a story. It's an experience. And somewhere between logic and belief... your silence might start agreeing with me.

I didn't even realize when it happened—when He stopped being just Krishna Calling and slowly became Kan Kan Mein Shri Krishn (Shri Krishna in every particle/existence).

From Krishna… to Krishn.

From a name I once heard… to a presence I now feel.

It is strange how faith doesn't announce its arrival. It shifts quietly, almost invisibly, like something within you realigning without permission. And then one day, you simply know—you are no longer searching for Him outside because you have started sensing Him everywhere.

This journey doesn't feel loud or dramatic. It feels intimate, almost cinematic in its silence—like something deeply personal unfolding beyond explanation, yet impossible to ignore.

This remains my favorite encounter—not the first one, but the one that every part of me still calls the closest to divine.

I was casually scrolling on Instagram when a reel suddenly appeared—Sourabh Raaj Jain speaking with calm intensity: "Yuddh karo, Parth" (Fight the battle, Parth/Arjuna).

And believe me, at that exact moment, I was standing at a crossroads in my own life—caught between fight or flight, between giving up or standing my ground. It felt as if life had paused for a second just to deliver that line directly to me.

Soon after, I came across the announcement of a live show titled Mere Krishn (My Krishna). And something within me made a silent promise—I would attend the first show… if I was guided there.

And perhaps that is the strange thing about destiny—when something is truly meant for you, life quietly begins moving you toward it. Doors open without explanation. Circumstances rearrange themselves. Even impossibilities begin to soften.

I somehow managed to get just one ticket—only one, but somehow it felt like it had been waiting for me all along. It was for the Mumbai show on 1st March. The last show. And the front seat.

Even now, when I think about it, it does not feel accidental.

It felt chosen.

Life did not take long to answer.

I usually attend such experiences alone. Especially after the Maha Kumbh Mela, I had begun exploring spiritual experiences in solitude—and strangely, that solitude never felt lonely. It felt revealing. Like meeting parts of myself I didn't even know existed.

That day, I dressed in a peacock-green saree. I even carried a mor pankh (peacock feather) with me—not planned, just instinct. A small offering, a quiet devotion, as if I might get even a second near my Krishn. My only intention was simple: to feel, to witness, to receive blessings.

The show began… and from the very first moment, it felt like something beyond a performance.

I cried for almost two hours straight.

Not gentle tears—no. Something deeper. Something uncontrollable. My eyes were so swollen by the end that the person sitting next to me had to offer water and a handkerchief. And in that moment, I understood—divine experiences are not watched; they are surrendered to.

On stage, I truly saw Krishn come alive in human form through Sourabh Raaj Jain. It was not acting anymore—it felt like a presence. Like memory. Like something eternal choosing to breathe through a body.

Pooja Sharma played Radha, and what an extraordinary performance it was—but I could not take my eyes off Krishna even for a second. Every time Radha appeared, I remember whispering to myself, "Aap tak toh pahunch hi nahi pa rahi…" (I cannot even reach you…) "I cannot even reach you because my eyes and soul are still with Him."

When the show ended, something unexpected happened. I got the chance to go backstage. No audience was allowed—I still do not know how that moment opened for me, but it did.

And suddenly… he was right there.

Close enough to be real. Yet impossible to feel ordinary.

Divine. Completely divine

By then, I had already watched his interviews, listened to his thoughts, and understood fragments of his journey. So I wasn't meeting a stranger—I was meeting a presence I had already begun believing in.

I asked someone behind me to capture a video. Only later did I realize that just beside him stood Ridhima Jain, but in that moment, my awareness had narrowed into something else entirely.

I stepped forward and hugged him without thinking. Without remembering he was an actor. Without remembering anything at all except the feeling.

A moment later, I pulled back, folded my hands, bowed, tried to touch his feet, and said only one thing:

"You are a medium… but a very strong one. Thank you for making us meet Krishna."

He smiled softly.

No arrogance. No distance. Only calm presence. And then he said:

"We are all mediums… even you are a medium. We just need to realize it."

In that moment, something inside me settled.

It did not feel like advice—it felt like remembrance. As if God had spoken to me directly, not through distance, but through understanding.

What struck me most about him was not just his portrayal of divinity, but his own being—grounded, humble, deeply composed, and quietly aware. There was no superiority in him, no separation from people—only stillness and grace, as if he understood the weight of what he carries, yet never claimed it as his own.

And truly, it makes sense why he is the one chosen to embody this role—because some people are not just actors playing characters. They feel placed in roles so that others can be guided through them. No wonder he was born and shaped in a way that allows so many of us to find direction through his presence.

Those words became a prayer for me.

Not something I recite… but something I live by.

Every time I doubt myself, I remember them.

Every time I feel lost, I return to them.

As if a divine conversation once happened just for me, and I was never meant to forget it. And as I walked away from that moment, something inside me was not overwhelmed anymore.

It was peaceful.

Not because I had met Krishn, but because I had been reminded… that perhaps, He was never away to begin with.

There are so many encounters with Shri Krishn that I could easily write an entire book on the ways I have felt His presence in my life.

But for now, let me take you through a few of the most significant moments

Not all at once… just enough for you to feel what I felt.

Krishn is a feeling.

When logic ends, reason fades, and rationality falls silent—that is where He begins.

He is not to be understood. He is to be experienced.

How Krishna Turned into Krishn for Me

I find myself utterly at a loss for words.

How does one even begin to articulate a love such as this? How does one attempt to give language to a feeling so vast, so consuming, that even the richest vocabulary seems insufficient before it?

What lives within my heart is not ordinary affection, nor a fleeting emotion softened by time. It is devotion—so profound that it belongs to no human being, neither living nor departed. It belongs to no earthly relationship, no worldly bond.

It belongs only and entirely to Shri Krishn.

If there exists a true meaning of love—Prem, Pyaar (love in its purest emotional and spiritual form)—then for me, it resides only in Him. Sometimes I wonder if I will ever be capable of experiencing such depth of love for anyone else in this lifetime. And the fact that I feel it so deeply speaks to the richness of my inner world.

It feels ancient.

Timeless.

As though my soul recognized Him long before this life ever began.

How do I even begin to explain the moment of standing before His idol in a temple?

The world simply dissolves.

The noise fades, movement disappears, and time itself seems to surrender its authority. Minutes stretch into what feels like hours, and I remain there—completely unaware of anything else.

And then the tears begin to fall.

Not of sorrow.

Not of pain.

But of something far deeper—a serenity so overwhelming that the heart struggles to contain it.

In those sacred moments, my thoughts fall silent. My soul feels recognized, acknowledged, understood—as though it has finally returned to a presence it has always known.

Sometimes it truly feels as if He is holding me, even though no hand touches mine.

How do I explain the strange paradox that when I close my eyes and think of Him, I find myself smiling and crying at the same time? How do I explain that the mere sight of Him awakens something so natural within me that it requires no thought at all?

My head bows.

My hands fold.

And from somewhere deep within me escapes a whisper so simple, yet so complete:

"Hey Mere Krishn" (Oh, my Krishna).

Nothing more. Nothing else is needed.

How do I explain that no matter how demanding my day becomes, no matter how exhausting life feels, my thoughts return to Him again and again? It is as though He walks beside me like a shadow—one that never leaves me, neither in the brightness of sunlight nor in the quiet of darkness.

And how do I explain that whenever the gentle sound of a flute reaches my ears, an involuntary smile finds its way to my face and heart?

And somewhere within me, a quiet voice always returns:

"My Krishn is here again."

Before sleep claims the night, my final thoughts belong to Him. Gratitude rises in my heart for countless blessings—many of which I may never fully comprehend.

And when dawn arrives, before the world demands anything from me, He is already the first thought that graces my mind.

When I offer water to Tulsi ji, I cannot help but smile and think of Him.

No matter the time zone I find myself in, my mornings begin with a cup of ginger tea and Krishn thoughts and bhajans—from Radha Raman by Sri Indresh Upadhyay Ji to Jaya Kishori Ji's So Dukh Kaisa Paave. I sit in stillness, letting my mind empty of everything but devotion and love for the Supreme. With this energy, I start my day.

Before leaving for work, I sometimes say softly:

"Bye, Krishn… take care."

As though the One who sustains the cosmos requires my concern. And yet, the heart insists.

Whenever I see animals—especially cows—something within me quietly feels that Krishn must surely be somewhere around.

Whenever life humbles me, when I lose or feel stuck, I look upward and ask:

"Ab kya seekhna chahte ho, Shri Krishn?" (What are You trying to teach me now, Lord Krishna?)

And when life grants me victory, I cannot help but smile and say:

"Harne doge kabhi ya nahi?" (Will You ever let me lose?)

And when someone attempts to deceive or manipulate me, I do not react. Somewhere within me, a quiet confidence rises, whispering:

"Kar lo lakh koshish…" (Try a thousand times…)

"Mera chaliya jab jawab dega…
Woh jab meri taraf se khelega… tab dekhenge." (My beloved Krishna, when He responds… when He plays on my behalf… then we will see.)

So I remain silent. Because when Krishn walks beside you, there is no urgency to fight every battle with your own hands. Some battles… some answers… are simply meant to be left to Him.

There are truths that cannot be taught—they were never meant to be learned. They live within us, silent and ancient, waiting for the moment we are ready to remember.

Krishna was never an arrival in my life. He was an awakening. The first time I felt Him, something inside me trembled—not with surprise, but with recognition. As though a door sealed for lifetimes had opened in an instant. As though a voice I had carried across births was calling me home.

This was not the beginning of devotion. This was the end of forgetting. A bond older than this body, older than memory, carried through yugas (cosmic ages in Hindu philosophy) like an unfinished prayer waiting to be completed.

Krishn did not come into my life. He returned when I was ready for Him—and claimed what was always His.

Meri Jhaai (My Grandmother): The First Messenger

Every soul is guided. Some through dreams, some through teachers, and a rare few through love that transcends lifetimes. My grandmother was not just a grandmother—she was my appointed guardian, the one who held my hand in this life exactly where she left it in the last.

She whispered Krishna's name into my life. Her presence always felt like a shield, her blessings older than her body. When she left the physical world, she did not leave me. She became a bridge between Him and me.

Sometimes I feel her presence in small moments—a warmth, an intuition, a quiet guidance. She and Krishn are not separate forces for me; they feel like two lamps lighting the same path.

Why Krishna Chooses Certain Souls

Not every soul is drawn to Krishna. Not every heart aches for Him. Those who feel Him deeply, tenderly, unbearably—they are rememberers.

Krishna chooses souls who have walked with Him before—those who have served, loved, or surrendered in other lifetimes. These souls carry a subtle imprint that awakens the moment the heart is ready.

When my tears fall without reason at His name… when His murti (idol form) feels alive… when the flute feels like memory and not sound—I know these are echoes.

Sometimes, He comes as intuition. Sometimes, as courage. Sometimes as softness in moments where I expect myself to break. Sometimes, as an inner voice telling me, "Not here, not this. Walk away."

He protects in ways only He can—quietly, invisibly, yet unmistakably.

There were moments in my life when the world expected me to fail, falter, or collapse. Yet something within kept me steady, safe, moving. That "something" was Him.

He shows Himself not through miracles, but through alignment. Through the way things fall into place when I stop resisting. Through the peace that arrives without logic.

He who is everywhere—how can He not be felt?

Bhav–Bhakti–Prem — The Trident of My Bond with Him

1. **Bhav — The Feeling:** My connection is not ritualistic. It is emotional. He is not a God I worship—He is the presence I breathe in.
2. **Bhakti — The Surrender:** Not the bhakti of rules, but the bhakti of trust. I do not ask Him for anything. I simply walk knowing He walks with me.
3. **Prem — The Eternal Bond :**This is not love as humans know it. It is a longing that is sweet, a pain that is comforting, a relationship where I can speak without speaking.

"My love for Krishn is not a secret—it is my nature."

Why I Cry When I Feel Him

People cry from pain. I cry from recognition.

There is a love so immense that the body cannot contain it. When the soul remembers what the mind cannot explain, it trembles—and it overflows.

I cry for Krishn not from sorrow, but because something within me awakens to a memory older than this life. A memory my lips cannot speak, yet my heart has carried in silence through lifetimes.

I feel protected by a presence my eyes cannot see, yet more real than anything I can touch. My heart quivers under the weight of something eternal—tender, vast, and unbearably intimate.

These tears are not a weakness. They are the soul recognizing its origin. Proof that this bond was never created—only remembered.

Sometimes, remembrance is too sacred for the body to hold without breaking into tears.

Why This Bond Feels So Ancient

Because it is. Because every life is a continuation, not a beginning. Because souls travel in threads, not fragments. Because He is the only constant across births. Energy knows no distance, and the soul always remembers its source.

If you are reading these words, you are already being guided toward Krishn. I am only a vessel, a channel for His energy. With all my heart, I pour love, faith, and surrender into these lines, so that each word may awaken the divine presence that has always lived within you—not through me, but through the light that has never left your soul.

I stood before God with questions that had no softness left in them.

Why was I chosen for struggle instead of security?
Why was I given silence where I needed support?
Why was my character forged through loss while others were cushioned by ease?

Why did I have to break before I was allowed to understand my own strength?

For years, I believed I was being tested unfairly. I believed I was unseen. I believed I was carrying more than my share.

I did not realize I was being constructed.

What felt like rejection was redirection. What felt like abandonment was protection. What felt like a delay was discipline.

I was not being punished. I was being prepared—to endure without bitterness, to lose without losing faith, to stand alone without ever being alone.

Today, I do not ask, "Why me?" Today, I say, "Thank You for trusting me." Thank you for giving me a life that demanded growth. Thank you for the weight that built capacity. Thank you for believing I could rise when I could not yet see how.

Everything I lacked created depth. Everything I lost created awareness. Everything that wounded me expanded me.

I was not born to live an ordinary life. I was born to shatter it, to transform it. Born so that every Sonia—the one who feels invisible, unheard, beaten down by silent wars—can see her scars and find fire instead of shame.

Born to serve, to bring light where darkness lingers, to open doors where hope has long been forgotten, to lift the weary, to ignite hearts grown cold, to awaken souls paralyzed by fear. Born to tell them: if I can rise, so can you.

Born to awaken devotion, to reveal the wisdom of Shri Krishna, to illuminate the Bhagavad Gita and Mahabharata, to spread joy, courage, and peace. If even a single soul finds their path because of my words, my life will have fulfilled its mission.

I know the hand that held me when I almost fell—Shri Krishn, steady, unwavering, divine. I am merely a vessel. My duty is clear: to follow my dharma (righteous duty), to serve, to guide, to lift others.

Spreading spiritual wisdom is the highest form of service—and I would choose it a thousand times over.

Call Him Krishna. Call Him Jesus Christ. Call Him Allah. Call Him Waheguru. Call it the Universe. The name may differ. The Source does not.

Until 2025, I was breathing through life. Now, I am living it consciously.

Surrender did not weaken me—it clarified me. Acceptance did not shrink me—it stabilized me.

I would not rewrite my journey. Not the nights that emptied me. Not the losses that reshaped me. Not the seasons that isolated me.

Because now I see the architecture behind it all. Every fracture was intentional. Every delay was strategic. Every tear was an initiation.

I was not unfortunate. I was selected—to rise without arrogance, to serve without ego, to become a bridge so that through my journey, others may meet their Krishn.

In every unseen protection, in every survival that defied logic, in every moment of loneliness—Kan Kan Mein Shri Krishn (Krishna in every particle of existence).

I was never surviving the fire—I was becoming the flame. Because in every particle of me, and in every particle of you, resides Shri Krishn.

We call Him Maakhan Chor (butter thief)—the butter thief. But He is more than that. He steals not butter, but burdens, pain, sorrow, fear, and ego. You do not notice it at first. One day, you simply wake up lighter, as if everything that never belonged to you has quietly been taken away.

There is no greater thief than Him. Once He steals your heart, there is no escape.

When Krishna holds your hand, He never lets go. The world may collapse, people may leave, trust may break—but Krishna remains. Silent. Steadfast. Unshakable.

He does not promise a life without trials. He promises you will never walk alone.

And being chosen by Krishna is not gentle. It is dismantling. He removes every comfort, every certainty, every illusion of control. Slowly, silently, everything you depended on falls away—until you are left alone, not to destroy you, but to prepare you.

To empty you of illusion, so He may fill you with something greater than life itself—a love infinite, consuming, transformative.

Then something awakens: surrender. Trust. Devotion.

A falling leaf becomes sacred. Silence begins to speak. Even strangers feel like blessings.

You realize—you were never abandoned. You were being prepared.

And once Krishna chooses you, your life is never ordinary again.

Jhaai and Shri Krishn's Love for Sonia

Her grandmother was never just a grandmother. She was a bridge between Sonia's known world and the path Shri Krishn was quietly preparing for her.

She taught Sonia love, patience, and care that asked for nothing in return. Through her warmth, Sonia first learned the tenderness of life, long before she knew she needed it.

While her grandmother held her hand in this world, Shri Krishn was already shaping her soul beyond what she could see.

She taught Sonia love. He taught her surrender.

She cared for her body and emotions. He tended to her spirit and unseen battles.

They were never separate forces. Her grandmother was the gentle doorway; Shri Krishn was the light beyond it. And through her, He guided Sonia home.

The First Stirring of Something Ancient

2021: The Storm That Came Unannounced

Two years had passed since Sonia had been forced to learn the cruel art of living without her grandmother—her Jhaai. Acceptance had not arrived with peace; it had come only with helplessness. There was no other way to survive the loss.

Grief had changed its form. Some days, memories pierced her heart, and she wept in silence. On other days, they arrived like a quiet blessing, making her smile at the love that once filled her life.

Time moved forward. Her career grew, her routine became stricter, and life demanded discipline. But Jhaai never truly left Sonia's world.

She kept her alive in small rituals.

In the summer heat, she made aam ka achaar (mango pickle) exactly the way Jhaai used to.

In winter, the kitchen once again carried the aroma of gajar-gobi ka achaar (carrot and cauliflower pickle).

She cooked sarson ka saag (mustard greens dish), wore Jhaai's sarees to work, and on every festival, recreated the same sweets with the same devotion.

Every morning, she slipped Jhaai's gold bangles onto her wrists. Their soft chime felt like protection—like a blessing—like Jhaai still walking beside her.

For two years, these small acts held her steady.

And then, in 2021—

A storm arrived.

Sudden.

Unannounced.

Unforgiving.

The kind that does not just disturb life… it shatters it.

Grief carries a dangerous illusion within it. When a heart is broken, even the smallest warmth can feel like salvation. A few gentle words… a little attention… a hand that seems to understand your pain—and suddenly, the wounded soul begins to worship the one who offered comfort.

In that fragile space between loneliness and healing, it becomes frighteningly easy to mistake kindness for destiny.

Sonia was standing in that very space.

There was someone she had known for a while. Slowly, almost unknowingly, she began to lean on him. His presence softened the silence within her. His concern felt like care. His attention felt like love.

Or at least, that is what her grieving heart chose to believe.

Perhaps it was love.

Or perhaps it was life quietly preparing its most brutal lesson.

Because what Sonia did not know then was that she was not walking into a love story. She was walking straight into the fiercest storm of her life.

A storm that would not simply hurt her—it would dismantle her. It would tear through every illusion she held, shatter the fragile pieces of her heart, and leave her standing in the ruins of everything she believed in.

This storm demanded something far greater than tears. It demanded her death—not of the body, but of the woman she had been until that moment.

Because sometimes, life destroys you with terrifying precision for only one reason: so that from the ashes of that devastation, an entirely new soul can rise.

But rebirth is never gentle. Before a new self is born, the old one must burn—slowly, painfully, mercilessly. Every belief, every attachment, every illusion must collapse.

And Sonia was about to learn that storms are never accidents. They are awakenings. They arrive like destruction… but leave behind transformation. And the woman who would emerge would no longer be the same Sonia the world once knew.

There are moments in life when something shifts so quietly that the world does not notice—but the soul does.

In 2021, Sonia felt the first ripple. It came without warning, like the first gust of wind brushing a battlefield before the conches are blown.

For twenty days, her world narrowed into a single universe: Mahabharat. Not modern retellings. Not polished versions. But the raw 1988 epic.

Sonia did not watch it like someone learning a story. She watched it like someone remembering it. Scene by scene, verse by verse, the rhythm of each lesson, the silences between the words stirred something ancient within her.

Krishna's words did not feel like philosophy. They felt like the truth her soul had always known.

And somewhere deep within, a quiet whisper arose:

"This is not new to you. You have walked with Him before."

At that time, Sonia could not understand that the universe was already preparing her for the darkest chapter of her life.

When the World Grew Dark

In 2022 and 2023, the storm came. Not all storms roar. Some arrive quietly, closing doors, dimming the light, tightening the air around the chest until even breathing feels heavy.

Sonia's storm was like that—nights that seemed endless, mornings that never truly began, days that passed like shadows.

She felt abandoned, unheard, unseen—the way Draupadi must have felt in the sabha (royal court assembly in the Mahabharata), standing in silence and finding no protection.

The world she once relied upon had turned into a place of quiet cruelty, where the soul is bruised, and the heart is tested beyond endurance.

Yet her parents and siblings remained unaware, not out of indifference but because Sonia chose to carry it alone. They saw her face, not her wounds; her routine, not her battles; the person she appeared to be, not the one collapsing inside.

But He saw.

Krishn saw.

Sonia was in a relationship that slowly began to consume her. Once, she believed she was loved, truly loved. She believed she had found her world in him—the man she imagined as her Ram, the one she would stand beside for life.

Loving him felt sacred, almost destined. She loved him with a sincerity that asked for nothing but love, safety, and respect. And for that love, she gave everything—patience when things became difficult, understanding when he pulled away, silence when her heart was full of words she could not speak.

Piece by piece, she began placing fragments of herself into a relationship she was desperate to protect, believing love meant enduring and devotion meant staying even when it hurt.

But love, when carried alone, cannot hold the weight of two hearts.

Slowly, almost invisibly, the man she trusted began becoming the very storm she once believed would protect her from all storms. The warmth faded into the distance, words once gentle began to cut, and comfort turned into absence.

Yet Sonia stayed.

She told herself every relationship had storms, every love had seasons. Love meant patience, love meant understanding, love meant staying. And so she stayed—through silence, emotional distance, and moments where her presence felt invisible—until she slowly realized she was no longer fighting for love, but for who he once was.

And in that silent war, she was losing herself.

What she believed was love had quietly become a cage. The man she trusted to hold her wings slowly began clipping them—not out of her fault, but because control replaced care. Affection turned into authority, and authority turned into domination.

Manipulation entered so gradually that it became normal. Gaslighting replaced understanding. Words turned sharp. The girl who once carried warmth, innocence, and quiet strength began to disappear. She stopped speaking for herself; even when she knew something was wrong, fear held her voice captive.

Yet she stayed—because she loved him, because she believed love meant endurance, because leaving felt like failure, because the world outside felt heavy with judgment, and because somewhere within her, she feared she could not live without him.

So she stayed, and this relationship became her silent Kurukshetra (battlefield of dharma and conflict, from the Mahabharata) of ego, control, and emotional collapse.

Sonia had always been ambitious, focused, and determined. She dreamed of building something meaningful, of making her family proud, of standing firmly on her own feet.

But somewhere along the way, that girl began to fade. Friends heard from her less, and family saw her less. Laughter became distant, joy unfamiliar. Sleep turned restless, food lost comfort, and days became mechanical. Each morning arrived with quiet dread.

She learned to live carefully—measuring every word, softening every reaction, bracing for storms before they arrived. But no matter how cautiously she moved, storms still came—sometimes in silence, sometimes in words, sometimes in wounds that left invisible marks.

And slowly, something within her continued to shrink. Her voice grew quieter, her presence smaller.

Until one day, she stood before a mirror and truly saw herself. Not with vanity, but with disbelief. The exhaustion in her eyes, the heaviness in her posture, the dull ache in her entire being—she looked unrecognizable.

The girl who once carried light now stood hollow, drained, and unfamiliar to herself. And as she looked at that reflection, the tears came—not loudly, not dramatically, but quietly… as though even they had no strength left to fight.

Sonia looked years older than she truly was. Her body carried a constant weariness, the kind that sleep could not fix. Her mind felt trapped in cycles of anxiety and self-doubt, replaying every word, every moment, wondering how she could have prevented the next eruption.

Over time, even the tears stopped coming. There is a point in suffering where a person no longer cries—not because the pain fades, but because the heart grows too tired to keep expressing it. And Sonia had reached that place where hope had quietly slipped away.

Until one day, something inside her shifted. Not anger. Not revenge. Just exhaustion—a deep, bone-weary exhaustion from living every moment of her life in fear.

And in that stillness, a realization surfaced with startling clarity. She was already broken, already emptied, already standing dangerously close to losing herself completely.

And when a person reaches that edge, something unexpected happens. Fear begins to loosen its grip. Because when someone believes there is nothing left to lose, a different kind of strength begins to rise—slowly, quietly, but undeniably.

For the first time in a very long time, Sonia made a decision within herself. Not from anger, but from the last surviving fragment of the girl she once was. And in that quiet moment, she promised herself she would no longer live in fear.

Draupadi's Echo in a Modern World

There were days when Sonia felt like Draupadi—not for the same reasons, but for the same silence, the same loneliness. The world around her was loud, judgment roared, and understanding was absent.

And yet, in that quiet, she understood something profound: Draupadi did not call out to the world. She called out to Krishna.

Her strength was never in who stood beside her, but in the one name she whispered when no one else answered.

And so, in the darkest hours—when sleep felt impossible and courage thinner than breath—Sonia would close her eyes and whisper only one name: "Krishna."

And like a quiet tide, He filled the room—not with thunder, not with miracles, not with dramatic signs, but with stillness, with clarity, with a faint, unwavering reassurance: "I am here."

The Rebirth of Courage

Then came 2024.

It did not arrive suddenly, not in one moment or one breath. It came like light slowly entering a room where the curtains had been closed for too long—gentle, persistent, inevitable.

The same Krishna who had silently held Sonia through her darkest hours now began reshaping her. She began speaking, even when her voice trembled. She began seeing the truth, even when it hurt. She began standing with dharma (righteousness), even when it isolated her.

That year, Sonia did not rise. She returned—to her strength, to clarity, to her path, to herself. Every tear, every silence, every collapse, every quiet awakening had only been preparation.

The Soul That Krishna Chooses

People often ask:
"Why does Sonia feel Krishna so deeply?"
"How does His presence overwhelm her so suddenly?"

The truth is simple.

Krishna chooses whom He chooses.

Not every soul hears Him in their heartbeat. Not every heart feels Him in every breath. Not everyone recognizes Him in their pain. But some souls carry ancient memories—old bonds that do not break, connections that wait across lifetimes.

For such souls, Krishna does not come once. He returns—again and again. Each birth a reminder. Each trial a lesson. Each fall, a promise.

And when He chooses, it is never without purpose—a message, a path, a calling already written.

Sonia's grandmother understood this long before she did. She saw what Sonia could not. Her blessings were never casual; they were directional. She was the hand that led Sonia to the door. And Krishna—the light beyond it.

Through her, He guided Sonia.
Through her, she found Him.
Through her, she came home.

My encounters with Shri Krishn

In May 2024, I was in Ludhiana. I was at the peak of my Krishn bhakti (devotional love toward Krishna) after my visits to Khatu Shyam Temple (a sacred pilgrimage site in Rajasthan,

India), where my first darshan (holy sighting of the deity) itself happened on Ekadashi (a spiritually significant fasting day in the Hindu calendar).

Despite knowing the story of Barbarik (a warrior from the Mahabharata known for his immense devotion and sacrifice), my experience inside the temple left me strangely empty. I went through darshan (holy viewing of the deity) multiple times, yet felt nothing, while others around me were in deep devotion and tears. I kept asking myself—why can I not feel what they feel?

Soon after, something shifted. Within 24 hours of that visit, something I had silently wished for came true. It was deeply personal, but it shook my disbelief in ways I cannot ignore.

Still, one question remained—why did I not feel God?

A few days later, in Ludhiana, I met a 17-year-old girl named Parul. She lived devotion in its purest form—speaking to Radha Krishn (Radha and Krishna), wearing a Tulsi mala (prayer beads made from holy basil), and offering everything in her daily life to Him. She wrote "Krishn" on my wrist with mehndi (henna), and the next morning brought handmade makhan (butter), saying simply, "I just know."

That night, I slept on the terrace, something I deeply love as it reminds me of my childhood and my Jhaai (grandmother). Around 3:30–4 a.m., I suddenly woke up.

And I felt Him.

Not through sight—but through presence.

A form passed by—sky blue, yellow dhoti (traditional garment), peacock-feather crown, flute in hand. Not fully visible, but unmistakably real in feeling.

And then, within me, a simple truth arose:

"You do not find Me outside. I am within you. The moment you remember Me, I am already there."

My mind became completely still. A deep peace filled me.

I tried to explain it later with logic, but nothing fit.

It was not imagination.

It was recognition.

I have always believed that Krishn is my Guru (spiritual guide). Irrespective of form, time, or place, He has guided me, protected me, and illuminated my path. In my heart, I am forever Arjuna (warrior prince from the Mahabharata who receives divine guidance from Krishna)—standing on the battlefield of life: confused, restless, uncertain—while Krishn, my eternal Saarthi (charioteer), steadies my hand, whispers wisdom, and shows me the way. Whenever I pray or even silently think of Him, I feel Him—not in statues or rituals, but alive within my heart, present, watching, and guiding.

And yet, life has its own way of revealing Him.

One Janmashtami (festival celebrating the birth of Krishna) in Delhi became unforgettable. The entire neighborhood was immersed in devotion—incense in the air, bhajans echoing through the streets, children dressed as Radha and Krishn, joy everywhere. I was fasting, visiting the temple, already attuned to the energy of the day.

During a Jhaankiya (processional devotional performance depicting scenes from Krishn's life), something unexpected happened. The boy playing Krishn walked straight toward me and pulled me into the center.

For a moment, I froze—but somewhere deep inside, I knew: how does one refuse when Krishn Himself calls?

We began to spin.

And everything else disappeared.

Marigold petals rained down like golden light. The crowd faded. The music blurred. In that moment, it felt like only He and I existed—dancing in a world made of stillness, joy, and something beyond understanding. I wasn't performing; I was simply being carried by something far greater than me.

When it ended, reality slowly returned—the crowd, the streets, the sound—but something had shifted within me. People gathered around, bhajans (devotional songs) rose again, and yet I remained in that lingering silence of what I had just felt: not imagination, not performance, but presence.

We returned home shortly after, just a short walk away. I went inside to change when my chachu (uncle) suddenly called out, "Sonia, jaldi bahar aa! Baal Gopal (child form of Krishn) aaye hain ghar mein!" (Sonia, come quickly! Baby Krishn has come to our home!)

I ran out without thinking.

And there He was—Baal Gopal—seated in a basket filled with rose petals, radiant beyond anything I had ever seen. A group had brought Him from house to house, and by grace, He had arrived at our doorstep.

The priest looked at me and asked softly, "Sonia, kya mangna chahti ho?" (Sonia, what do you wish for?)

My voice faltered. "Mere paas sab kuch hai… aur inhe pata hai mujhe kya dena hai. Jo denge, mujhe manzoor hai." (I have everything… and He knows what I need. Whatever He gives, I accept.)

Then came the question, "Inhe godi mein logi?" (Will you hold Him in your lap?)

In that instant, something in me simply surrendered.

I nodded.

When He was placed in my arms, everything changed.

Time dissolved.

I felt a love so complete, so quiet, so overwhelming that words cannot hold it. It was not ordinary emotion—it was fullness. As if something within me that had always been searching had finally returned home.

I held Him like a mother holds her child—not as imagination, but as an experience that felt more real than anything else in that moment. Every breath felt sacred. Every heartbeat felt witnessed.

And in that silence, I understood something without needing explanation:

Krishn does not arrive in life.
He reveals Himself within it.

There are endless encounters with Krishn. I am still learning, still absorbing the depth of His love, still understanding what it truly means to surrender to something eternal. And I believe that as long as I am alive, my journey with Krishn bhakti (devotion toward Krishn) will only deepen, expand, and become richer with time.

This is not the end.
It is the beginning of something far more meaningful.
From here onward and upward.

Did Sonia finally reach Vrindavan? (sacred land of Krishn's pastimes)
Did love ever find her again—not the kind that breaks you, but the kind that heals you?
Did Jhaai ever find her way back to Sonia once more?

Perhaps some answers are too eternal for just one lifetime. Or perhaps… they were never meant to be answered at all.

Until then, this story rests here—between grief and grace, between loss and devotion, between the woman Sonia once was… and the soul she is still becoming.

Meri Jhaai (My Grandmother) is not an ending. It is a beginning that refuses to end.

And somewhere, in every particle of existence—Kan Kan Mein Shri Krishn (Krishn in every particle of existence).

But understand this—

What you have read is not the whole story. Not even close.

There are moments that were never written. Truths that were never fully spoken. And a silence that still carries weight far beyond these words.

Because some chapters are not revealed when they happen—they are revealed only when the soul is ready to recognize them.

So if you think this story has ended here, ask yourself carefully…

Why does it still feel like something is waiting to unfold?

Why does the silence after these words not feel empty—but alive?

And what if Sonia's journey was never just about what happened to her, but about what is still happening beyond her understanding?

Because some endings are not endings at all. They are thresholds.

And once you cross them in your mind, there is no returning to who you were before.

So when the next book opens, it will not begin gently. It will begin like a memory you suddenly realize you were always part of—but only now are ready to see clearly.

And by then, you will not be reading the story anymore.

You will be inside it.

To be continued in the next book...

NOTE: If, in any part of this journey, any word has unintentionally caused hurt to anyone—living or departed—I offer my deepest apologies. That was never my intention. This writing comes only from emotion, memory, and reflection, and I seek forgiveness for anything that may have been misunderstood or felt otherwise.

Insta id: anjalinsethi
e-mail: Anjalinsethi@gmail.com

www.ingramcontent.com/pod-product-compliance
Lightning Source LLC
LaVergne TN
LVHW090302210926
848480LV00001B/103